THE SHEPHERD AND THE HORNED GIRL

THE SHEPHERD AND THE HORNED GIRL

TALES OF THE SHEPHERD

BOOK ONE

BREANNA BRIGHT

This work is dedicated to Shawn Lohman, who invented the monster that inspired this story.

CHAPTER 1

A GIRL AND A SHEPHERD SEARCH FOR
SOMEONE

Ruby stared out her window, watching the fog creep with finger-like tendrils over the cliff's edge and onto the mainland. It cascaded in from the ocean, carrying dark things inside, things her mother said would eat her if she ever wandered into the fog. A bundle of garlic, bay leaf, and mandrake was tied to her windowsill, twirling slowly like a hanged man.

The twilight sky faded further, hiding the ocean and the fog in darkness. Still, Ruby stared at the horizon, as she had every evening for a month, waiting to see if her father's boat might appear.

She wondered how long she would keep looking, how many years would it take for her to accept that he was gone and not coming back. Like so many other sailors, taken by the fog, never seen again, eaten by the monsters within.

Now, the ocean was swallowed by nightfall. If she opened her window she could hear it, but she didn't dare. The fog would get in. She could see the white mist pressing against the glass, as if trying to find a place where it could slip through.

Ruby laid back in her bed, ginger hair fanning out over her pillow. Something ate away at her from the inside out, chewing at her stomach.

Dad...

The fog...

What do I do?

Then there was a knock at the door. Ruby turned her head and felt—no, somehow *knew*—that it was for her.

She stood up, walking past her mom's bedroom, always sleeping, to the front door. When she opened it, some fog crept in and swirled up against her feet like a cat.

On the other side of the door stood a monster.

~

*I*vas saw the creature for the first time when the fog rolled in and concealed the world in blue.

Ivas knew better than to enter the fog—everyone did— but one of his sheep had run away while he had guided his herd into the barn for the night. It was only a lamb, so he couldn't leave it to the dark. In all his thirty years he had never lost a sheep, not to wolves, not to disease, and certainly not to the fog. It wasn't happening this night.

Using a walking stick and a flashlight to feel his way through the rocky terrain, Ivas braved the surreal evening. He kept his beam low. The light was useless against the fog, so he used it to watch his feet and make sure he didn't step off a cliff.

Legends said that the mysterious fog that rolled in from the ocean carried malevolent things within it. Others said the fog had a mind of its own and would twist about any who traveled in it, making them lose their way so that they were forever trapped, disappearing in the morning.

Ivas was not a superstitious man. Having lived alone in

the countryside for most of his life, he was rarely bothered by the tales of the elderly. But even he felt the supernatural presence of the fog, so thick no light could penetrate it. Coming to shore no matter the weather, it was hard to ignore the warnings of the stories.

That night, he felt safer since he was accompanied by his dog, who—due to Ivas's lack of creativity—was named Blanc. She was a Berger Blanc Suisse the color of snow, which made her glow in the ethereal fog. She ran safely ahead of Ivas, guided by her animal eyes and nose, tracking the wayward lamb. Her excited whines alerted Ivas which direction he needed to go. At last, she sent out a triumphant yelp as she found their evader, and Ivas could hear her paws pounding the ground as she took off. Ivas followed as quickly as he could.

He followed Blanc's whines until—much to his surprise— the fog broke and he entered a clearing. Ivas sighed with relief. These blissful but odd gaps were said to carry strange monsters within, but Ivas was too grateful to see again to take the story seriously.

His torch lit up the area, and Ivas saw with surprise that he had walked all the way to the Mclaven farm, a trek that usually took an hour at least. He could smell the sea that lay beyond the cliffs, and there was the little stone cottage where the Mclaven's lived. Nearby was a wagon with a missing tire, hay still stored inside it, and settled in that hay was his wayward lamb. Blanc sniffed at the little animal and gave Ivas a cheerful expression. Her ears pointed straight up, alert and happy, and her glinting black eyes and black lips made it look like she was smiling. Ivas put the flashlight in his pocket and went to his knees to pick up the animal.

If he hadn't knelt that moment, the creature might have seen him.

When he rose back up with the lamb in his arms, *it* was

there. The creature—for it lacked any detail that could be mistaken for human—was hunched forward long ways, with a tattered wool cloak covering its body and face like a cloth over a table. From its cloak protruded thin black legs, like those of a spider, with coils of bells wrapped around them, making ghostly music with each step, so faint it might not have been real. Around its body was a leather strap holding a pouch that was bulging with many scrolls, all tied with different colored ribbons.

As terror and confusion began to overwhelm him, Ivas was also haunted by familiarity, some distant memory from childhood that had been hidden away in the dark under-the-bed recesses of his mind that was suddenly and violently returning, begging him to remember.

Ivas was not a creative man, not one for seeing shapes in shadows; his eyes were reliable to the point that he believed anything they showed him, including this creature, which now approached the cottage. Ivas remained frozen, staring at it so hard he feared the creature would feel his gaze. He was still standing, Blanc at his feet, lamb in his arms. He felt so obvious and vulnerable, but the thing did not notice him. It approached the cottage, the bells around its legs making an eerie sound.

Ivas stared in shock. It briefly occurred to him that he should shout a warning to the people inside, but his fear wouldn't allow it. The part of his mind that cared only for self-preservation kept him weighted down, kept him silent, and he selfishly let it. Slowly, Ivas sank to the ground, to his knees. Blanc licked his face, but Ivas didn't blink. He stared at the creature from over the top of the wagon.

To Ivas's horror, the door opened and a young girl with hair like leaves in the autumn stepped outside. The evening wind flapped against her nightgown as she stepped out onto the dew-soaked grass, staring at the monster before her. The fog crept in closer, spiraling around their legs. She seemed so young, with a tangle of freckles across her pale face.

Ivas expected her to scream, for the creature was far larger than her. It would not have even fit through the front door. But she did not. Instead, she stared up at the thing with wide, trance-like eyes. The creature stepped forward, staring down at her, spider legs penetrating the mist that covered the ground.

Stop...stop him! Ivas shot up, clutching the lamb in his trembling arms. He opened his mouth to shout, but no sound came out. He couldn't bring himself to draw the monster's attention. Blanc whined at his feet.

The creature reached into its pouch and took a scroll tied with a red ribbon from inside it. The thing handed the paper to the girl, and she let it sit in her palms, staring at it as if it had fallen from the sky.

She took the red ribbon in her fingers, and it fell away with a single tug. The ribbon fluttered to her feet in a stream of red and the wind scooped it up and dragged it toward Ivas. He watched it flit and swirl through the grass to his hiding place. He looked down as it slipped under the wagon and settled next to his foot, tangling around his ankle. He snatched it up quickly.

When he looked up, the creature was staring directly at him. A flash of eyes glinted from the darkness of its hood.

The shepherd stumbled back, mouth trembling with the need to scream. Tears pricked at his eyes.

Coming...coming for you...

The creature took a step toward him, cloak dragging the ground, bells whispering.

Ivas's eyes darted to the girl. He felt he should do something, but his feet were already pulling him away. He saw a flash of tears against her pale face, then the cascade of her red hair as she started to fall, knees hitting the ground.

Ivas heard a scream, but he couldn't tell who was making the sound. The fog pushed forward in a gust of wind. The creature towered over him like a thundercloud, and Ivas felt as if he were falling into the darkness of its cloak, tumbling down out of the reach of sanity.

Ribbon tangled in his fingers, lamb clutched in his arms, Ivas ran. He was swept up in the swirling blue, heart pounding. He looked over his shoulder, but, even if the creature was following him, he couldn't see it for the fog.

Ivas knew that running was bad, panicking was bad. As a man far from his youth, he shouldn't feel so afraid, but his heart was screaming, drowning out the sounds of common sense, and he only wanted his home. Of course, it cost him, and his foot found a hole that made him slip. His ankle twisted beneath him and his knee struck the rocks. The lamb cried. Ivas whimpered, pursing his mouth shut so he wouldn't shout. He couldn't let anything hear him, let alone a sound of injury and distress, just the thing to attract predators.

He didn't wait but used the adrenaline and the fear to push himself up and keep limping. "Blanc, stand." He risked the command.

Blanc returned to him, tail wagging, happy to assist.

"Walk on."

Blanc turned and walked steadily ahead, staying in the flashlight beam. With her pure white coat, she was like a specter in the dark. Ivas moved as fast as he could, pain shooting up his leg every time he put weight on it. Each flash of pain was a punishment for his bad decisions.

The walk was longer now with the extra burden and Ivas's fear of running into the spider-like messenger. He heard a sound in the darkness and went to his knees, turning off his flashlight so that nothing could see it. He remained that way until he could stand it no longer, then clicked on the light and limped on.

Ivas had always considered himself a steady man. He was cool-headed, had trained Blanc himself, and dealt with sheep all the time. The fog was in his head, tricking him, making him make mistakes. That's how it claimed you was how the stories always went. Some fool-hearted soul took on the fog, and the fog always won.

Tears began to fall down Ivas's cheeks, for he truly believed he would not get home that night, and that he would run through the fog forever. Then Blanc began to whine and yelp as she found the scent of home.

"Oh, Blanc. Oh, you wonderful girl." Ivas wiped his face, adjusting the lamb so he could get to his sleeve, and jogged on until he saw the shadow of his home and the towering black silhouette of the barn. His lights were still burning in the windows.

Ivas tossed the lamb into the barn without ceremony, frightening the sheep, who all started to bleat. He ignored them and limped inside the house, shredding off his clothes and boots. He locked the door and pulled the curtains on all the windows before going to his bedroom.

Ivas collapsed onto the bed, too full of misery and exhaustion to be afraid. It was all right now, he could sleep. If the thing found him, he wouldn't even feel it, he would just sleep. But the cries of the lambs echoed through the house. And when he closed his eyes, images of the cloaked creature flashed in his head. Ivas shuddered.

What about...

He slipped off the bed and opened his bedroom door, giving a sharp whistle. Blanc bounded up the stairs excitedly, and he motioned her into his room. Blanc hesitated, remembering the rules of where she was and wasn't allowed to go, but Ivas insisted. He picked her up and carried her to the bed, holding her close under the blankets. Happy for the attention, Blanc settled in next to him, and Ivas slept briefly and fitfully.

~

It was early morning at the town dock. So early that only a grey glow of sun shyly hinted on the horizon. The air tasted like dampness and salt, and there was nothing to hear except for the creaking of the boat as Tess stepped onboard.

Tess liked being out before anyone else, even the other sailors and fishermen—fisher*people*, she corrected herself. She was a rare breed, but there were plenty of wives and daughters who took to the sea. Mrs. Pendlebrook had taken over for her husband a few months ago when he had fallen ill and had kept on boating since.

There was still fog on the water, but Tess wasn't worried. The sun would clear it up soon, and it was too low to hold any creatures that the stories suggested. She smiled at that, taking pride in her lack of superstition. All the other sailors practically reveled in good luck and bad luck. Tess always rolled her eyes, scoffed, and made a point of ignoring any rituals the others took part in.

She started up her catboat, the *Ocean Scorn,* and the motor came to life with a watery rumble. She smiled at the sound and took a walk over the deck, checking the ties, listening for any sounds she wasn't used to. She knew the *Ocean Scorn* so well, she just had to touch it to sense if anything was wrong.

As the first white rays of sun peaked through the misted morning, other sailors started to appear, sleepily heading for their rigs. Tess was all ready to leave by then and hoisted the anchor. She drove out of the bay, watching the low fog disperse as she hit the waves of the deep water. Tess tilted her head toward the sky and breathed in the salty air.

She loved this part, loved everything about sailing her own boat. She had been doing it since childhood, and it all felt as natural as breathing.

Then a shadow fell, and Tess felt a cold shiver run up her spine.

She shifted the controls so that the engine idled and stepped to the bow, around the boom so that she could get a better look, not sure if her eyes were showing her the truth.

The fog was there, sitting on the ocean like an overcast wall blocking her path. She hadn't seen it in the dark, but now it was clear and looming. Tess tasted wind on her tongue and realized her mouth had dropped open in shock. She craned her head up, watching the wall of mist continue toward the clouds like a castle with never-ending towers.

Tess could see nothing beyond it. The fog didn't seem to end in any direction. For the first time in her life, she felt a tremble in her hand, a pounding in her chest. Not the kind that came with the challenge of a storm or the excitement of a good catch. This was fear, the kind that made her wish she had given her boat a woman's name instead of something so rebellious, the kind that made her remember how she had never christened it. Tess truly felt in danger, staring at the fog.

She ran back to the steering wheel, shifted the engine, and turned around.

CHAPTER 2

THE SHEPHERD RECEIVES A VISIT

By late morning, the sky was blue and the sun was bright, giving no indication of the ominous night before.

Ivas let himself sleep in for the first time in many years. This was the first day he decided that chores could wait. When he did get out of bed, he found that his ankle was nicely swollen and purple. Luckily, all shepherds eventually found themselves with physical ailments, and there was a cane leftover from his grandfather that Ivas could use to get around. Ivas got out of bed and dressed himself in fresh clothes. He brewed strong coffee and ate a hardboiled egg to wake himself up. Despite the extra sleep, he felt worn and heavy. He felt followed. Haunted.

Blanc followed Ivas through the house excitedly, for she normally stayed outside on warm nights. She happily bounded outward as they entered the early morning. Ivas winced at the rising sun and pulled his hat over his forehead. Together, they went to the barn and released the sheep. There were seven Valais Blacknose, each with a colored ear tag. They left the barn with no protest, bleating a good morning to them as they entered the field, quietly looking for a spot to stand and graze. Ivas counted and they were all there, including the little lost lamb.

The Valais Blacknose were a unique type of sheep with thick locks of wool that curled like the hair of a little girl. It fell over their eyes much like an English Sheepdog. Their noses and ears were black as coal, and the horns, for those that had them, curled just like their wool. As far as sheep went, they were probably the most pleasant to look at.

Some of the sheep came up to Ivas with familiarity. They sniffed at his hands and licked his pants. The bellwether announced his presence with the clanging of the bell around his neck. The other sheep stayed relatively close to him. They filled the air with sweet little bleats and settled against the green landscape like awkward clouds.

Though the air was filled with that sweet morning smell that always accompanied the early hours of day, and the grazing sheep were a relaxing sight, it did little to settle Ivas's mind. He felt as if it were still the night and that something was hiding in the shadows. He shivered, and Blanc looked at him with friendly eyes.

It was just a dream, he told himself, despite knowing better. *Everything is fine now, Just don't...think about it.*

Ivas sat on the wooden fence and hooked his foot around a post so that he wouldn't fall off. He pulled a bar of soap and a spoon out of his pocket and started to carve a shape. His skill with carving was about as good as his skill with naming things, but Ivas enjoyed the activity. It was a therapeutic way to spend an afternoon while watching the sheep. His bathroom sink was lined with little soap animals waiting to meet their scrubbing fate.

Just as Ivas was starting to get the shape of a bear, he heard the crunch of dirt and gravel as tires approached. Ivas jumped and turned a little too sharply, slipping off the fence and dropping his carving. Blanc barked and the sheep rose their heads in alarm, the bellwether's bell jingling.

The bells jingled. It had bells on its legs.

Ivas's heart pounded and he took deep breaths to calm himself down. He recognized the ancient truck that approached. There were few people that he did not know, for the area was tight knit. And even Ivas, who was in minor solitude in the farmlands, was close with the community.

The rusted truck came to a sputtering stop and a man stepped out of the driver's side. It was the sheriff. His name was Jack Cries, but everyone just called him Jack, or Sheriff if they were in trouble. Jack waved to him from the dirt road, and Ivas walked forward to meet him, leaving his soap carving abandoned in the grass.

"Morning, Ivas." Jack spoke like a blunt piece of wood, his tone conveying everything his words didn't. He looked tired, and Ivas's heart began to pound again. He clutched his cane tightly. Jack had a full, well-groomed beard and layers of shirts and flannel over his slim figure. He rarely dressed in his official uniform. That, paired with his already untraditional physic, made him look more like a wannabe lumberjack. His thick glasses didn't help.

"Want coffee, Jack?" Ivas asked.

Jack sighed. "I would love coffee, but I'd better just have water, lots of work to do."

"What's going on?"

They walked back to Ivas's house together, a small dwelling made of stone that he had inherited from his grandpa. The story was that his great-grandfather had carried the stones from the seashore himself, dragging them by wagon over the rolling hills to this very spot until he had constructed the house. Ivas found the story a little far-fetched, even as a child.

"The hell happened to your leg?" Jack asked, distracted

from Ivas's question. They went inside and Jack took a seat at the table.

Ivas opened his mouth to explain, but no words came out. *There was a hole, and the dark, and the fog...*

The cup he was filling with water trembled out of his hand, clanging into the sink. Jack jumped.

"Sorry." Ivas breathed and tried again. He handed the cup over and the sheriff drank it down. Ivas stared at him as he gulped.

Something happened, something happened...

He could feel his eyes going dry and had to remind himself to blink.

Jack emptied the cup and sighed. "I'm running the rounds, Ivas. A kid went missing last night."

The girl...

"Which one?"

You left her...

"You know the Mclavens? Your neighbors? Their daughter, Ruby. The mom came to me this morning, said her room was empty. No note, no packed bag. Just gone."

Ivas gripped the edge of the countertop. He felt his stomach clench with nausea and his extremities tremble with an icy coldness. "Redhead?" he whispered.

"Yeah."

I left her...

"I saw her last night." The words tumbled out of Ivas's mouth as he tried to swallow his panic. It was a bold move telling the truth, but Ivas didn't hesitate. It was one thing to be the last person to see a missing girl, but an entirely other thing to be caught lying about it.

Jack's head jerked around in surprise. He set his cup down and reached into his back pocket for a pen and notebook. "You did? Where?"

"At her house. One of my sheep got out, so I went after it.

Blanc and I did. I found it at the Mclaven's place and I saw—Ruby, you said?—I saw her standing outside."

Jack started writing everything down. "What time was this?"

"Oh hell…" Ivas concentrated, trying to think, but memories of the creature and Ruby collapsing kept filling his head. He had noticed the lamb gone at sunset. It took about an hour to walk to the Mclaven's place, maybe an hour and a half with the fog. "Around nine o'clock? Nine-thirty? I think. It was hard to tell in the fog."

Jack raised an eyebrow. "That's right, the fog came in last night. You were out in that mess?"

"It was a lamb that got out."

Jack nodded, understanding. "Is that what happened to your leg?"

Ivas nodded. He still hadn't looked Jack in the eye.

"So, what else? Did she go off on a walk? Was anyone else there?"

Someone else...

"All I saw was that she was still in pajamas. She stepped out on her porch for a moment and then she went back inside. I left. That's all I saw."

Jack frowned. "That's it? She just stepped outside for no reason?"

Ivas rallied. "I thought it was strange too, but I didn't say anything. I didn't want to scare her, you know? She just seemed…deep in thought. Maybe she just couldn't sleep." It was a half-truth.

Jack considered this and appeared to believe Ivas. He released a heavy sigh. "I'm a little worried about this one, Ivas. I'm hoping maybe she was just off with a boyfriend or something, but with the fog, I do worry."

"What's the plan?"

"I'm going out to the other farms now, see what else I can

find. If she's not back by sunset, I'll have to put together a search party. Think you can help?"

"Of course."

He noticed Jack's stern expression as he tapped his pen against the table. A shadow fell over his brow. Ivas finally met his gaze.

"I'm sure it's nothing, Jack, you know how kids are. Remember when we were kids?"

The two men smiled, recalling their boyhood days. "I remember all those ghost stories you told me about the fog," Jack said.

"I was just trying to scare you."

"It still gives me shivers, you know? I'm not ashamed to admit it."

Ivas admitted that it didn't give him pride knowing that. Ghost stories were just supposed to be fun, but with the fog that rolled onto their shore, the ghost stories were too real.

And after what Ivas saw…

"They scare me too."

Ivas put his hands in his pockets, worried about any tell they might give away. He was keeping something from Jack, and he didn't need the sheriff suspicious of him.

When he put his hands in his pockets, he felt a familiar thread of silk. The smooth fabric gave him a jolt, making the night before even more real. He clutched the ribbon, realizing what he had—a clue that the sheriff didn't.

"Alright, I still have a ways to go, but I want to see you tomorrow. I need to get a full statement if Ruby doesn't come back, alright?"

"Alright." Ivas squeezed the ribbon tightly.

Jack stood up and Ivas followed him out. Blanc wagged her tail at them, escorting Jack to his truck.

"Let me know if you think of anything else," Jack said.

"I will. And don't worry, Jack, I'm sure she's okay."

Jack sighed. He seemed very old to Ivas, very far from the carefree boy he had grown up with.

"She's just fifteen, Ivas…"

Ivas didn't answer. He felt his throat swelling as a lump formed.

Jack started his car and waved goodbye. The truck disappeared in the cloud of yellow dust. Ivas waited until it had disappeared behind the hills before allowing himself to relax his body.

"Fifteen…" Ivas said to himself. Blanc looked at him expectantly and wagged her tail when he sighed.

Should have done something…

"What am I going to do, Blanc?"

She answered with a happy dog-smile.

Leave it, a dark part of Ivas's mind said. *Tend to your sheep and let it fade into a nightmare.*

Ivas pulled the ribbon out of his pocket and stared at it. The little river of silk was bright red. Like a Christmas bow, it had been wrapped around that piece of paper that the girl, Ruby, had received. What had it been? What did it mean?

Ivas put the ribbon back in his pocket and looked at Blanc. "Watch the sheep, girl. I have to run an errand."

Blanc sat obediently next to the fence and looked out at the herd. With her there, Ivas had no worries about thieves or wild animals taking any of them while he was away. He went to the little wooden shed next to the house and found his bicycle in there, surrounded by tools and junk that should be thrown away but never would be because they might come in handy someday. His bike had once been red, but all the paint had faded to the silver metal underneath. He took care of it enough to keep the rust at bay.

Ivas had found no use for a car. Well, there was plenty use for one, but he just didn't want to maintain it, buy gas, fix it up, or pay the cost. The bicycle got him to town and back, and that was all he really needed. Everything else could be solved by borrowing a vehicle from someone else.

Ivas dressed warmly for the months had turned gold with autumn and the ocean pushed cold winds to the shore. Donning a cap, cardigan, and scarf, he pedaled off down the road toward town. It wasn't hard with the bad ankle; he simply let that leg hang while the other did the work.

The landscape rolled out around him into cascading green hills, overcast skies, and snakes of stone walls that no longer held back anything, their stones having fallen away so that they were only relics. Ivas weaved up and over the hills, standing up on the pedals to get to the top, then enjoying the ride down. The whip of ocean air increased as he got closer to town.

The dirt road soon turned to cobbles as Ivas came upon Loch Lamond, a little port-side village made up of stone shops and houses. It looked as if it were part of the land-scape, nestled down in the natural slope of the cliffside.

Once in town, he got off his bike to walk, using it to support himself. The streets were fairly empty. Most business would be going on at the dock by now, so it surprised him to see restaurants opening and people already gathering on porches outside, drinking tea and chatting. Such idleness was reserved for the evening when all work was done. Yet there was a tenseness in the air, and Ivas realized that by now the entire town must have found out about Ruby. Her family would have come in looking for her, asking if anyone had seen her before going to Jack. Gossip lingered at every corner and doorway, and Ivas found himself getting back on his bike to escape it all quickly.

He left the main road in favor of more narrow alleyways and side streets until he reached a very quiet and subtle part of town, a poorer district with tiny homes and apartments reserved for the elderly. Ivas rolled his bike to the end of the lane until he reached a little brown house at the end where Old Popper lived.

Old Popper was one of the older residents in the area. Deep into his seventies, the man was still amazingly sharp and had a good memory, one that served well in Old Popper's new occupation, that of local storyteller.

Formerly the town librarian, Old Popper's life was all about stories. In fact, this was the very man who had told Ivas the ghost stories that had scared their sheriff so. If anyone knew about what lay in the fog, it was Old Popper.

Ivas knocked loudly on the door, which opened immediately, surprising Ivas so much he stumbled forward, almost knocking over the tiny old man before him.

"Easy there! I haven't even invited you in yet."

"Sorry there, Old— Mister Poppermill. Do you remember me? I'm Ivas Sbarge."

Old Popper narrowed his eyes to see better and cackled. "Sbarge's kid, the sheep farmer."

"That's right. I'm sorry to bother you."

"No bother, young lad. At my age a visitor is a blessing and I shall hold you hostage with long ramblings and stories about 'the good old days.'"

"Actually, I *have* come for a story."

Old Popper grinned, excited to have a customer to his official trade. "I remember you. Scrawny lad with the white pup and a funny hat. What was that hat?"

Ivas felt his cheeks turn pink. "It was an elf hat for Christmas. Mother knitted it too big."

Old Popper laughed so hard he went into a fit of coughing. "A Christmas hat! You wore that thing all year. I knew I remembered you! You did love my little tellings at Hallow's Eve. Come for some more, have you?"

"Yes. I need you to find a story for me."

Old Popper grinned. "Then yer in the right place."

CHAPTER 3

THE SHEPHERD HEARS A STORY

The town had a library, but any local looking for real literature went to Old Popper. Inside that tiny brown cottage of his was an array of books that would give any scholar a dropped jaw and fluttery heart. From floor to ceiling there were bookshelves that Old Popper had built into the walls himself, and they were stuffed cleanly with an impressive collection of hardbacks, some so old you couldn't see the titles anymore, other's so new Ivas wondered how Old Popper had obtained them. There were stacks of books on the dining table, books lining the fireplace mantle, books on the stairs leading to the second floor. After retiring from his librarian life, Old Popper had attempted to open a bookstore. He purchased all the books, but never got around to actually investing in a store. Instead, he sold books and told stories from his own house.

"What story are you seeking? Adventure? I recall you particularly enjoyed my telling of the feared pirate Captain Girshwin."

"I'm looking for something very specific, and I don't

think it'll be in any book. I want to know about local legends, things involving the fog."

"Oh, aye, the fog. I got a thousand stories in me head just about the fog, carrying all sorts of supernatural heebie-jeebies from the sea. They hid in the fog, creeping onto the shore, slipping into the moors and the farms."

Everyone knew the story about the fog. Every child was raised on it, warned about what hid in the misty depths. There were those, like Ivas, that realized that these stories were just covers for the truth, meant to scare people from walking in the fog and accidentally stepping off a cliff. But in a small town that had been raised on ghost stories, superstition ran deep in the roots, and there were those that took the creatures of the fog very seriously.

"Were there any stories about a creature that…walked on the legs of a spider and carried letters in a bag?"

Old Popper frowned. "Spider? Letters? There's the one if it found you it would drag you back to the sea…"

"No, no." Ivas sighed. "This creature is a…I'm not sure. It has all these scrolls."

A light flickered in Old Popper's eye and he smiled with revelation. "I do recall a tale of a messenger. It had naught to do with the fog, but it was an old story of a messenger who carried letters and scrolls. 'E was the servant of death."

"The servant of death?"

Old Popper smirked at Ivas, eyes twinkling almost tauntingly. "Come on, we're going to need some tea for this story."

Ivas followed Old Popper to the kitchen in the back. There were no books back there, just a small kitchenette with a wood stove and a tiny wooden table covered in mail and paperwork. Old Popper cleared it off and Ivas sat down. The old man went to work, setting water to boil on the stove.

"I never told this story to the kids, thought it was a bit

too scary. I didn't like to bring death into it, and quite frankly it wasn't as interesting as the others. The ghost pirates, squid monsters, Loch Ness, you know, everyone likes a good monster story."

"This one isn't a monster?"

"Not in the same light. He didn't drag people off to their doom or haunt them from the sea. No, he just delivered messages."

"From death?"

"Hey, am I telling this story or you?"

The kettle whistled loudly and Old Popper found a couple of mismatched cups, into which went the hot water and tea bags. Ivas let his seep into a deep auburn color while Old Popper sipped his and settled into his chair comfortably.

"It's like I say, when you tell a story, you have to start from the beginning. How's yer tea?"

"Fine."

"Biscuit?"

Ivas almost said no, but the thought of sugar suddenly sent his stomach into a frenzy and he said, "Yes, please."

Old Popper grabbed a tin off the cupboard and popped it open. Ivas helped himself, shoving little rounds of short-bread into his mouth.

"It was my grandfather what told me this story when I was a lad, that's how old it is. It's been around longer than any of my Halloween tales, even if it's not told as much."

Ivas nodded. He stirred his tea and the clink of spoon on porcelain was the only sound as Old Popper gathered his memories and laid the story out in pictures in his mind.

"When a human met death for the first time, it was not an easy affair, not like it is now. There was a lot of confusion, and both sides weren't sure what they were supposed to do. When the very first death occurred, the man who died put up quite a fuss. He didn't take well to being told he wouldn't see his family again and would have to go somewhere far away and different from what he had ever known. He insisted that Death let him return and say his final goodbyes to his family and let them know what had happened to him, for you see no one had ever died before and no one really knew what to make of it.

"Death was uncertain about this. He was very absolute in his decisions, but being that it was his first time as well, he decided to let the man return to explain the situation and give his farewells. Death gave him until nightfall, and then they would have to return to the afterlife.

"Well, life is a hard thing to give up. You get addicted to the breathing and the heartbeats, you see, and the man didn't want to leave. He found that there wasn't enough time to say what he needed to say. So when night came, he tried to hide from Death and ran into the fog, but no one escapes Death.

"But poor Death, he didn't quite know what to do. He was just trying to do his job and this man was putting up such a row about it that Death said, 'Fine, you just stay here, see if I care.' As punishment, Death turned him into a horrible creature with spiny legs and black hair, a creature of the night that was neither living nor dead. The creature wandered the fog between the two worlds with no place to stay.

"When a human died for the second time and saw what happened to the first guy, he went right on his merry way. I'm sure you can imagine.

"As Death became more prominent and entered the natural cycle of life, the creature found a use for itself in the ever-growing amount of souls in the underworld. Legend goes that for a price—for a great price—the souls of the dead can give the creature one last message to the living, and he would deliver it to whomever they choose. One last good-bye, just like he got."

Old Popper paused to take a drink of tea, and Ivas realized he had let his sit. He quickly gulped down the strong brew so as not to be rude.

"What's the price?"

"Hmm?"

"What's the price for delivering a message?"

"A piece of your eternity trapped in limbo, I suppose. You can't break the rules like that without someone getting angry, and that's usually the last punishment for someone who's already died."

"What message could be so important?" Ivas wondered, touching the ribbon in his pocket.

"What, indeed?"

A moment of silence passed as they sipped their tea. If the thing he had seen last night was just a messenger, would it have taken Ruby? Or was it there to warn her?

"So, did you see it?" Old Popper interrupted his thoughts.

"What? No—"

"Did he deliver a message to you?" Old Popper winked.

"I was just...remembering the story from my boy days and wanted to hear it again."

"Lad, I never told anyone that story— Do you hear that?" Old Popper raised his hand to silence Ivas and both men remained still. As Ivas adjusted his hearing, he noticed the sound too, a bellowing echo from far away.

"Is that the boat horns?" Ivas wondered, standing up. He grabbed his cane and headed for the door.

"It's far too early for the boats to be back," Old Popper noted. He followed Ivas to the door and they both stepped out. In the street, Ivas clearly heard the boat horns sounding from the bay.

"Something must have happened," Ivas said. "Shall we go see?"

"Go on ahead, lad, I'll have to find my shoes. Probably just a storm rolling in."

They waved at each other and Ivas mounted his bike again, pedaling toward the port.

"You owe me one!" Old Popper suddenly shouted. Ivas skidded to a stop in surprise, looking back.

"How's that?"

"A story, eye for an eye, and it sounds like you've got a whopper up your sleeve."

Ivas didn't answer but quickly rode away.

~

The port was small, reserved for fishing boats and some trade. By the time Ivas arrived it was packed with people, and the bay was traffic jammed as the boats came back into port all at the same time. The air was filled with shouts.

Ivas limped closer, eager for news. If a storm were coming, he would have to prepare and secure his sheep. He didn't bother trying to stop one of the hectic bystanders, instead following the port down to the end where he saw the *Ocean Scorn* had already docked. On its deck, Captain Tess Burlock was busy tying things down. Ivas waved at her and she waved back.

Tess was another one of Ivas's schoolmates. Daughter to a fisherman, she had taken over the boat as captain after her father became too old. Her brown hair was boyishly short to save it against the high sea winds, and she was bundled up tightly in rubber shoes and layers of clothes. She jumped off the boat to meet Ivas.

"You're too young to cripple yourself," she said, nodding to his cane.

"Just a sprain. What's going on?"

"The fog, it's still out on the water." Tess looked him in the eye, seeming uncharacteristically suspenseful. Ivas stared back and she realized he wanted her to continue. "It's just… so thick. It was like a wall, Ivas, just this tall wall of white. No one wants to go out in that."

"You've gone out in the fog before."

"Usually it wouldn't bother me, but it's so thick, it might be carrying a storm behind it. Everyone's just being cautious since that boat disappeared last month. And the fog is… Well, you know."

"Cautious about what?"

A boat disappeared…

"It's just been strange lately. Everyone is nervous about something. Remember when the shrimper Mr. Crass lost his bait and all the dead fish washed up on shore? No one would go out for a week. Everyone's just spooked."

I forgot about…

"Wait, a boat disappeared? Did I know that?"

Tess shrugged. "It happens sometimes, Ivas. My dad told me about all the horrible things that can happen to you out on the sea and no one would ever know."

Ivas rubbed the back of his neck and leaned against a post, suddenly feeling tired. "Nothing to worry about, then?"

Tess shrugged again. "Probably not, but be prepared anyway. You all right, Ivas?"

"It's been a long…everything."

"Let's get something to eat, then, my treat. Meet me at Cuppa in fifteen minutes. I need to change." She motioned to her wet coveralls and Ivas nodded in agreement. They parted ways, leaving the ramshackle bay.

~

*C*uppa Tea was a favorite cafe for locals. It was quiet and run by a sweet widow named Brenda Kindlestrike. Cuppa had all the charm without the pretentiousness. There was always a fireplace roaring, so it was nice and warm when Ivas stepped in. He stripped himself of his layers and sat down at a table. The cafe was empty at that hour, past breakfast and not yet lunchtime.

"Ivas Sbarge, is that you?" Brenda smiled at him, the fire reflecting off her little glasses.

"How are you, Ms. Kindlestrike?"

"Oh fine, just fine. Heard the boat horns going off. Something wrong?"

"Just some odd weather, nothing to worry about."

"That's dreadful, a storm coming and little Ruby still lost." Brenda shook her head and rubbed her arms, a nervous twitch.

"Yeah." Ivas reached into his pocket and touched the ribbon again.

"So, are you wanting tea? Coffee? I've got soup boiling up that'll take the chill off."

"Just bring me one of each and we'll see how we do from there," Ivas said.

Brenda laughed, slapping his shoulder. She carried the laughter back into the kitchen, wiping her eyes and giggling.

As Brenda disappeared, Tess arrived. She was dressed more comfortably in a sweater with a skirt and tights. Her hair was smoothed down with a bow.

"Did you order?"

"Yeah, got you a tea."

"Perfect, I'm freezing." She moved her chair next to Ivas so that she was closer to the fire. As the quiet sank in, filled only by the cracking wood, Ivas noted the troubled expression on Tess's face as thoughts that had been pushed aside now occupied her mind.

"Ivas, could I put my head on your shoulder?"

"Sure, that's okay."

She rested her cheek there and looped an arm around his. "I feel really silly, Ivas. I let the fog scare me."

Ivas found himself resting his cheek on her head. "It scares me too, Tess."

"I swore I wouldn't be like my parents, with their weird rules and superstitions, but being out there on the water… It was like the sky had fallen. The fog was so thick and so high, it was like a wall trapping me in. I felt so small next to it, and… For a moment, it seemed like anything could be in there. All those ghost stories seemed so real."

"I know what you mean."

"And then the news about Ruby Mclaven." Tess shivered. "Everyone says the fog took her away in the night. It's bringing back all the old fears."

She shook her head. "I let it scare me. It's just fog." She sighed and picked herself up, but Ivas didn't want her to stop. He didn't realize how much he needed to hold something, like a child needing a teddy bear.

"It's not safe anyway. You did the right thing turning back," Ivas said.

Brenda appeared with a tray and beamed at them. "Oh, hi there, Tess. Ivas didn't say anything about you coming. Want something to eat?"

"Give me the gooiest, cinnamoniest roll you have, Ms. Kindlestrike."

"You kids are too cute."

Tess held the tea under her nose, breathing in the warm fumes while Ivas braved the hot brew of his soup, taking in spoonfuls of potato and cheddar. They let the conversation rest while they ate, soaking in the warmth and the smells so that it took them far away from the fog.

"Do you want a ride back to your place?" Tess asked after she had taken her last bite of cinnamon roll. "Don't want you to have to ride your bike with the bad leg."

Ivas looked at her, going from her eyes to her pink bow. He would have liked a ride, but he didn't want to be left alone at his farm. To have the pleasure of her company only to watch her drive away. It was better to ease into aloneness again.

"No, thank you. I'll be fine."

Tess sighed. "Will you just do it? You have to use a cane. Your leg will just get worse. Just take the ride."

Ivas said, "Autumn beckons me, the sea winds blow, I must go to her, to the cliffsides, and tell her my woe."

Tess stared at him, lips opening. Then, on an impulse, he leaned forward and kissed her forehead. "You're my best friend, you know that?"

Tess blinked at him and touched her head. "Since when do you give kisses?"

"I feel full of poetry." He stood and left, making a beat with the thump of his cane. Tess quickly went after him, coming to his side as they went through the door.

"Ivas…"

He looked at her, but Tess seemed to have trouble finding what to say. Eventually she just gave him an annoyed smile and said, "You're my best friend, too."

Ivas gave the kickstand on his bike a nudge and tucked the cane under his arm. With a farewell wave to Tess, he rode off down the street, back out of town.

CHAPTER 4

THE SHEPHERD GOES TO A MAGIC PLACE

*A*s he neared the edge of Loch Lamond, where the stone path became dirt again, he heard a sound through the wind, high-pitched and flowing. It was a song. Up over the hill, Ivas saw a group of children moving through the tall grass, boys and girls of varying ages. They each carried a basket, and they were all singing the same song in eerie unison.

"Gather up the bay leaves, the dill, and the mandrake, gather up the periwinkle, do it for our sake. The garlic for the night, the hyssop burning bright, nettle though it pricks us, holly but no Christmas, the mistletoe is hiding, but the fern here is thriving. Gather up the bay leaves, the dill, and the mandrake..."

The song continued like that, forever in a loop as the children gathered the leaves and roots that the lyrics required. Ivas had sung that very song as a child. All the plants were used as protectants against evil forces, and it was the children that gathered them for their homes. It was a way to teach them, and the song was easy to remember. They all sang it together like a shopping list so as not to forget, going down the list as they went through the fields toward the forest until each plant was found, or at least the ones in season.

"They *are* spooked," Ivas muttered to himself. The children's voices were surreal, echoing against the overcast sky. Tess was right, everyone was scared.

The fog took her...

They were taking precautions, going back to the old beliefs.

Everyone says the fog took her...

". . . Nettle though it pricks us, holly but no Christmas, the mistletoe is hiding, but the fern here is thriving..."

The song followed him into the countryside, no matter how fast he pedaled.

And suddenly he was there again.

~

All around him, the world had become shades of fall. Orange pumpkins dotted the hillsides, and the horizon was cozy with golds and reds. Leaves flitted by his bike—whispering something he didn't catch—and swirled away.

This autumn was the same from his childhood. He could smell the freshly plucked bay leaves, and the harsh prick of the holly. He was just a kid of fourteen then, singing the song.

And Tess was there too, her hair still long, singing along with him.

"Gather up the bay leaves, the dill, and the mandrake..." young Tess sang.

Ivas sat down, hidden in the tall grass. She stopped and looked back. "What's wrong?"

"Nothing."

That wasn't true. His grandpa was sick again and had sent him away to pick the herbs. He was the only child out that day because the warm weather had kept the fog at bay. Tess had shown pity and joined him.

"Want to do something else?"

"There's nothing to do in this town," Ivas grumbled.

"I could ask Dad to take us out in the boat." Tess's father often took the two of them out together, along with any other friends who were curious about fishing.

"No, I don't feel like it."

"I could show you a new place."

"There's no such thing as 'new' around here." Ivas was determined to stay unhappy.

"No, really, I found this place in the forest." Tess looked around to make sure no one was listening, then she leaned forward and whispered, "I think it's magic."

Ivas gave her a dubious look.

"I'll take you there," Tess said, ignoring his doubt. "But you have to promise not to tell anyone."

A secret, now that had perked the young Ivas's interest. "Sure, gotta be better than doing this all day."

So Tess had taken him to the secret place.

That's right, secret. Ivas turned his bike off-trail, the memory coming back to him. It wasn't far, his leg could take it.

~

Tess had called the secret place Floborough Deep. She had taken him to the forest, leading him through a mass of yellow and brown until they reached a little clearing where the stone ruins of a building sat, rotting away. This was not completely unusual, for Ivas often stumbled upon broken walls of destroyed homes, but this was indeed special. The building was completely gone except for a stone staircase that still twisted up one remaining wall. It swirled up a complete story before ending to empty air.

The staircase stood by itself in the clearing. Pools of water had formed here and there, and they had turned gold from all the leaves that floated on their surface.

It was a simple walk, but unless you knew the way, there was no other way to find the place. Tess had sat down on the bottom step and hugged her knees.

"I love this place. Can you feel it?"

"Feel what?"

"The magic. I can feel it, like a heartbeat."

Ivas thought about making fun of her, calling her weird, but she was too sincere to make fun of. Ivas sat next to her.

"Let's climb up. I want to see what it's like at the top."

"Oh no, Ivas, please don't. I'm so worried it'll break or fall away, and then it'll be gone forever. Just leave it for now. Isn't it wonderful? Isn't it enough that we have it? Our secret place?"

Ivas considered it, staring up at the top silently.

"I write poetry here. It's so quiet, it helps me think."

"That is…so lame." Ivas smiled to show he was joking. Tess smiled back to show that she knew very well how lame she was.

"It is pretty," Ivas admitted. Some leaves drifted down from the branches of the giant tree, so gentle, the most harmless thing he had ever seen. He wanted to cry. There was no ocean wind here, the forest cut it out. All was still, all was deep.

Tess said, "I feel full of poetry."

"Grandpa's sick again," Ivas whispered.

"He'll be okay."

"Yeah, he'll be okay. But one day he won't be okay—and it'll just be me."

"You could come live with me and my dad."

That didn't sound too bad to Ivas, but he worried that he would be sent away from their little village, away from Jack and Tess. That maybe he had a horrible relative living somewhere else who would have to take him in.

"If Grandpa dies and they try to send me away, will you hide me?" Ivas asked. "No matter what?"

"Of course!" Tess's eyes brightened, shining but dutifully serious. "I won't let them take you, I swear."

She grabbed his hand and squeezed it tight. "There's the boat, there's Floborough Deep, plenty of places for you to stay."

Ivas smiled, feeling better.

"You can sleep here. We'll build you a tent around the stairs. Or we can build a house up in the tree!"

"Yeah, with a rope ladder, and only people that know the password can get up."

They made plans and plotted Ivas's future, even began constructing a lean-to for him to live in later. Of course, Grandpa lived for several more years, passing just in time for Ivas to care for himself. Everything was left to him, the farm and cottage, the savings Grandpa had leftover. He wasn't sent away and he didn't have to live in Floborough Deep. He just kept living his life as if nothing had changed.

He remembered that day too.

How Grandpa had finally managed to get out of bed after days of staying indoors.

"Grandpa, I let the sheep out."

Grandpa had patted his shoulder. "You're a good boy, Ivas."

Then he went outside for a walk.

Ivas found him that evening, lying in the grass on one of the hillsides, and had to leave him there until the doctor could come and take him away.

Ivas stopped his bike when he reached Floborough Deep. It was just like the day Tess had first showed it to him, shrouded in autumn leaves, still and yet…heavy.

The stairway was tall and untouched, leading to nowhere. Out of use and time with only the sentiment of a little girl leaving it to stand.

Ivas pulled the red ribbon out of his pocket and stared at it. It seemed so normal.

"A message from the dead, and then she disappeared," Ivas said to himself, "and I was the last one to see her."

The one who let her get taken.

Ivas shut his eyes, trying to push away the guilt that sat in his stomach like a heavy stone.

Behind closed eyelids, he saw the creature again, remembered the horrible fear that had controlled him, made him run while Ruby fell, left to the mercy of the fog.

Coward.

The forest didn't seem so safe and beautiful all of a sudden.

If they come, will you hide me?

Ivas put the ribbon away and got back on his bike.

I won't let them take you, I swear.

Ivas pedaled as fast as he could, swerving through the trees. He had to get back to the farm. The sheep would be waiting.

CHAPTER 5

THE SHEPARD GETS A VISIT

ack home, Ivas's cottage sat quietly, and Blanc was in the middle of a nap, sleeping on a bed of leaves. Most of the sheep had joined her in sleep, lying down in a big pile. At the sound of his bike, Blanc immediately perked up and ran out happily to meet him. Everything was safe.

"You're a good girl, Blanc."

She wagged her tail in agreement.

Woken, the sheep went up to the fence, bleating at Ivas. He passed by them, rubbing their noses. They licked his hand in return. With Blanc at his feet, Ivas circled the fence, checking for breaks. When he had made a full circle back to the barn, he replenished the water and added some hay to the feeding trough. Grass was getting short in the cooler season.

As the Valais Blacknose gathered for the treat, Ivas checked the ewes for signs of pregnancy. So far there was nothing. The little lost lamb from the night before was the only newcomer, having presented herself odd and late at the end of summer rather than in the spring. Still, there was plenty of autumn left for mating. Ivas tried to keep things simple with only one or two lambs a year. Right now, the males and females shared the pasture, but once a ewe was pregnant, he would separate them again.

Still, things happened, and he looked suspiciously at Little Lost who, until last night, had been the biggest mystery on the farm.

Chores taken care of, Ivas was left alone with his thoughts again. He stepped out of the barn into the empty farm, staring out at the fields. They seemed to roll on forever. Maybe if he stared out long enough, he would see her red hair against the grass. She would stick out easily. How does someone get lost out here? There was no place to hide, and with the cliffs there was nowhere to go.

Ivas was so lost in his own thoughts he didn't hear Blanc start to growl. As he turned, something struck him over the head so hard that he went to his knees. The world turned grey and his ears rang. The pain was overwhelming, and Ivas found himself wishing he would just blackout, but he remained very much conscious, clutching his head, lying in the dirt.

When the ringing abated, he could hear Blanc barking and someone yelling. Slowly, things became more clear and his vision came back.

"Ruby! Ruby, are you here?"

Ivas followed the sound, turning his head to see a woman running around his farm. She went into the barn, startling the sheep, who bleated in fear and ran away. Now Blanc was on full alert, getting into attack mode.

"That'll do," Ivas snapped.

Blanc retreated, coming to his side, but her fur was raised and her ears were laid back in warning.

"Ruby!" Now the woman was going into his house, and

Ivas finally recognized her as Mrs. Mclaven. She had red hair too.

Ivas pushed himself up on unsteady feet. His head gave a warning ring, and he clutched his cane to keep from falling again. Easy now, Ivas started for the house. He could hear the woman Mclaven yelling and pushing things over.

"What, in the name of God, are you doing?" Ivas thundered with a voice he recognized as his grandfather's. He stood in the doorway, glaring at the woman. She was holding a wrench as her weapon and had knocked aside some pieces of furniture, including his kitchen table and a bookcase. She glared back at him.

"I'm looking for my daughter. Sherriff said you were the last person to see her. Right, a lonely little sheep farmer, wandering through the fog at night? I know what you were doing. Were the sheep not enough for you?"

Ivas snatched up a mug she had knocked over and smashed it against the countertop, shattering the porcelain with a horrible noise. The lady Mclaven screamed and jumped away, just as scared as he was. He stormed up to her, trying to slow down, trying to remind himself why she was here. She was mad, but then the only thing that mattered had been taken from her. She held her trembling wrench.

He said, "Then search, search high and low. Don't leave anything. If you leave a single corner, it will haunt you, so look. And when you're done, come outside to me with your apology or I will drag you into town myself and let everyone see what a madwoman you are. Now, search."

Mrs. Mclaven did look mad, her wild eyes on him, too scared to move. Ivas turned his back on her, stepping back outside. He heard Mrs. Mclaven resume her search behind him.

Ivas went outside to wait. He calmed the sheep, then sat in the grass. She stayed a long time, checking the basement and the attic. She came outside to search the barn, then the shed. Then she went into the house and searched again.

Ivas remained where he was, staring out at the horizon. His head throbbed and started to swell, making a nice goose-egg on his skull. Ivas shut his eyes and lowered his head, trying to soften the pain.

At last, the lady Mclaven came outside. She walked up to him, but he didn't rise.

"Did you search it all?" he demanded.

He saw her nod in the corner of his eye.

"Are you satisfied? Don't leave unless you are."

After a moment she said, "I'm sorry."

He glared at her.

"I'm *sorry*. Please try to understand, I *am* a madwoman. I've been sitting in my house all day, waiting for Ruby to come home, and it has driven me mad. Jack told me you saw her last night, and at first I thought that was a good thing, but with each hour, my thoughts grew more dark, and I thought of all the farmers out here, lonely, disgusting farmers, how any of them could have her right now…"

She sat down next to him, hugging her knees. Ivas relaxed his gaze. He touched his goose-egg and felt something of admiration for her.

"Let me ask you something, Mrs. Mclaven."

"Hannah."

"Hannah, have you been through Ruby's room? Searched through your house? Did you happen to see a letter? Like a scroll?"

"Why?"

"Because I saw her with one last night. She was reading it on the porch. The paper looked old and was rolled up."

Hannah shook her head. "I didn't, but I'll check again. What could it have been?"

Ivas didn't answer.

"Not a love letter," Hannah said to herself. "Jack kept mentioning that she might have run off with a boyfriend, but Ruby hasn't been with any of her friends lately, she won't even go into town. Ever since her father disappeared she's been different, recluse, not that I blame her. We all need time."

"I didn't hear about that. I'm sorry," Ivas said. "Wait…the boat. That's right. Your husband was a sailor. It was his boat that disappeared."

Hannah nodded. "What could possibly want to punish my family so?"

"You're not being punished, Hannah," Ivas said. "These are our burdens."

She looked at him, and Ivas looked back.

"Your parents died," she said, remembering. "This was your grandfather's farm. You came to live with him."

Ivas nodded.

"I met you when you first came here. Do you remember?"

"Back then there were no faces, no names. It was just me, alone, only the grief."

"Did it ever get easier? Does it ever go away?"

"No, it just…learns to live with you. It becomes something more than grief and becomes a part of you instead."

"I really am—"

"Don't be sorry, just use it. Use it to find her."

Hannah's eyes widened, and she nodded. For the first time, tears threatened to come, pushing out all the useless things she didn't need. She hefted her wrench and stood up. "I have more farmhouses to search."

Ivas actually found himself smiling as she walked away.

That's not it.

His smile disappeared when she did.

The fog is coming.

He reached into his pocket one last time and touched the

ribbon.

You know, you know...

"She's not mine to find."

You know

You know.

~

vas was inside eating, holding an ice pack to his head, when Jack arrived. Blanc started barking before he heard the puttering of the truck. He looked up from the oatmeal he had been trying to force himself to eat and was grateful for the distraction.

He stood up and was outside before Jack was out of the truck.

"What's the word, Jack?"

Jack's gaze was all the answer he needed. "I heard Hannah Mclaven paid you a visit."

Ivas raised an eyebrow. "How'd you know that?"

"She was caught searching through the Marpoles' house. She apparently hit every home this side of town searching for Ruby. I guess she convinced herself someone kidnapped her."

Ivas shrugged. "She could have been right. Did you arrest her?"

"Of course not. She's just upset, and who can blame her? But are you all right? She confessed to knocking you over the head."

"I've had worse. One of the sheep kicked me in the groin once. I'll take a knock to the head any day."

Jack sighed. "It's getting out of hand, Ivas. No one has seen this kid. I've got my deputy organizing a search party, but there's a storm coming, so everything is rushed, everything's a mess. I don't know what to do…"

"At least you're looking," Ivas said. "You're doing all you can."

"Fuck, Ivas," Jack ran a hand through his hair and stumbled forward. Ivas quickly caught him.

"You okay?"

"I'm so tired…"

"Have you eaten?"

"Why? What time is it?"

"God, Jack." Ivas forced his friend into the cottage and heaved him to the table. Jack accepted the untouched bowl of oatmeal. The sheriff took small bites at first, but in moments the bowl was empty and Ivas began searching for something else.

"I let this happen, Ivas. This is my town, my responsibility."

Ivas poured a glass of milk and made a sandwich. Jack accepted the food and ate steadily.

"You can't protect everyone."

"I just never thought I would have to deal with anything like this. Not in this town, you know?"

Ivas poured a second glass and drank the milk deeply. When he lowered his glass, he saw that Jack was close to tears. He had removed his glasses and was clutching his sandwich so tight the bread was torn.

"Jack, do you remember that time I disappeared? When we were kids?"

Jack took a moment to answer, trying to steady his voice. "When you first moved here."

"That's right. It was right after my grandpa died and I had run away because I thought something bad would happen."

No.

"I thought the lawyers and social workers would come back and take me away."

That's not it.

"I had forgotten," Jack said. "You were gone too. For a day…"

"Three days."

The fog.

"I hid out for three days before it started raining and I had to go back to the cottage."

Jack stared at him. "Tess's place. You hid at Tess's special place."

"You remember."

"I'm sorry, it just took me a minute. Wow, three days. We were only seventeen." Jack chuckled. "I remember now. I had to go to the ruins, that old staircase, and leave food for you. We made a big deal about it, like it was a secret mission."

"But it was all okay in the end, right? I didn't have to leave, all that ruckus for nothing."

Jack smiled. "Thanks, Ivas."

"We'll get through this, too."

Jack nodded and heaved a heavy sigh. "Then I guess I'd better get back to work. Thanks for the sandwich."

"No problem." Ivas snatched an apple off the counter and tossed it at Jack. The sheriff juggled it in the air haphazardly before getting a grip. "Save that for later."

"Thanks. Oh, don't forget about the search party."

"What time is that?"

"The Mclaven's and their family are already searching, but everyone is meeting at the crack of dawn tomorrow morning for a formal search."

Ivas walked Jack out and the two men parted ways again. Blanc chased his car away, and the sheep watched curiously from the field.

Ivas felt suddenly drained, tired, yet not sleepy. Between the bike ride and the drama of small-town life, he felt as if all the energy had been taken from him, and there was nothing to do but wait for it to come back. He decided to let Blanc inside again, not wanting to be alone, and finally forced himself to eat some lunch.

His home was still in disarray from Hannah Mclaven's search, and he found himself wandering about, studying the items that had been knocked from their place. A lot of it was stuff that had been stored away for so many years he had forgotten it even existed. In his bedroom there was a shoebox that had been pulled out from under his bed, the lid thrown aside. Inside was an assortment of items: dried-up bay leaves, small rocks, coins, keys that didn't go to anything. Ivas had forgotten about the box. It held a collection from his childhood. It seemed so important back then.

Ivas shook his head as if to dislodge a thought. He pushed the box back under the bed with his foot and quickly walked away.

Back in the living room, most of the books had fallen from the shelf as Hannah had pulled it away from the wall. Perhaps she expected to find a hidden doorway there. He picked them up absentmindedly—dictionaries and almanacs mostly. Ivas wasn't much of a reader aside from the books required at school, most of which had been depressing tales of people long since gone. This was what he assumed most books to be, so he stayed away from them.

There was one work of fiction in his arsenal that Ivas had forgotten about until he found it on the floor. He didn't know the name of the book. The cover and first few pages had been lost, fallen from their spine like autumn leaves. The rest was soon to follow, the remaining pages clinging to the string that sewed them together. Ivas knew if he tried reading the book it would probably fall apart, its very purpose destroying it. The book had been his grandfather's, who had probably found it at a library sale. It was the only book Ivas could remember him reading.

The scent of the old pages stirred Ivas's memory, taking

him back to his childhood when he had sat on his grandpa's lap, listening to him read the story. Ivas remembered now. It was when he had first moved in and couldn't sleep. He had horrible nightmares. So Grandpa, who didn't know any stories or songs himself, read this one.

Ivas found himself sitting, sprawled-legged on the floor, staring at the novel, and his throat was swelling with the chore of holding back tears.

You know...

Grandpa didn't die lying on a hill, and Ivas had not hidden out in Floborough Deep for three days. The day Grandpa died had actually been a foggy night.

The nightmare...

Yes, Ivas's nightmare.

Suddenly, it was back, the memory charging in so hard Ivas cried out and Blanc came to his side. Ivas clutched his hair because he needed something to hang onto. The tears were streaming now, and he was gasping for air. Ivas stumbled to his hands and knees, scrambling to get outside. He had to run.

He slammed the door shut so that Blanc wouldn't follow him and ran. The sheep looked up in concern as he ran, sobbing now. He ran until the house was far away and the only sound was the win, and all he could see was the nothingness of the countryside. One of the little stone walls appeared and he tried to jump it, but stumbled forward, hitting the grass.

He stayed there, burying his face in the cool crunch of the leaves that had fallen there.

He remembered where he had seen the creature, why it haunted his memory. The time when he had first come to Loch Lamond. The time with no names or faces now returning, gushing in like water through a crack in a ship. Ivas could only lie there and sink.

CHAPTER 6

THE SHEPHERD REMEMBERS

Ivas's parents were dead, and he was to live with his grandfather. Grandpa wasn't a stranger. They had visited the old man often, and he even gave fairly good presents, but he suddenly seemed like a stranger to little Ivas, someone permanent who would have to care for him and discipline him. Even in the days to come, Ivas knew that that was the most scared he had ever been, and ever would be.

Grandfather's solution to Ivas's grief was to keep him busy with work, and Ivas accepted this because as long as he was doing something he wasn't missing his parents as much. He followed Grandpa around the farm, helping him with chores, and cleaning the house. He fell in love with the friendly Valis Blacknose who knocked him down with greetings. Grandpa also had a pure white Berger Blanc Suisse dog, though Ivas was warned that she was strictly a working dog and not for playing.

That changed when she had puppies. But that was later.

"Don't go out into the fog at night," Grandpa had warned. "It's full of all sorts of ghastly things."

But for Ivas, who had grown up in the city, Grandpa's warning felt like an invitation. It wasn't only farm work that Ivas used to deal with his grief. Out in the countryside of Loch Lamond, the air shivered with possibilities and hummed with thousands of stories—legends of fairies, monsters on the moor, hidden treasure lost by a sunken ship waiting to be found on one of the many adjacent islands. There was a dead circle of grass where nothing grew. It was said to be a portal to another world. Ivas drank it all up, listening to Old Popper's stories at Halloween time, learning all about the local legends. There were even rumors of a witch living in the village. Out on the moors, in the ancient cemetery, off the seaside cliffs, and in the shadowy forests, it all seemed possible. Every story felt absolutely true.

Ivas wanted it to be true. He even went to the dead circle and tried to cross through the portal but did not succeed. His friends told him that it had to be done at midnight during a certain moon, and even Ivas wasn't willing to go out in the wilderness at that hour. Ivas wanted it to be true, wanted his life to be more than dead parents and a sheep farm. He wanted magic.

He had also taken to collecting things. It started with the gathering song, when he would keep bay leaves and cloves of garlic. He found other things like four-leaf clovers and animal-shaped rocks. Old coins and shiny quartz. He started saving these in a box under his bed in case any had magical properties that could help him.

The fog was the most promising lead he had. Even the adults took the fog seriously. His grandpa taught him the gathering song so that Ivas knew which herbs he needed to protect the house. The fog didn't come every night of course —sometimes it wouldn't show up for months—but when it did, they doused every light, even the one in a person's heart.

That's when the nightmares came. At least, Ivas had

thought them to be nightmares, had tricked himself into thinking that's all it was. When the fog rolled in, a creature in a cloak with large spider legs would come to his window and tap on the glass.

Ivas was afraid at first. He would go to his grandpa's room to hide. His grandpa was patient, telling him there was nothing to fear. That the things in the fog couldn't come inside; they didn't like the light. He would turn on the lights and whisper to him that everything was alright, that it was just a nightmare.

Of course, it wasn't. Ivas sobbed into the leaves, choking on them. It had come for him, just as it came for Ruby.

And Ivas had opened the door.

After the first initial shock, Ivas had felt drawn to the Messenger, as if a familiar voice was calling for him to come outside.

The bells. The sound of the bells...

And Ivas, who was so eager for the promise of the paranormal, went to the door.

"Stay here. Don't go out into the mist," his grandpa had said.

"But something's out there." Ivas took the doorknob in his hand.

"Ivas, stop!"

"I have to see what it wants. It's been watching me."

So, his grandpa found the pistol that he owned strictly for keeping wolves away from his sheep. He didn't like to use it, and wouldn't if he could avoid it.

"Then take my hand. We'll go out together."

He had clutched Grandpa's wrist tightly with both hands as the two of them stepped out the door. The fog enveloped them immediately. Only three steps away, Ivas lost sight of the cottage. There were no sounds, was no movement. Ivas realized that the thing could be standing right in front of them and they wouldn't know. He tried to find it, but the Messenger was gone.

"Let's go back," he begged.

"This is the fog, Ivas. Do you understand now?"

"Yes, yes. I want to go…"

"This is what it does. It gets inside you, makes you afraid of all the things you do not know."

Grandpa looked down at his pistol and tossed it away. It was as if it had never existed.

"Grandpa, I want to go home."

"Then go, find it if you can." Grandpa pulled his hand away, and Ivas started to scream.

"Don't!"

"I can't go with you, Love." He sounded truly melancholy by that fact, but held by it.

"What do you mean? It's right here…" Ivas stepped back, arms outstretched, reaching for the door he knew was right behind him. They hadn't even left the stoop. And yet the air remained empty. Ivas couldn't even feel the entryway under his feet. And now those three steps had cost him again.

Grandpa was gone.

Ivas began to scream for him, stumbling around blindly. There was nothing in the fog but him.

And then there was something in the fog, and Ivas wished he was alone again.

A shadow appeared, briefly, in the shape of the cloaked creature that had haunted his window. Ivas saw it and ran the other way, his screams taken from him.

Into the fog he ran.

~

*I*vas lifted himself from the ground, worn out. The sun was setting and he had to get back home, had to put the sheep away.

Ivas limped back over the countryside. It seemed a much farther walk now, and his ankle complained from the earlier mistreatment.

Remember...

"No," Ivas whispered to himself.

Remember...

"If I remember, I'll never go back."

His farm came into view. He could hear Blanc's whines as he approached the front door and quickly let her out. She wagged her tail at him happily, immediately forgiving him.

"Sorry, Blanc," he said, rubbing her pointed ears. "Come on, we've got work to do."

They gathered up the sheep. Blanc was flawless, rounding them up to Ivas's commands, and the sheep were obedient, filing back into the barn. Ivas made sure Little Lost was present, then locked up the barn. Then he sat on the fence and watched the horizon.

The fog crawled in from the sea, climbing up the cliffs and rolling onto land. In Loch Lamond, doors were shut and windows were locked. No one was taking chances this night. Except for Ivas, who watched it come. The fog came in low, creeping along the ground, but it would rise as the sun set. Ivas only had a short amount of daylight left.

He pushed himself off the fence. Blanc watched, confused but ready.

"Let's take a walk, Blanc."

Ivas went to the house and found his cane. Already the chill of night was taking the place of warm autumn sun, and Ivas began searching for something warm to wear. Stored away in the same place he had found the cane was more of his grandfather's belongings, one of which was an old serape made of the very wool that came from the Valis Blacknose. It was incredibly warm, and Ivas wrapped it around himself, securing it in place with a large button on the shoulder. He expected to be hit with the scent of his grandfather, but years of storage had given the garment an antique-ish smell.

Ivas packed a knapsack with a flashlight, a large kitchen knife for defense, and food, then stepped outside into the twilight where Blanc waited.

Ivas walked as quickly as he could, wanting to get to the Mclaven farm before the rest of the dark fell into place. Blanc jogged along ahead of him, seeming to know where they were headed. The fog was overtaking him, and Ivas turned on his flashlight, though the light bounced against the whiteness, almost useless.

Of course, he couldn't outrace the dark, and by the time they reached the Mclaven's, the fog had settled in. Ivas was almost on top of the house before he saw the porch light. He scanned the windows briefly, but no one was there. He suspected that Hannah was still out looking or staying with a friend.

Ivas went to his knees in front of the door—the very spot the messenger had stood—and called Blanc to him. She waited hopefully as Ivas reached into his pocket and presented her with the red ribbon.

Blanc sniffed at the silky fabric, then her nosed darted to the ground, sniffing about the front steps. Ivas nodded encouragingly. After a moment of deciding, Blanc found a trail and began to follow it, and Ivas followed her.

It wouldn't work in the day. There are no monsters in the closet when the sun is up, no witches at high noon. Some things could only be found in the fog. Ivas had driven away the memory of what these things were, but they had not forgotten him.

CHAPTER 7

THE SHEPHERD GOES INTO THE FOG

What time was it here? And how long did they walk? Ivas could only follow Blanc, seeing only her fluffy white tail floating ahead of him at the end of his flashlight beam. The fog was so thick he could push it around him like water. It rippled and wafted from his fingers.

You know what waits here...

Ivas pushed those feelings away and kept walking, eyes on that fluffy white tail that had never failed him before. He told himself not to think about it, to just walk, and walk, and eventually he would get somewhere.

Blanc stopped and whimpered, but it wasn't her successful whine that said she found something. Something else was here. Ivas quickly put his hand on Blanc's back to comfort her.

"That'll do, Blanc. Easy." His voice trembled like his hand. He slowly went to his knees as the will slipped out of them. He could hear it now, something walking toward them. Each footstep felt like it stepped on his heart, and Ivas wrapped his arms around Blanc and shut his eyes tight.

"Sbarge's kid," a voice said.

Ivas gasped and almost ran, snapping his eyes open. He fell back and Blanc straightened up, growling a warning.

It was Old Popper.

But…it wasn't. It couldn't be.

"I didn't tell you the whole story." The old storyteller seemed sad. Ivas struggled to catch his breath and got to his feet again.

"Is that you? Is the fog tricking me?"

"It's full of tricks, but none so cunning as the ones your brain plays on you."

"What are you doing here?"

"The story, there's more to it."

"What is it? Are you trying to warn me? Have you seen the girl?" Ivas was having trouble concentrating on just one problem. Old Popper looked at him with large, sympathetic eyes.

"Oh, Ivas, you're still just a boy, lost in the fog."

Then Ivas snapped. "No! I'm doing it right this time." He held out the ribbon determinedly. "This one…not this one."

Old Popper sighed then walked away, immediately disappearing. Ivas didn't call after or try to follow. He gave the ribbon to Blanc again. "Find her, Blanc. You can do it. We can't let the fog stop us."

Blanc sniffed, made a circle around them with her nose pressed to the ground, and relocated the trail.

And so, they walked.

And Ivas started to hear things.

He hugged himself, clutching his forearms in a tight grip. He kept his eyes locked on Blanc while the sounds of scurries and footsteps mocked him from both sides, daring him to turn his head and look away, just for a second.

Don't look. Don't look…

His breath came in short, sharp gasps.

Don't stop. Don't stop...

He could practically feel the movement, as if it was creeping along his skin. There was a sudden thump that made him cry out, then the horrifying sound of something behind him, following. Tears came to his eyes.

But Blanc kept moving forward, no barking or even a perk of her triangle ears, as if nothing was there.

Nothing *was* there.

Ivas slowly lowered his arms, turning his hands to fists instead. He kept his eyes straight ahead, still not daring to look away from Blanc.

There was a rumbling, like thunder, and this time Blanc stopped and turned her head.

"Don't look, Blanc. Keep on the trail."

After a moment, Blanc obeyed. The rumbling continued, soft and far away.

"Just keep going." His voice came out in a frightened whisper.

Suddenly, Ivas was struck from the side. He felt a large mass plummet into his ribs and he toppled over, rolling through the dew-covered grass. The flashlight fell from his hand and rolled away.

"Blanc!" He called for her, trying to maintain his sense of direction while also fighting off whatever had struck him. Ivas threw his fists, but after a moment found that there was nothing there.

"Blanc! Here!"

He sat there, waiting for his dog to come, but she did not. He couldn't even see the light of his flashlight. Ivas felt as if he were shrinking in on himself, becoming a child again. He hugged his knees and fought tears.

He was alone now. He never really realized what that word meant until that moment. It was like the sound of a music box. Worse than being in a crowd where no one sees you. He was like all the other forgotten things, left in the fog.

~

"What are you doing here?"

The shepherd screamed and covered his head in response, trembling uncontrollably. He wished he had a blanket to hide under as it seemed the only appropriate response. The voice that spoke belonged to something very large. The sound was so big that it seemed to encase Ivas. A voice like that… There was no running, only hoping that it would not see you.

"You who cowers yet braves the mist, what are you doing here?"

"Leave me alone!"

"You did not come here for no reason. Everything enters for a reason, yet you seem like someone who is lost."

"No, I'm not lost." Ivas finally found the nerve to speak but did not move. "It's everyone else that is lost."

"So, you are here seeking something."

The voice, though big, seemed more gentle now, and Ivas risked raising his head. The fog swirled about but had retreated, allowing Ivas to see a little.

"Y…yes."

He could see the black shape of something moving about, circling him, with no distinguishable features, only that it was large. So very overwhelmingly big that Ivas couldn't stand it.

"Who are you?" Ivas asked.

"A lost thing. Something hidden away. But *you* can see me."

"No!"

Something came for him, shooting out of the fog and

rushing toward him. Ivas screamed and turned to scramble away. He felt large fingers grasp and wrap around his little body. The fingers bound him and lifted him off the ground. Ivas closed his eyes.

"Open your eyes."

"No!"

"What are you afraid you'll see?"

"Let me go! I have to find her! I have to find the girl!"

The thing hesitated. Its grip loosened and Ivas wiggled one of his arms free so he could hang onto the large hand that bound him.

Carefully, slowly, he opened his eyes.

Some of the fog had cleared, and he saw he was only a few feet off the ground. The thing that held him was lying down. He could see its arm disappear into the fog, through which he could barely make out a face looking down at him. Its eyes glowed like lighthouses. The rest was shadow.

"Can you see?" the thing asked.

"I-I-I can't see anything in this fog; it's too dark."

The thing opened its hand so that Ivas sat in its palm. He looked up at its face now, drawn by the glow of its eyes.

"I have learned to see," it said.

"Who are you?"

"I have never needed to call myself anything."

"Then, do you know what this place is?"

"This place? It is a fog of breath on a cold day—full of what is unspoken and what is constantly told. A place where some things hide and some things get lost. It is full of things no one remembers, and things no one can forget."

"And...you are a lost thing?"

"I'm only lost if someone is trying to find me. I don't think I am lost anymore."

"How did you end up here, in this place?"

The giant didn't answer, but it stared at Ivas, as if it had never seen anything so remarkable. Ivas felt himself turn red and looked away, burdened by its gaze.

"You are looking for someone lost," it said instead.

"Yes, a girl with red hair."

He saw movement as the giant's other hand went to its face and plucked one of the lights from its head. Ivas gasped and backed away, but the thing held it out to him, and Ivas saw it was only a lantern.

"Take one of my eyes, then."

Ivas carefully did so. It seemed like a normal, old-fashioned lantern with a beam of blue light falling out of its port. The thing turned its hand and Ivas slid off, back to the ground.

"I want something in return, a trade, something I'll return when you find your way back to me."

Ivas looked down at himself, trying to think of what he had that would be of value.

"I want your fear, traveler. I see it is a heavy burden on you. I shall keep it until you return my eye."

"M-m-my fear?"

"You will miss it more than you think."

The giant hand reached for him and Ivas flinched away, expecting pain. Two fingers touched the top of his head and Ivas felt a distinct tugging, as if the creature were pulling out his hair. It yanked, and Ivas felt something come loose. He cried out, more in surprise than pain, and saw that the creature held a small squirming thing between its fingers. Before Ivas could make out details, the thing cupped the fear in its hand and pulled it away.

"Until then, traveler."

The giant rose—Ivas could hear it all around him—and the fog consumed it, wrapping around the creature and filling in the shadows it left behind. Ivas was alone, holding his lantern and feeling oddly empty. It was not as if his fear had been replaced with bravery, only that it had been taken away with a hole in its place.

His tears dried and his trembling stopped. Ivas found that he could face the fog without any of the dread. It was a relief, but also left him with a terrible longing. The giant was right, he did miss the fear. Without it, the rest of his mind was left dangling, as if a hole had been punched in a spider's web and the strands were no longer connected properly. It was hard to be happy without the contrast of fear. It was hard to be sad without the motivation of fear, and his anger seemed to have dissipated entirely with nothing to fuel it. Ivas found that he wanted his fear back very badly, but he needed the creature's eye, and it was right about it being a burden. For now, he walked quickly and determinedly. There were no sounds or shadows playing tricks on him. Ivas only concentrated on what he had to do.

The lantern light cut through the fog nicely. Ivas could now see several feet ahead of himself. He walked quickly, sending out whistles into the night, trying to call Blanc. Without his fear, he didn't consider what else his whistles could be calling.

~

As he walked, the lantern began to reveal things Ivas didn't recognize. Trees sprouted up from the fog, suddenly appearing, then being swallowed up by the white as he passed. These trees were naked and had large, twisted roots. They all seemed dead and ready to collapse. Things were looking at him from the trees. He could see their eyes flash, but they did not bother him.

He heard a sound and stopped so that his footsteps wouldn't interfere. He trained his ears carefully, and the sound came again. Some strange echo that he couldn't identify. At first, he thought it was Blanc's barking, then maybe the cry of a girl. Ivas followed the noise, trying to get closer so he could make it out. As he walked, the noise didn't become any clearer. He wondered if he was imagining it right as he stepped into air and began to fall.

Ivas cried out in surprise and a nauseating jolt shot up through his stomach as he fell. Half his body went down, but the other stayed on solid ground. Ivas grabbed hold of the grass and rocks and quickly rolled himself away from whatever he had fallen over. After catching his breath, Ivas stood and used the lantern to see what had happened.

The light revealed a long cliff edge, beyond which lay the ocean. He could hear the water now, echoing up at him, full of sounds that his mind had been fooled by.

It had tricked him, the fog. Ivas looked behind and saw that, indeed, the trees that had made him think he had entered the woods were gone. These were the long, empty cliffs of the island, and he had almost fallen over them.

Had that been Ruby's fate? The stories said that the fog liked to keep those that wandered into it. Ivas began to finally realize that it was already too late. If the fog had taken Ruby the night before, then she was probably lost forever. When the sun rose, would he disappear with the fog as well?

Feeling the hopelessness of his situation, Ivas turned away and started walking along the cliffside. At least this way he knew where he was.

Ivas wished he had his fear back. It was better to be afraid than to feel like this. He stopped for a moment and looked out to where the sea was, wondering when the sun would come up. *If* it would ever come up.

For a moment, Ivas just stood there, hands hanging at his sides. His fingers went loose and the lantern slid from them, touching the ground with a thump.

Autumn beckons me. The sea winds blow...

Ivas stepped forward. He could feel where the ground fell away at the tips of his toes. Down below, the waves whispered.

I must go to her, to the cliffsides, and tell her my woe...

Without his fear, death seemed like an easy companion. Ivas needed something more than the fear to keep the feelings at bay.

"Ruby might still be out there," he whispered to himself, "just like..."

Grandpa.

And then, without the fear to hold it back, the rest of that night reappeared in Ivas's memory, and that was reason enough.

~

Little Ivas, only a lad of seventeen, ran into the fog. Lost from his grandfather, fleeing the cloaked figure that had been coming to his window. That haunted his nightmares.

But there had been a worse monster in the fog that night.

A worse monster—

"Come here, little boy..."

~

Ivas heard the clink of metal and spun around. The rocks loosened under his feet from the abrupt movement. He saw a claw reaching for his lantern, so with a shout he lunged forward and grabbed it back.

A chuckle echoed back at him from the fog and a voice spoke.

"I remember you, little boy."

Come here, little boy...

"You've come back to me."

I've come for you.

Because he had no fear, Ivas shined his lantern on the creature. The light glinted off its white teeth, which grinned at him. It shined on its sparkling eyes and revealed a body that resided in the nightmares of children—a twisted, writhing thing with skin that looked like a mixture of tree bark and sharp spikes of fur.

As a boy, it had found Ivas in the fog and pinned him down like a cat playing with a mouse. It laughed every time Ivas had screamed and would let him get away for another chase.

This time, when Ivas did not react appropriately frightened, the creature frowned. "Not a little boy now, no. Not little. Where did your fear go, boy?"

Then it grinned again. "I'll just have to put some back in you."

It struck, darting at Ivas with remarkable speed. Ivas watched it come and held up his lantern so that the light shined directly into the monster's eyes. He saw it wince and took his chance, dropping the lantern and ducking to the side so that the creature stumbled past him, its vision compromised by the excess of light and dark.

Ivas thought back, remembering how he had escaped last time.

The place...

He charged forward and slammed his body into the monster's side so that it tumbled back to the edge of the cliff.

Tess's magical place...

The thing raised its arm and shoved Ivas off. Ivas felt his feet leave the ground for a second before he struck the earth again. He laid down on the ground and remained still.

The monster found its bearings, and Ivas heard stones

from the cliffside fall away into the ocean. He had been so close. His lantern lay several feet away, tipped on its side.

"The dark won't hide you from me," the creature warned. "My eyes know only darkness."

Ivas remained still. He could possibly outrun it, but not without leaving the lantern behind. Fighting it would mean losing. Without his fear there was no panic, only that sinking hopelessness coming back into his heart.

The creature was coming upon him, chuckling to itself, happy to see its prey cowering on the ground.

"That's better," it purred. It pounced on Ivas, whipping him over onto his back. Ivas cried out and tried to scramble away. It pinned down his chest, laughing. Ivas fought back, throwing a punch at its head, but the thing pulled away. Instead, Ivas wrapped his arms around its legs and shoved it over.

It fell, and Ivas jumped to his feet, running for the lantern. Something hit him harshly in the back, sending Ivas to his stomach again. The thing laughed gleefully. Ivas felt its foot grind down into the small of his back, and he cried out in pain.

And because he had no fear, Ivas said, "Do it, you useless creature. Finish what you started years ago." And he found that he meant it.

The creature laughed through its teeth. "Do what? Kill you? But dead things don't scream, don't run. The fog is so still, but you are full of life. Fight for it, boy."

It tossed Ivas over so that he looked up at it.

Fight...

It grabbed his leg in its teeth and dragged him across the grass toward the cliffside.

But nothing hurts...

It lifted Ivas up and held him over the cliff so that Ivas dangled above the night-covered ocean.

It never hurt...

When Ivas didn't scream or struggle, the monster gave him a frustrated shake.

"If you drop me there won't even be a body to play with," Ivas said.

Defeated, the monster tossed him back to the land. Ivas pushed himself to his feet and glared at the monster.

"Can you even hurt me?"

The thing glared back at him and with a loud, angry roar, it struck Ivas in the head, sending him sprawling. Ivas clamored to his feet and ran for the lantern.

"You are mine, boy. I'll keep you in the fog for as long as it takes. You will fear me."

Ivas heard it running toward him, felt its teeth wrapping around his waist as he picked up the lantern and shined it in the thing's eyes. The monster dropped him and backed away, suddenly realizing…

"The eye."

Ivas held the lantern high, letting it dangle over his head. The monster sulked away, but Ivas saw it smirk in the shadows the lantern left behind.

"Not all light is salvation," it said.

Ivas turned away, back to the fog.

"Did you not hear me, boy?"

Ivas heard its feet galloping toward him. No time to turn, no time to run.

"You belong to me!"

Ivas stiffened, waiting for the connection, but nothing touched him. A horrible sound took place instead, filling the fog with a terrible racket. A tearing, snarling noise. Ivas turned and saw a ghost upon the black monster.

No...

Blood appeared on the white, and it seemed less like an actual physical being than a ball of fury and growls, but under it all, Ivas saw Blanc, consumed by her animal instinct to kill and protect. It would have frightened Ivas to see her that way if he could have felt such a thing. Her white fur stood up to a point, her triangle ears flat against her head, and her eyes black. Blood stained her teeth and mussel.

The monster was not accustomed to such fearlessness, and when it was finally able to tear itself out of Blanc's jaws, it fled. Blanc went after it.

"Blanc! Come!"

Ivas held her in the beam of the lantern before the mist could take her again. Blanc stopped, and slowly her fur went down, her ears went up, and her growls faded away. When she turned back to Ivas, she was the kind sheep-herder again, eyes friendly and tail wagging.

Ivas went to his knees and put his arms around her, burying his face in her fur. He wished he could feel afraid so that he could have relief now and feel the full effects of gratitude that Blanc deserved. Still, something burned inside him, casting out the hopelessness. Something stronger than the fear that the giant had not taken

"You sweet girl."

She licked his ear and ran her nose through his hair, sniffing about fondly. Then she stopped, and Ivas felt her body stiffen.

He let her go and turned, first seeing a set of thin, spider-like legs, which disappeared into a tattered cloak. The sound of bells filled up the fog.

The messenger...

Ivas stared up at the creature. It towered over him, staring down from the shadows of its hood. Ivas couldn't see its face, but he felt it looking at him.

Messenger for the dead...

It was just as the night before, a bag of letters strapped to its side, bells tied about its legs, whispering softly in the fog.

Ivas remained on the ground, caged by its legs. Even without his fear, it took a moment to find the words.

"Where is… Please, I have to find the girl. You gave her a message. The girl with red hair."

The messenger came forward, walking straight over Ivas. Its cloak billowed around him in a tent as it walked over him. Ivas stood once it had passed and retrieved the lantern. Blanc stood at his side, and the two followed the messenger into the fog without word or sign that it intended to help them.

~

*H*ow long did they walk? There was no time here. Ivas was sure that the sun must have risen and he had disappeared along with the fog.

He and Blanc followed the Messenger, who stood out among the mist. Wisps of white fled its step, giving brief clearing to their journey. Ivas recognized things like grass and trees as they passed, grateful to see shapes in such a blurred world. His lantern aided the clarity even more, placing light in the dark.

"Can you understand me?" Ivas asked, overwhelmed by curiosity. "Can you speak?"

The creature did not answer. Ivas watched its strange, pointed legs carry it with grace, the soft whisper of bells filling each step. Its cloak was so worn out and discolored that it rippled and flowed like silk yet kept the rest of the Messenger hidden from sight.

Ivas jogged ahead, catching up with the Messenger so that they walked side by side. Ivas peered up at the strange being, holding his lantern aloft to try and catch a glimpse of what was under the hood. Without fear, the curiosity was in control. The Messenger didn't seem offended as Ivas took a closer look.

From the depths of the hood something flashed, like the reflection of animal eyes, and something inside Ivas, something stronger than fear—survival instinct, perhaps—made him lower the lantern again.

The Messenger stopped and Ivas looked around, piercing through the fog with the lantern. He could see trees. The glimpses of autumn colors were startling in the night. His foot splashed in a pool of water.

"I know this place," Ivas said.

It was Floborough Deep, Tess's special place. A place to hide, to be safe.

Promise me...

Ivas made circles, spinning the light around and around.

Don't let them take me away...

The light fell on a set of stone steps and Ivas froze.

Them.

He went to the stairs and tested his foot on the stone. It seemed solid enough. He looked at the Messenger, seeking a sign of confirmation, but the supernatural postman remained stubbornly mute.

This is where she found you.

Ivas remembered now. After escaping the creature, this was where Jack and Tess had found him three days later. Floborough Deep, a place of poetry, of safety, where Tess swore she could feel something, everything, like a heartbeat.

Ivas raised the lantern above his head, lighting up the spiraling staircase in front of him, and started to ascend. Blanc and the Messenger remained behind.

In the daylight, the stairs were only a story tall, but Ivas felt he was climbing much higher.

Then, suddenly, the fog cleared.

Ivas gasped at the sudden change. Suddenly, his lantern

shined bright, and the constant feeling of whiteness, as if he were walking through a wall, was lifted.

He was on top of the fog. All around him, the mist flowed out like an ocean, as if he were sitting in the clouds. Up above, the sky was black and full of stars. Ivas could have been above the clouds themselves, a hundred feet in the sky. He breathed in the air, untainted by humidity. It was that perfect crispness that comes with an autumn day. Breathing in was like taking a bite of a fresh apple.

He stood on a small island of stone, the top of the staircase where a small bit of the second floor still remained.

Someone else was there as well.

At first, he thought it was another creature. It had sharp horns, like deer antlers on its head, and claws coming out of its fingertips. When it heard him arrive, it turned its head and he saw animal eyes glowing yellow.

But a familiar head of red hair was tangled in the antlers, and surrounding the frightening eyes was the soft face of a girl, still plump with adolescence. She wore an oversized brown sweater and a long wool skirt.

"Ruby," Ivas said gently. He set the lantern down. It glowed comfortably like a fireplace. "Are you all right?"

She stared at him and bared her teeth, showing off fangs. "Stay away."

Ivas took a step forward. "I'm here to help you."

"You're just another monster," Ruby hissed, "the fog trying to trick me."

"…You may be right," he confessed, "but I'm not here to hurt you. Don't you want to go home?"

"No, I haven't found him yet."

"Found who?" Ivas approached her. Ruby backed away until her feet touched the edge of the ruins. She put herself on all fours and growled like an animal. For a moment, Ivas only saw horns and teeth and animal eyes.

"Stay away from me!"

Ivas sank to his knees in front of her and took her clawed hands. At his touch, Ruby sank to her knees as well, her body dripping like a candle. Ivas saw a flash of light in her eyes as tears coated them. He gripped her hands tight.

"Did the fog do this to you?"

"No," her voiced rasped, as if she had just woken up. "I wished for it."

She held up her claws, showing them off. They were sharp and shiny against her still-human hands.

"I wished for horns and claws. I wished for fangs and strength. I wanted to be scarier than the things that scared me."

Scarier...

Ivas squeezed her hands tightly. "You don't need these, Ruby. You shouldn't even be here. Did the Messenger take you?"

She finally looked him in the eye. "No... That is, I went into the fog myself. He showed me this place when I became lost."

"Why did you come here?" Ivas's brow wrinkled, finding the idea inconceivable. "What would possibly..."

She reached into her pocket and pulled out the scroll, the one the Messenger had delivered to her.

"It's from my father."

The boat disappeared...

"He disappeared last month. He went out on his boat and never came back. But this letter...it's from him."

Her hand started to tremble as she looked at the scroll. "It's his handwriting, his signature."

"What does it say?"

Ruby swallowed. Her voice was heavy and cracking, like ice with too much weight. "It says... He said...to run."

"To run?"

"Run as far from the fog as you can. Because something is coming, and it knows how to keep people here. It knows how to find the lost things and make them its own. But you won't die, because even death can't find you in the fog. Dad can't die."

She tightened her fist, crumpling up the letter. "My dad is stuck in here somewhere. He's trapped."

"Can I see?" Ivas opened his hand for the letter. Ruby passed it over, but when Ivas unrolled it, he saw only a blank page.

"There's nothing here."

Ruby looked again. "Maybe only I can read it since it's for me."

Do you hear...

He handed it back to her. "What's coming, Ruby?"

She read her letter, the last words from her father. "All it says is...run. It's coming. It has taken me. It hides in the fog."

...the thunder?

"It will consume all in the fog."

I hear...

"Run, Pumpkin—" At the familiar pet name, her tears fell. "There is no lightning in the fog."

Ivas frowned. "No lightning?"

...hear...

"What does that mean?"

"There's no thunder without lightning," Ruby said.

"But...I can hear the—"

Something rose out of the fog just then, like a mountain in the shape of a man. Tendrils of mist rolled off its body like beads of water. Ivas recognized the single glowing eye staring at them. He turned his head to look at the lantern, which blinked.

"You were watching..."

He couldn't see, but he could practically feel the giant

smirking with triumph. "Why take one when I can have two?"

It reached over their heads—its giant hand like a storm cloud covering the stars—and plucked back its eye, placing the lantern in its head. With its other hand it snatched up Ivas, giant fingers binding his body.

"And for you, I have a gift." A cruel smile plagued its dark face, and it held up a squirming worm-like thing between its fingers. Ivas only watched without conviction as the giant placed the fear back into his head.

He could feel it crawling through him, into his ear, up his nose, even his eyes. The rush of terror was overwhelming. Every tremble that had been waiting in his bones, every scream that hadn't left his lungs, all the fear from what he had encountered, suddenly rose, and Ivas began to scream, thrashing in the thing's hand, tears streaming down his cheeks. There was no room for rational thought, only panic, and the need to run.

The giant laughed, its voice rolling over the fog like distant thunder. It looked down at Ruby, who stood up, feeling her claws lengthen and her horns grow. The fog curled up at her feet.

"Stay away from me."

"I'll take you while there is still you left to be had," the giant rumbled. His free hand came for her. Ruby looked to Ivas, but he was too distressed to be of any help. With no other choice, she turned and ran, reentering the fog as she galloped down the spiral stairway, going at a momentum that threatened to send her tumbling.

At the bottom, she hit the ground running and did not stop. She heard a dog barking but could not see anything. She was at the mercy of the fog now. Thunder crashed all around her as the giant pursued. Looking over her shoulder, she could see the glow of its eyes above.

"Why did you come here, little one? Were you not looking for me?"

"Stay away!" Ruby screamed before realizing the risk in such an error. Taking a different strategy, she darted to the side and dived onto her stomach, hoping that perhaps the giant would miss her. She lay still on the ground.

"Everything enters for a reason."

Ruby risked looking up. She could see the giant, standing so tall its shoulders disappeared out of view, but its back was to her.

"Do you seek something?"

"Don't listen to it!" Ruby heard Ivas's voice echo down. "He just wants more!" A cry of pain cut off his warning.

"Come out, little one. I know what you seek."

Ruby looked about the fog, hoping to see the familiar shadow of the messenger. It had found her when she first entered the fog and had acted as a guide, taking her to the safety of the stairway. But now, Ruby could feel the power of the fog beckoning her. She had her horns and claws, which she dug into the soft earth. She could hear Ivas's cries from high above, his pleads to be released, and somewhere she heard her father's voice too. Lost and alone.

But she was here.

She was scary too.

Ruby felt it before she saw it, the giant hand reaching down for her. Its lantern eyes had seen her through the dark. Ruby didn't run. She rose and raised her arm in a blocking stance, seizing the giant's wrist.

Except it wasn't a giant anymore. Whether Ruby had become larger or it had become smaller, she wasn't sure. But now they stood at the same height, and Ruby stared at it with yellow, inhuman eyes. She dug her claws into its skin and bared her fangs.

"Where is the other human?" she demanded in a voice that wasn't quite hers.

The glow of its eyes narrowed. "The fog is vast. If you let it, it will swallow everything."

She struck it with her other hand, claws gashing against its flesh, and the monster tumbled back, making the ground quake as it landed.

"Give the man to me."

"The fog is but the cold breath of a god. Just wait until the rest of that god catches up."

The giant turned away from her, trying to slip away, and Ruby could see that it still held Ivas in its hands, like a child clutching a favorite toy. She grabbed its wrists and twisted until the thing gave in and dropped the shepherd. Ruby pressed her horns to the giant's skull, temped to push them in, but the part of her that wasn't scarier than the monsters shied away from such an act and she shoved it away instead, letting it disappear into the fog.

Ruby spotted Ivas on the ground—she found it was getting easier to see—and scooped him up in her hands. He was tiny now, trembling, and full of heat and sweat despite the cold night. Ruby found herself hanging onto him. There was something warm and soothing about him. She wanted to eat him and care for him at the same time. She felt at odds, yet strangely comforted.

Ivas looked up at her and touched her thumb between his hands.

"R-Ruby, it's okay now. I found you. You're not lost anymore. I came here looking for *you*."

She stared at him with yellow eyes. "But...Dad's still in here. I made the monster go away. I can save him."

"You can, but not like this. It's time to go home."

She shook her head. "Not without Daddy."

Daddy. The word seemed so silly, yet it slipped from her

lips as if desperate to remind her of something. "He's in here."

"But *you* don't need to be." Ivas pinched her thumb between his little fingers. "Ruby, your mom is so worried. She wants you back. We need to go back now, or the fog will eat us up too."

"But…but…"

"Ruby, look at what you've turned into. What would your father think?"

That hurt more than she wanted it to. She wanted to be angry. She wanted to toss Ivas away and storm off in giant strides in search of what she came for, but he was no longer sitting in her palm. He was standing over her, holding her in his arms, and she was crying like a scared little girl.

Because she was. She wanted her mom. She wanted to go home. More than anything, she wanted the fog to go away.

And this man had found her.

She felt Ivas grab her horns, and pain struck as he started to bend and tug at them. She cried out and fought back, but he wouldn't let go, even as her claws shredded his serape. With these arms he had wrestled sheep, hauled wool, carried wood and stone, and now all his strength went into those horns.

"Let them go. You are not a monster."

Ruby yielded, and with a great and terrible *snap* the horns broke off, splintering from her skull. Ruby felt it in her head and all the way down her back. She screamed as the pain overwhelmed her and she fainted from it.

Ivas caught her and lifted the girl over his shoulders as he had with Little Lost not one night ago.

When he looked up, he saw that familiar white shape of Blanc. Her tail didn't wag, and her eyes were hard. She was working now.

"Walk on, Blanc."

At the familiar command, Blanc turned and guided Ivas back to safety. He kept his eyes on her and followed. The lantern was gone, his flashlight was gone. Now it was only the darkness and fog and the ghostly shape of Blanc leading him onward.

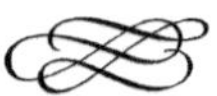

CHAPTER 8

THE SHEPARD LEARNS ABOUT THE DEAD GOD

Ivas woke in the fallen leaves. The hearth-scent of them filled his nose. The golden sun pierced his eyes with a gentle ferocity, but he did not flinch away. It was the most beautiful thing he had ever seen, a sight forgotten in the fog.

Ruby was clutched against him. They were wrapped together in his serape. They were covered in dew, and it was the typical cold morning of fall. But that sun, like golden syrup, Ivas soaked it in. It glimmered between the leaves, turning them to fire.

Ivas didn't remember climbing the stairs to the ruins, but that was where they were, safe on top away from the fog. Everything hurt from lying on the stones, but Ruby was safe, and so was Blanc. The sun was up. Ivas could not have asked for more.

He shook the girl awake and she looked at him with sleep-crusted eyes. She wiped her nose on her sleeve and tried to sit up, but her body trembled. Ivas noted that what remained of her horns still sat in splintered stumps on her head, but her brown eyes were warm and gentle, her hands soft and human. Together they struggled up, and Ivas helped her down the stairs.

"I want to go home," Ruby whispered. Her voice cracked, sore and dry.

"My house is closer. We'll stop there first."

Blanc ran ahead, getting wet in the morning dew. Ivas and Ruby trudged along behind her.

"Your house?" Ruby asked.

"Mmhmm. I live up the road from you. I have the sheep farm."

"Oh, yeah." Ruby recalled seeing Ivas around town; everyone knew everyone in Loch Lamond. "What's your name?" she asked.

"Ivas Sbarge."

"And you…you came looking for me?"

Ivas guided Ruby around a rock in their path.

"Why? Do I know you?" Ruby felt guilty, worried she was forgetting Ivas from an important part of her life.

"No, you don't know me. We're just neighbors."

"But you went into the fog… Why?"

"Because I was the only one who knew."

Ivas was too tired to explain further, and Ruby let the matter rest. They continued their journey, wordless and weary. Ivas concentrated on his steps, one after the other. If he thought about the long walk back to his house, it only made him want to collapse again. Single steps were easier.

Eventually, they did get back to his home, and the dawn was still young. He could hear the sheep bleating from the barn, and the responsibility outweighed his want for rest. He put Ruby inside first, then he and Blanc released the sheep into the field. They happily jogged out, looking for places to graze.

Blanc stayed with the sheep and Ivas went gratefully inside. Ruby had made herself at home, starting a fire in the fireplace and wrapping herself in a blanket. Her boots and skirt were tossed aside, wet and dirty. She laid down on the couch and closed her eyes. Ivas didn't bother her but went to his bedroom and changed clothes as well. His grandfather's serape was damaged, so he set it aside. He looked at his bed longingly but knew that it was only the comfort he wanted. He would never be able to sleep. Even in the light of day, his head was full of the fog.

Instead, he went to the kitchen and went to work cooking. Ivas didn't have an appetite, but Ruby had been gone for almost two days. Sure enough, the smell of bacon stirred her and she came sleepily into the kitchen, still wrapped up, and sat at the table.

"I saw the Messenger deliver your scroll," Ivas said, picking up where the conversation had left off. He shoved bacon strips into his mouth in an effort to wake up. He produced the red ribbon and handed it to Ruby. "I used that to have Blanc track you."

"But why would you go into the fog all by yourself?" Ruby played with the ribbon, running it between her fingers, then tying it in a bow around her wrist. This was a complicated task with only one hand, but Ruby seemed calm having the distraction.

"It's a long story, but I know what's *really* in the fog."

Ruby shivered at the memory and dropped the bacon that was on its way to her mouth. "I want to go home," she murmured.

"We need to think of a story for your mother," Ivas said. He set a cup of tea in front of her, and she sipped at the soothing liquid, her voice returning to normal.

Ruby's eyes narrowed as her sleepy mind began to function on real thoughts again. The problem wasn't that no one would believe them—that Ruby had been taken by the fog and come out again. They most certainly would.

"People will talk. They'll want to know at first, but then they'll be just as scared of you as they are of the fog."

Ruby rested her head on the table. "What could I possibly say?"

"We could say you ran off with a boy, got lost…"

"No. Mom wouldn't buy it. I'll tell her I went to Balliecroy to…get away. I'll be in trouble, but it's better than being the haunted girl who survived the fog."

Ivas nodded. Balliecroy was a neighboring city about half a day's walk from Loch Lamond. It offered some amenities that their little village didn't. It made sense that Ruby would run away there.

She touched her tender head, breaking off some of the splintered antler that was rotting off there. It was swollen and painful, but she continued picking at it, trying to get back to normal.

"What do I do?" she asked.

"You go home and move on with your life like the rest of us," Ivas said, almost bitterly.

"But Dad is trapped there. He said something was coming, and so did the giant."

Ivas shuddered, wishing she wouldn't even mention it. "That's not your concern. You're just a child. Go home to your mother."

What could she say? Weak and tired, Ruby ate the bacon he put in front of her, tears falling and plinking on the ceramic plate.

"I—I tried, right?" She looked at Ivas, eyes begging for an answer. Every part of her screamed that it was her fault, that she should have tried *harder*.

"I tried…I tried to find him. I went into the fog… I tried!"

Ivas reached across the table to touch her hand, and she trembled under his fingertips. Her eyes were full of water, but she didn't blink.

He knew what he should have told her. *Of course you tried. You did what no child should have done, should never have to do, because you love him. And no matter what I say, the fact that you failed will stay with you forever. You won't remember all the times he said, "I love you." You'll only remember this.*

"Did you really think you could save him from the fog?" he asked.

Tears dripped. "My dad is trapped. He's in pain…"

What could he say that would make it better? What words could possibly take away the guilt?

"So is your mom, and you can help her right now by going home and showing her you're okay."

Ruby nodded, her body finally slumping and tears slowing. She sank back into her chair.

"When you're ready, go back home, take your punishment, and make things right with her. She's torn this countryside apart looking for you."

"She…she has?"

"Yes." Ivas rubbed his head where the bump Hannah had given him was still healing. "The only thing that matters to your mom and dad, Ruby, is that you're safe. Isn't that why your dad sent you the letter? Not to save him, but so that you could run?"

She nodded in defeat, then slowly looked up. "But I don't want to run. If something is coming, then shouldn't we do something?"

"Go home, Ruby," Ivas said. "You've had a long night."

❧

Ruby did go home, walking through the fields that separated her home from Ivas's. The air was cold, but the sun was warm, and they each had a new appreciation for the colors of a new day. Ivas had placed his cap over

Ruby's head to hide the stubs of horns that protruded from her skull. Her clothes were muddy and tangled with dead leaves. She certainly looked as if she had hiked a two-day journey. Ivas walked with her for a while until they came in sight of her house. The search party was gathered there, organized by Jack. Ruby's mom stood next to the sheriff, straight and emotionless. Ruby's eyes watered at the sight of them. All these townspeople gathered to find her.

Ivas squeezed her shoulder in farewell. "You're always welcome at my cottage…if you need to get away."

Ruby nodded, then continued on alone to accept her fate. Her mother spotted her immediately—the single red-head coming over the hill—and ran to meet her, taking them both to the ground in a tight hug.

Ivas went back to his cottage, unseen by anyone; they were all in awe at the girl's reappearance. Ivas went home and collapsed into his bed, falling asleep before he could even take off his boots.

~

*R*uby was aware of everyone's eyes on her as Hannah collapsed around her, body crumbling, being held up by Ruby. The girl hugged her back, but her eyes darted toward the search party. She could name every person gathered there—over a dozen at least. Several elementary school teachers, the woman who used to babysit her, Mrs. Kindlestrike who ran the local cafe, many of her father's comrades—sailors and old men with concern filling their eyes. None were immediate family members. All of Ruby's relatives lived in towns much bigger than theirs and very far away.

Shoulders relaxed and voices murmured. Some nodded in that "I told you so" manner. The sheriff, Jack, was there as well, arms crossed and expression hard. He seemed as hurt as her mom but was trying to hide it. He walked up to them.

"Ruby, are you all right?"

She nodded, realizing she couldn't answer because there was a lump in her throat. If she tried to speak, she would just cry. Her mother was trembling all around her and Ruby could hardly stand it.

She forgot that grown-ups felt pain too. They hid it so well—at least from children.

"Where were you?" Jack asked.

Ruby took a deep breath, shrugging her mom off in the process. Hannah finally pulled herself away but still clutched Ruby's shirt as if she might run away again.

"Balliecroy," she said. "I-I'm sorry. I left you a note…" The idea struck her suddenly, a way to maybe alleviate some of the punishment that awaited her.

"There was no note," Hannah rasped. She seemed like she wanted to scream.

"I…I taped it to the door. It must have been blown away."

Hannah's grip on Ruby's shirt tightened.

"I'm sorry." Ruby's voice broke and tears flowed with surprising quickness. She really was. She didn't want to see her mother in this much pain, to cause such a fuss in her small town. "I'm sorry. I just started walking. I didn't mean to go so far." That part was very much true. When she had first wandered into the fog, she had never meant to go so far at all.

"I…I just wanted to get away from the sea." She quivered, staring at the ground, tears falling like rainfall into the dirt. "I kept thinking I saw his boat. I kept thinking he would come back. I just wanted to get away—"

Now she was sobbing and couldn't speak anymore. There was no lie in her words now. Hannah pulled her back into her arms, only now she was collected again, not trembling anymore. A shield for her daughter, not a mother on the brink of insanity. But then, Ruby wondered if that was what motherhood always was.

Jack had finally relaxed, uncrossing his arms. Part of him was worried that Ruby would have a kidnapping story to tell, a horror that she had escaped from, but it was just as Ivas had said, all a misunderstanding.

He turned to the crowd and waved his hands. "It's alright, everyone! Ruby is safe. Thank you for sparing your time to come out, but let's give them some space now."

Everyone meandered away, some pausing to chat with each other, others ready to get back to their own lives. Some were brave enough to approach Ruby and Hannah, patting their shoulders and telling them that they were glad Ruby was okay. Mrs. Kindlestrike promised to bring some food over later.

Hannah kept a firm hold on her daughter and guided her back toward the house. They went inside to a deep quiet. Ruby went to the kitchen table and sat down, suddenly feeling very tired, while Hannah kept sighing and wiping her eyes, as if she couldn't catch her breath. She walked to the counter, then opened the fridge, but didn't actually take anything.

"You..." She started to speak but stopped and shook her head, as if she couldn't decide what to say.

"I know," Ruby looked down shamefully.

After a few moments, wrestling with whether to scold her daughter or smother her with kisses, Hannah found the words she was looking for. "Maybe getting away isn't such a bad idea."

Ruby looked up.

"My sister offered us a place to stay for a while if we need to. I've been...distracting myself with work, but I know you've been skipping school. And if it's what you need...we can go."

Ruby's cheeks burned. How did her mom know she had been skipping class? This town was too small.

"I'm sorry," she said again. "I just...I couldn't sit through class. Everyone else is still living their lives like everything is normal and I can't stand it."

Hannah finally stopped pacing and sat down at the table, taking Ruby's hand and looking at her in a way that Ruby had never seen before. When Hannah whispered, "I understand," Ruby knew that she truly did.

"But I don't want to leave," Ruby added. "It...doesn't do any good. It still hurts."

Hannah squeezed her hand more tightly. "I know."

"When I was...walking back, someone said you had been looking for me. 'Tearing up the countryside.'"

Hannah frowned. "Who said that?"

"Our neighbor, Ivas Sbarge."

Hannah laughed, an abrupt, barking laugh that made Ruby jump.

Edge of insanity...

"Ruby... If..." She sighed, struggling for words again. "Even if you disappeared forever, there would never be a moment I would stop looking for you."

Those words struck something in Ruby's heart and clung there like a spider web, sticking and tickling her no matter how hard she tried to wipe it away. It was a haunting feeling that she couldn't shake.

"Why don't you go take a shower and a nap. You look exhausted."

Ruby nodded. Now that she mentioned it, she did feel soul-crushingly tired. She stood up, pausing to give her mother a soft kiss on the forehead. Hannah squeezed her hand and kissed it before letting her go.

"Where'd you get that hat?" Hannah asked.

Ruby turned back and smiled a little. "I found it on the road. Do you like it?"

Hannah allowed a soft little laugh to puff through her nose and shook her head in disbelief. Hats. As if she hadn't been living a nightmare for the past two days.

"It's a little big, but kind of cute."

Ruby tipped the brim in thanks and made her way to the bathroom. She made sure the door was locked securely before taking off Ivas's cap and staring at herself in the mirror. Brown eyes and a scatter of freckles. The stubs of her horns still very prominent in the tangle of her hair. She touched them and was comforted by their solidness, the knowledge that it was all *real*.

She reached into the pocket of her jacket and squeezed the scroll that had led to all of this, the last message from her father.

She had been so close...

Her breath was sharp and quick. She shut her eyes and felt her teeth grinding against themselves as the guilt and the anger returned, drowning out Ivas's words about letting it go and living her life. *She* had entered the fog. *She* had survived. There was an itch under her fingernails and in her gums.

Danger was coming, and her father was still out there.

There would never be a moment I would stop looking for you.

Ruby opened her eyes again and noticed that her horns had begun to heal.

~

*I*vas woke to the sheep screaming.

He startled awake to a grey afternoon. His head felt heavy and groggy, but he could hear the sheep's cries and Blanc barking. He forced himself out of bed, aching and wanting only to sleep it all away.

Outside, some dark clouds had moved in and the temperature had dropped. What startled Ivas was the appearance of fog, patches of white hovering over the grass as they might in the early morning. His heart pounded with fear as he ran to the barn to get the sheep to safety.

"Here, Blanc!" he called.

Blanc went to work rounding the sheep up, but they didn't need much encouragement. Ivas opened the door and they all quickly filed in. Ivas looked up and spotted what Blanc had been barking at and had caused the sheep's fright.

The Messenger was standing at the fence, half shrouded in a pocket of fog. Though the incredulous hood still covered its body, Ivas felt that it was looking at him.

Once the sheep were inside, Ivas shut the door and latched it. Blanc stayed at his legs, still in work mode. Her triangle ears were pointed straight up as she watched the supernatural visitor.

"What are you doing here?" Ivas asked.

The Messenger, of course, did not answer. All was silent except for the flap of the Messenger's tattered cloak. If it was here, if the fog had come in this early, then something was wrong.

"Come on, Blanc." Ivas motioned the dog to the cottage and put her inside where she would be safe. Looking back at the field, he saw that the patch of fog had drifted away and the Messenger was gone. With a tired sigh, he grabbed his bicycle and started pedaling toward town. He needed answers.

∾

*I*vas pedaled with ferocity toward town, leaving a dust trail behind him. Seeing the Messenger gave him a shot of adrenaline. He was glad to have his fear back. Soon, the dirt trail turned to cobblestones as he entered town. The port-side village was quiet enough, but Ivas could sense the unease. He saw familiar plants hanging from windows and doorways—garlic, holly, bay leaves, all things of protection. Tendrils of fog rolled in from the water and he shivered. But people were out. He saw them visiting in homes and cafes, gossiping about Ruby, no doubt. Ivas kept riding until he reached Old Popper's place.

The door opened on the first knock.

"Sbarge," Old Popper said, eyeing Ivas almost suspiciously. "I thought you'd come. I had a...very strange dream about you."

"You did?"

"Yes, in the fog."

"We need to talk."

"I'll put the kettle on."

Ivas settled in, comforted by the books and the smell of tea brewing. Old Popper brought in two mugs and Ivas drank his down quickly. Old Popper refilled it.

"Yes, a very strange dream," Old Popper said thoughtfully, continuing the conversation as if they had only just paused it. "You were in the fog, and I had something important to tell you."

"What is the fog, Mr. Poppermill?" Ivas asked. "Surely there's a tale."

Old Popper smirked. "I've already given you a story just yesterday that you still owe me for."

"And this time I will owe you double," Ivas said. "I promise to give you a story, but I really don't have the time now."

Old Popper sat back thoughtfully, trying to decide if he wanted to test Ivas further. In the end, he let it go. "Alright, but it better be a whopper."

"It is, trust me." Ivas sighed.

"So, you want a story about the fog? There's lots of them, most of which you've already heard."

"But what's the first story?" Ivas insisted. "The earliest you can remember? Please, think."

Old Popper gave him an uncharacteristically firm glare. "Just cause I can't remember doesn't mean I'm not thinking."

He stood up and went to a bookshelf. "I keep a record of stories, you know. Local legends and the like. There is one I know of…"

Old Popper found a leather-bound journal and flipped through the pages. It was well worn in that good kind of way that spoke of a book's healthy life. He smiled. "Oh yes, I love these old stories."

"Does it say where the fog came from?"

"Not a lot of origin stories as far as local legends go. They just sort of pop up one day, like flowers, and no one asks how they got there. People just enjoy them." Old Popper flipped through the pages, giving his thumb a lick.

A memory clicked in Ivas's head. "Is there a story about… a god?"

Old Popper stopped turning and, after a pause, snapped the book shut. "Oh, *that* story."

Ivas didn't notice that he was balanced on the edge of the chair. "What is it?"

"An old Pagan tale, tossed around before this land was properly settled. I guess as far as 'origin' stories go, the stories of the fog started with that one." Old Popper sighed and leaned back in his chair, thinking. "Lots of details have been lost of course, I just know the bits and pieces I've picked up over the years. There was a legend of a god, you see, a dark god that lived beyond the horizon of the sea. He was said to carry the sins of man so that they would not be burdened by them. But when the old god finally died, he exhaled his final breath in the form of the fog, and that breath carried all the monsters and sins of man within it and flowed back to shore to haunt mankind."

Ivas slipped and repositioned himself in his seat. "But what killed him? What could kill a god?"

Old Popper shrugged. "Maybe all the sins poisoned him."

"But it said—" Ivas stopped before he said more. He was remembering the words of the giant despite his best efforts to repress the memory.

Wait until the rest of that god catches up...

"But then," Old Popper continued, "gods can't really die, can they? In all the mythologies, they go to sleep or get trapped. There was another story about a hungry god." Old Popper used his Halloween-story voice. "I think I've told this one before, about the town that disappeared?"

Ivas nodded. Everyone knew the story of the disappearing village. "Yeah, you said that one night the fog rolled in and swallowed an entire village."

Old Popper nodded. "Every house was gone, every pet, farm animal, and human being. Only the roads and flower beds remained."

This was a popular story Ivas was familiar with. There was even a rumor that you could find this village down the shore. As a boy, Ivas had friends who claimed to have found the leftover cobblestone streets of the village that disappeared.

"Perhaps it was this god that ate it," Old Popper concluded.

Ivas felt his stomach sink. Suddenly, he was in the kitchen, heaving up the tea Old Popper had served him.

"There now, lad. My tea isn't that bad, is it?"

"Sorry," Ivas gasped. "I'm just…not feeling too well."

"Why don't you lie down a spell?" Old Popper patted Ivas's shoulder. "Come upstairs, you can use my bed."

Ivas honestly wanted nothing more than to lie down, but he wanted to lie down in his own bed. "Thank you, no, I have to get back. The sheep need to be put away." Ivas wiped his mouth and took a drink of water Old Popper offered.

"Is that story true?" Ivas asked, almost begging. "It can't be. It's just fiction."

"I don't know, lad. I heard that story from a traveler years ago. He told it to me when he learned about our superstition of the fog. Said his family lived there and when he came to visit it was all gone. He thought he must have gone mad or lost his way, but others confirmed that the village had once stood there but had disappeared one night in the fog."

"What happened to this traveler?"

"Moved far away from the shore, too scared to stay. Went back to where he came from."

"Do *you* think he spoke the truth? Or was it just fiction between two storytellers?"

"I don't like to turn my opinion to stone. It was possibly a lie. It wasn't in the papers. But then, who would report such a thing? The journalist would be a laughingstock. But I will say that—personally—I did believe him. He had fear in his eyes. He told it in a halting way, the same in which a man speaks of war. He at least believed it was true."

Ivas shivered.

"Maybe that's enough ghost stories for a while," Old Popper said.

"I think you're right. Thank you, though."

"Be careful, Ivas. It might just be stories, but even metaphorically, you shouldn't wander too deep in the fog."

～

*A*fter a brief rest in Old Popper's reclining chair, Ivas left the book-filled home and ran into Tess. She was walking down the street, dressed in her boat clothes and looking very spooked.

"You okay?"

Tess jumped at Ivas's voice, then broke into a relieved sigh. "Oh, Ivas, I'm glad to see you. I've been worried. I heard Ruby came back home?"

Ivas nodded. "Yes, turns out she just wandered off to the next village."

"Thank goodness, everyone has been so worried, so… paranoid. I'm just glad everyone is safe." She hugged his arm.

"Everything okay?"

"No, not really. I mean, I'm okay, it's just…"

"The fog?"

"How did you know?"

"It came in early today. Is the water bad?"

Tess stared down at her hands and shrugged. "The wall is still there. It's…closer."

"Closer?"

"I'm sure of it. The other sailors think so too. It hasn't gone away; it just stays on the water getting a little closer to shore."

"You sound like one of Old Popper's ghost stories."

"You haven't seen it," Tess said darkly. "You try looking at a wall of fog and not think of ghost stories."

"Hey, I didn't mean anything by it," Ivas said quickly. "Trust me, I know. On foggy nights when I'm all alone on the farm…I know."

Tess shuddered. "Let's not talk about it. I need a fireplace and something warm to drink. Want to come?"

"I can't, it's going to get dark soon." There was already mist curling up along the cobblestones.

"Maybe I'll drive up and check on you later."

"That's… Don't trouble yourself. Stay home where it's safe. I'll see you tomorrow. Raincheck."

"You sure?"

Tess seemed like she needed the company as badly as he wanted it. Tess saw the conflict in his face and smiled gently.

"I'll stop by later. We'll have some tea and you can make a fire."

Just the idea of having warmth and company made Ivas relax. His shoulders sank and he nodded. "That sounds good."

Now in higher spirits, Tess beamed. "Great! I'll bring some food. It'll be so nice to get away from the water. Can't wait to see Blanc."

Ivas smiled too. Tess was already dancing away, but he stopped her.

"Tess?"

"Hmm?"

"You're sure about the fog? That it was closer?"

She nodded. "Yesterday, I could still see Abbey Bluff. Now, the wall…the fog, I mean, almost covers it. You ever get a bad feeling about something? Like something bad is coming?"

"Don't say that. Everything is fine."

Tess nodded. "You're right. I've lived in this town too long. The kids have been out in the fields, singing that fucking song."

～

The song seemed to still be echoing in the soft evening shadows as Tess walked down the cobblestone road toward home. It was a blessedly short walk from the dock to her apartment above Linda Haverford's flower shop. Also, the town nursery, florist, and gardening store. Linda kept busy being the only flower game in town, not only raising trees and plants, but arranging flowers for the various special occasions the town celebrated. She made a killing during the spring festival every year. Sometimes Tess helped out during busy seasons. Valentine's Day and the annual sweetheart dance earned Tess a couple free months of rent because Linda always needed an extra pair of hands.

Tess admired the woman the same way she admired her father, growing up and watching him work. She recognized the way Linda's hands made magical things happen. The way Linda made plants grow was the same way her father made his boat sail. Sure, there was logic and a scientific technique behind it all, but there was also a sort of magic, a way their hands moved, pushing soil and tying knots in that quick, professional way that matched a magician's quick movements making things appear from behind ears.

Tess had grown up with the notion that masculinity was strength. That if she wanted to be like her father, she had to embrace the "tomboy" culture, and she spent her teenage years in oversized t-shirts and dirty pants, rolling her eyes at girls who wore makeup and cooed over boys.

But when she had turned nineteen and decided to move out of her parents' house—much to her mom and dad's protest—she realized how wrong she was. As a young kid barely getting by, Linda cut her some slack by having Tess work part-time in the shop, and Tess realized that even things considered "feminine" took the same dedication as anything else. A special skill, a passion that Tess admired. After a while, she found that she really enjoyed wearing dresses and putting a bow in her short hair. She even developed a crush on her friend Jack, but found that she really preferred just being friends. The same went with Ivas. The dating pool was pretty shallow in such a small town.

But there were other ports, other towns, and Tess found that she was sailing further and further away each time she took her boat out. She had already traveled to the closest shore-side city, and eventually, when she got tired of Loch Lamond, she would see the world.

But for now, she was very much content with her life and her superstitious little town. She loved living above the flower shop, constantly smelling the fragrance of various plants and enjoying the site of the tree nursery hidden on the other side. That was the view from her apartment—a little thing with a single bedroom, a kitchen the same size as her bathroom, and a living room mostly devoid of furniture but filled with books with pictures of faraway places. Tess had all her favorites bookmarked, and once she had the money saved up, she planned on visiting every single one.

She tossed her wet boat clothes aside and put on a long skirt and boots instead. Tess had enjoyed a summer of pretty skirts, but the autumn coldness was forcing her back into pants and scarves.

When she was changed, Tess found a microwave dinner and ate her meal at the window, admiring the countryside, or trying to at least. The fog was already creeping in, giving her the shivers.

She kept thinking about the wall on the water, kept trying to shake it off, but found herself wondering if Linda had a batch of garlic she could hang at her window instead. Tess hated feeling so scared. Being a sailor, that was the one thing she learned to never be because when you were scared you panicked, made irrational decisions.

But still, the fog loomed…

Tess sighed and threw away the little plastic tray that still held half her dinner. She hated those things anyway. It was too quiet in her apartment, and she didn't feel like watching TV. Was it too early to go see Ivas? Who cared. It wasn't like the old sheep farmer had anything going on. She needed company tonight.

Tess grabbed her jacket and car keys and left the apartment. The shop was already empty as she passed by on the stairs. Linda usually closed up early during the cold months. She preferred to go to her house, where her own impressive garden grew to perfection.

Tess's truck—given to her by her dad as a high school graduation gift—sat in a little parking spot next to the nursery. She didn't drive it a lot, but it was handy for supply runs out of town and was constantly being borrowed by people needing to move or farmers needing an extra vehicle to haul something. There was lots of sharing in this little village, from superstitions to the flu.

Tess started up the old pickup and backed out onto the cobblestone street. It was a brief, bumpy ride to the dirt road out of town. Twilight was settling on the horizon. The fog was illuminated by her headlights in an uncomforting way. The further she drove, the denser the mist became, and Tess suddenly found herself turning off onto a side road, away from Ivas's house.

She would get there, but as much as she hated to admit it, she *was* scared, and she needed something to get her back out on the water. Tess needed a good luck charm, a talisman. Tess needed…to see a witch.

Her eyes locked on the silhouette of the old, abandoned lighthouse on Beacon Point and followed it to a familiar road that wasn't really a road, just a dent in the tall grass.

She followed this to a tiny cottage clinging to life on the edge of the sea. One day, after years of erosion or a strong hurricane, it would fall in. By the time she reached it, the fog was thick and prominent. Tess's heart pounded, and she knew in her heart that this was what she needed to do. In the morning, she would feel silly and kick herself for being so irrational, but at that moment, the dark seemed full of monsters, and she felt like a child wanting the hallway door to be left open.

In the dark and the fog, she believed it all. The ghost stories, the urban legends, the fear. She believed in witchcraft.

Tess stepped out of her car, leaving the headlights on, and felt the dampness of the fog as the mist wrapped around her, seeming to grab and bind her very body. She saw the light from the cottage as a door opened, and she ran for her life.

~

*I*vas found himself becoming oddly…angry. The closer he got to his cottage, the darker the sky became, and it was irritating Ivas, as if the weather was becoming spooky on purpose just to frighten him.

He was grateful to see the cottage with its windows glowing warmly and noted worriedly that Blanc wasn't running up to meet him. Ivas gave a whistle and Blanc darted from the field where he finally noticed Ruby. She leaned against the wooden fence, face half-covered by Ivas's hat. She had changed out of her wool skirt into pants and a heavy coat. Her orange hair was untangled and clean, indicating she had gotten a shower and a nap, something Ivas wished he had time for. She raised a hand to him, and Ivas joined her against the fence.

"Is everything all right?" he asked.

"I, umm, wanted to return your hat. And…where are your sheep?"

"I put them away early. Something startled them."

Ruby's eyes widened. "Was it the Messenger?"

Ivas raised an eyebrow. "Yeah. How did—?"

"I saw him this afternoon, hidden in a patch of fog. He didn't deliver a message, though, just watched me."

Ivas nodded, confirming that he'd had the same experience.

"I think he's trying to warn us," Ruby said.

Ivas shivered, painfully aware of the dark clouds and thickening fog. "Let's have this conversation inside."

The three of them went into the cottage where Ivas bolted the door. Blanc pranced around the house happily while Ruby sat at the table.

"Are you hungry?" Ivas asked. He moved into the living room and worked on making a fire in the fireplace.

"Oh. I haven't really thought about it. I don't think I've eaten at all today."

Ivas struck a match and set it to some kindling. He coaxed the fire with twigs and branches before adding large logs. The heat hit him comfortably and he remained crouched in front of it for a moment, letting feeling come back to his cheeks. When his fingers stopped tingling, he stood up and returned to the kitchen.

"Well, I don't have much, but I'll do what I can." Ivas pulled out a carton of eggs and began filling a pot with water. "How are you even here? I figured your mother would have locked you in your room."

"She tried, but I told her I was going to bed and snuck out the window. I know it's a shitty thing to do, but I had to talk to you about this."

"'This?' This is nothing. This is not a reason to sneak out of your house and worry your moth—"

Ivas was cut off when Ruby removed her hat, showing him the horns that were growing from her head. The horns had healed themselves and grown a couple of inches.

"Oh."

"It's the fog," Ruby said. "I think it's affecting me."

"You have to fight them. Don't go…big on me again."

She blinked wide-eyed at him. "Big?"

The water started to boil and Ivas plopped the eggs into the pot.

"I heard a story today. I visited Old Popper and he told me about a village that disappeared one night."

"I know the one. They say the fog took the whole town away."

"Your father said something was coming. The giant warned us of a god. I think your message was right, something big is coming."

The eggs danced in their boiling pot. Ivas found a chunk of cheese in the fridge and cut that up along with some bread. It was a poor bachelor's meal, and he tried to find something more healthy he could offer Ruby. He found a couple of apples and cut those up as well.

"What should we do?"

"As your father instructed. Run. Tell your mother anything you need to. I'm sure after what happened she'll take you anywhere you want to go. I'll convince who I can as well and we'll leave the shores until the fog recedes again."

"But…" Ruby seemed torn. She was at the age of hope. She had been told stories of heroes, the fairy tales with morals about not giving up. She hadn't grown old into the reality of stories. She knew only of heroes, not the other characters, the so-called villains. "We can't run."

"It's quite easy, actually," Ivas said. He turned off the stove and scooped the eggs out with a spoon. "And it's the only thing we can do."

"But that's not fair." She was at the age where there was still such a thing as fairness. "Our whole village could disappear and everyone in it. We know about it, that must mean we can do something."

"Like what? How do you fight mist? How does a mortal take on a god?"

"You *did* fight the mist. You went in and came back out. These horns on my head call to the fog. I challenged the giant and won. We aren't mere morals, Ivas."

Ivas tapped one of the eggs against the counter, concentrating too hard on the task.

Ruby kept on. "How did you know I was in the fog? What made you come after me? You don't even know me!"

Ivas slammed the egg, squashing it on the countertop. "Be quiet! This isn't the same."

"Why not? Why did you go after me? You'd do it for one stupid girl but not a whole village?"

"You're not a stupid girl. Please stop—"

"You saw the Messenger too!"

"Shut up!"

Ruby's mouth snapped shut, but she glared at him. Ivas trembled. He realized he was trying not to cry.

"I've seen—I'm sorry—I've seen the Messenger since I was a child. He kept trying to visit me, and I knew what he wanted, but I wouldn't let him in. I knew he was trying to deliver something. You felt it too, right? When he came to your door?"

Ruby nodded. "I heard a knock and…I thought I was dreaming. I thought it was my father visiting me."

"I thought it was my parents," Ivas said. "My parents died when I was a child, but I didn't want to open the door to them. I didn't want to hear what they had to say because I thought it was my fault."

Tears ran down Ivas's cheeks. He stared at the counter, at the cheese and apples. He could hear Ruby breathing heavily behind him.

"I thought they were coming to haunt me, to tell me everything I did wrong. I wanted to destroy the Messenger, and that's how I lost my grandfather too. He went into the fog for me and died there. I almost died as well, but I made it to the morning. I don't know how."

He wiped his eyes and looked at her. Ruby's expression had softened.

"I saw you too, that night the Messenger delivered your father's letter, and I thought...I couldn't have another dead person on my heart."

Grandpa...

Ivas trembled and the tears ran down his cheeks. "If I had the chance to save just one..."

Mom... Dad...

"I just... I couldn't...not if I had the chance. I could have saved them and I didn't."

Ruby stepped forward, taking his hand and squeezing it. Ivas squeezed back.

"Thank you," Ruby said.

The words, spoken softly and perfectly, struck the back of his knees and Ivas sank to the ground. Ruby stood over him, still holding his hand.

"I blame myself too," Ruby said. "That's why I went into the fog after Dad. I should have stopped him that morning from going out on the boat. Should have woken up and told him I loved him, should have given him a longer hug when he tucked me in."

Ivas felt something wet drip on his hand and realized she was crying too.

"Why does it seem we're always trying to live for the dead?"

Ruby sat down next to him and they stayed that way in silence for a moment, having no answers.

Ivas thought to himself that he should take her away, force her and her mother to leave.

Save just one...

But then he thought about how the fear had held him back before. How, without it, in the fog, he had finally been able to save someone.

"My friend, Tess, she has a boat," Ivas said carefully. "Perhaps tomorrow we could venture out and take a closer look."

"Really?"

Ivas nodded. "There might be a way to stop it. Maybe the answer is in the stories."

Ruby smiled a little. She looked out the window and sighed. "It's dark out. I didn't even realize."

Ivas stood up for a better look. Even with the shadows, the heavy veil of fog was obvious. "It's too dangerous to leave the house. Will you be okay tonight? If we leave early, we can sneak you back…"

As Ivas spoke, Ruby's eyes grew large and she began to tremble. She was staring at something behind him. The room filled up with a bright blue light. Ivas turned his head back to the window and saw two lantern-glowing eyes staring back. A low chuckle rumbled through the house, making the glass in the windowpanes shudder. The giant straightened up, and Ivas watched its dark form circle the house, passing by windows with deep thundering footsteps.

Ivas moved toward Ruby, to comfort her, but froze when he saw that her fear had denigrated into anger. He could visibly see her horns lengthen.

"Ruby, it's okay. He can't hurt us in here. The fog can't touch us."

Ruby nodded but kept her narrow eyes on the source of the footsteps.

"Come out, little one," the giant rumbled.

Ruby opened her mouth to answer, but Ivas quickly placed his palm over her lips. "No, don't answer. Ignore it. Don't invite it in."

Ruby closed her eyes and took a deep breath, nodding.

"The fog is calling you. Can you hear it?" the giant continued.

Ruby touched her horns.

"The monster's inside," the giant said.

Ivas took Ruby's arm and led her into the living room. There was one window there, which he quickly pulled the curtains on. He pulled Ruby down by the fireplace.

"Don't listen to it. You're not a monster."

Ruby smirked a little, touching her horns again. "There are monsters inside all of us." She motioned to the window. "They were all human once."

"What about you, shepherd?" the giant coaxed. "Will you come to find what you lost?"

We forgot something.

Ivas stiffened suddenly, remembering.

"We have your woman, shepherd."

"Tess!" Ivas jumped up, startling Ruby.

"Who?"

"My friend Tess, she was coming here tonight. Shit!"

"Maybe it's a bluff."

"How would they know she was coming?" Ivas thought quickly, remembering the fog curled around their feet in town. Could the fog spy on them? Even so, Tess still hadn't arrived. She could have easily been taken in the short walk from her car to the house.

"What should we do?"

Ruby stood up and Ivas saw claws forming on her fingertips.

"No, wait." Ivas put a hand on her shoulder, easing her back toward the fireplace. If she changed, Ivas wasn't sure if he could get her to become human again. "Stay here. I have an idea."

Ivas put on his work gloves, thinking quickly.

"What are you doing?" Ruby demanded.

"They don't like light, they don't like the warmth, so…" Ivas reached into the fireplace and grabbed one of the burning logs. Ruby's eyes widened. Ivas could feel the heat of the burning wood soaking through his glove, so he moved quickly, going to the door and stepping outside into the mist. Blanc followed and he let her. She didn't seem affected by the fog, but he could feel it wrapping around him like a blanket, slipping into his eyes and ears and into his mind.

"Tess!" Ivas shouted to the dark, holding the burning log aloft. "Tess, where are you?"

The only response was the deep chuckle of the giant. "Your little flame doesn't scare me."

"Then come get me," Ivas challenged, wishing his voice didn't quiver as he said it. Blanc stayed by his side, barking at the shadow, white hair spiked up like a cat's.

He saw the dark form of the giant come forward, a large human-shaped shadow against the blue of the fog. Ivas immediately wanted to drop the flame and run, but the thought of Tess kept his feet weighted to their spot.

"Where is the other? The horned one? I have not finished with her."

"She's just as eager to finish you," Ivas said, "but let Tess go. She's not lost, she doesn't belong in the fog."

The giant smirked. "She seeks what is lost to her just as you did, shepherd."

Ivas saw a wave of darkness come out of the fog toward him. The hand of the giant with fingers like the bars of a cage. Ivas cried out and swung the flame at the hand. The giant flinched. Ivas felt the impact as the log made contact. A rainfall of sparks burst between them, floating up into the fog.

"Let her go or I'll shove this down your throat!"

"You dare threaten me?" the giant's voice thundered around him. Its hand came forward again, striking Ivas in the chest. The breath was knocked out of his lungs and Ivas fell onto his back, gasping for air. The log fell from his hands, sending sparks and embers glowing across the ground. Ivas reached for it, but the giant was already standing above him, reaching for him. In his panic, Ivas lost his grip on the log and screamed.

A brilliant sparkle of white light suddenly appeared, casting comforting beams through the fog, lighting up the dark. The giant retreated, stumbling away from the source, which Ivas couldn't make out.

"Come...back..." Ivas gasped for words, still trying to get his lungs to breathe air again. "Wait... Tess!"

Hands grabbed him and forced him to his feet. "No! Make him give her back!"

He was forced to move. Ivas didn't fight back. He couldn't see. The shock of white light had blinded him, his chest throbbed with pain, and he could barely take in a breath. He let the foreign hands push him on until he felt hard wood beneath his boots and saw the warm yellow light of his home. Ruby was to his left, holding his arm, and on his right...

"Tess!"

Her short hair was a mess, but she smiled reassuringly. Ivas grabbed her arm. "You're okay. You're not hurt...?"

"I'm fine. Everything's okay."

Ruby stood up and shut the door, locking it in place. Blanc glared at it, barking loud bursts of warning. Ruby patted her head until she calmed down.

"Are you hurt?" Tess asked.

"My chest is killing me. I hope I didn't break a rib." Ivas grunted. Tess helped him to the living room and laid him down on the couch.

"Just lay still for now. We'll get you to a doctor tomorrow."

"What happened? I saw a light. The giant had you…"

Tess reached into her shirt and pulled out a necklace. Connected to a long chain was a glass bottle that shined with a strange liquid.

No, it wasn't quite liquid, it almost looked like…

Light.

Like a shining bit of reflective water had been plucked from a river and placed in a bottle.

"I could see just fine as I was driving up," Tess explained. "I saw your cottage lights, but the minute I stepped out of the car, it was like the fog spun me around and I couldn't see anything even though I knew your house was just a few yards away. I kept walking in that direction, but I wasn't getting anywhere. Then I saw your light, I heard you calling for me, and then…"

Tess trailed off and hugged herself, looking at the ground. Ivas recognized the look in her eyes as they became unfocused and lost.

"Hey, it's alright." Ivas took her hand. Tess squeezed it tightly.

"There was…something in the fog. It was coming for you."

Ivas nodded.

"But I had this." Tess held up the bottle, laughing a little. "I thought I was being so stupid."

"What is it?"

"It's… I went to a witch."

"What?"

"I know. I felt so silly, but I just needed something to… put me at ease. The fog on the water scared me so much, I needed some comfort, even if it wasn't real. So, I went to a witch and she gave me this. She said it was a drop of moonlight, that it would light up any darkness, even the fog, and cast away any evil there."

"That was the light I saw?"

"I opened the bottle and it let out beams just like moon-light. It scared that...thing away, and I saw you and the cottage in front of me all along."

"I saw it too," Ruby said. She stood in the living room door, listening silently. Blanc had retired to the fireplace, which told Ivas that the giant must have moved on. "I watched from the window for your fire. When it went out, I came outside. I saw you by the moonlight and dragged you back in."

Tess looked up at Ruby and her mouth dropped. Ivas quickly squeezed her arm to quiet her.

"It's okay. This is Ruby Mclaven, remember? The girl that disappeared."

"Yeah, but..." Tess stared at Ruby's horns in shock. Ruby held her head up defiantly.

"When Ruby came out of the fog she... Well..." Ivas motioned toward her. The horns spoke for themselves.

"I don't understand," Tess said. "What have you two been doing?"

"We haven't done anything," Ruby said sharply. "Ivas saved my life. I got a little souvenir from the fog, but Ivas is helping me fix it."

"The fog did that to you?" Tess's voice filled with sympathy. "Oh my god. I always thought it was just stories, just stupid..."

"Easy." Ivas tried to hold her, but it was too late. Tess went on her hands and knees, hyperventilating.

"Are you going to be sick?"

Tess shook her head. Ivas rubbed her back. "Ruby, could you grab her some water?"

While the faucet ran, Tess started to catch her breath. "I'm a sailor, I don't get sick."

"Of course not."

"Ruby… That monster…"

"I know. But it's all okay. You had your…moonlight?" Ivas touched her necklace.

Tess nodded and grabbed the vial in her hand, squeezing it tightly like a talisman. "That's right. I thought it was just a lucky charm, like a rabbit's foot. I didn't think that it was real. That any of this was real."

Ivas stared at the bottle around Tess's neck. "You said you got this from a witch?"

Ruby reentered the room, and Tess sat up to accept the water. After several long gulps, she seemed to calm down. "That's right. I went to the sea witch who lives by the shore."

"What witch is this? I've never heard of her."

Tess smiled. "She keeps to herself, but I knew her secret."

"Like a real witch with the pointy hat?" Ruby asked.

"No, nothing like that," Tess said. "I thought if anyone could give me something to beat the fog, she could."

Ivas sat up, testing his ribs, and took the bottle in his fingers. He studied it more closely. "And it worked."

Ruby smiled, her eyes twinkling with the same idea that was forming in Ivas's mind. "If the moonlight worked, then…"

"Maybe she can help us."

CHAPTER 9

THE TRIO VISITS A WITCH BY THE SEA

Sleep came fitfully for the trio. No one was willing to go fully asleep, but in the early hours of morning, they managed to pass out from exhaustion, Tess on Ivas's bed, Ruby on the couch, and Ivas piling up with blankets and pillows on the floor. Blanc was happy for his company.

Ruby woke up first, while it was still dark. She rose out of Ivas's bed, stiff and sleepy, but with a sense of urgency. She needed to get home before her mom woke up. Blanc looked up at Ruby as she entered the living room. She gave her a sweet, dog-smile and wagged her tail gently.

"Shh." Ruby put a finger to her lips. Blanc went still and returned her head to Ivas's lap. The shepherd snored, unaware. Ruby continued her journey through the house but paused in the kitchen. After rummaging through some drawers, she found a scrap piece of paper and pen and wrote out a note to let them know where she would be. She laid it on the counter and left through the front door.

There was just enough dawn to see by, and fog hung in heavy patches across the landscape, but there was no malice to it, just an early morning eeriness. Ruby was aware of an ache in her head as she walked across the hillside toward home. She kept reaching up under Ivas's hat—which she had borrowed again—to stroke the horns growing there. They were definitely longer now. It was going to be hard to hide them.

The sun was high enough to turn the landscape golden when Ruby reached home. The dew gave the air a wet leaf smell, and as the sky turned blue, the air became crisp and cool. Ruby found that her bedroom window was still cracked open from her departure and slid back inside. The house was quiet and warm. Ruby sighed with relief, throwing off her dirty clothes and collapsing onto the bed.

As tired as she felt, however, sleep didn't come. She kept touching her horns, thinking of witches and moonlight and giants. Ruby reached under her pillow where she had hidden her father's message. She read it over and over again; she must have read it a hundred times by now. Tears pricked her eyes as she read the word "Pumpkin."

She read his warning to run.

But Ruby wasn't going to run. Tess had a boat. Tess knew a witch.

Ruby was going to save him.

She hid the letter away again and gave up on sleep. She could smell coffee, which meant her mom was up. Ruby got dressed, pulling on some pants, her old, familiar boots, and a jacket to keep away the autumn breeze. She brushed her teeth, then wandered down the hall into the kitchen, where her mom sat at the table, an empty coffee cup set aside. She was staring out the window with an expression that made Ruby's stomach clench.

"Mom?" she asked tentatively. Hannah's eyes were full of pain, yet her face was still with apathy. She turned her head slowly toward Ruby and sighed. Shoulder's sagging in defeat.

"Sit down, Honey."

To her mom, Ruby was "Honey," to her dad, "Pumpkin."

"Mom…" Ruby couldn't sit down. Her hand flew to her mouth, where she began to rub her fingernails against her lips. It was a bad habit she had as a child, one she had broken a long time ago, but now she immediately fell back into it, enjoying the smoothness of her nails against her lips.

"Leave your lips alone," Hannah murmured. She took a deep breath and picked up her cup, even though there was nothing in it. "I got a call from the coast guard this morning."

Ruby could practically hear the blood rushing in her ears. The coast guard? Call? She hadn't even heard the phone ring…

"They've had to call off the search for your dad's boat… because of the fog." She was holding her cup too tight. Ruby pressed her fingers against her mouth.

"They don't think they're going to search anymore…" Hannah's mouth remained open, as if to continue, but no words came out. She brought the cup to her lips, but of course it was empty. Hannah made an ugly noise of frustration and threw the cup into a corner. The handle broke off with a little *clink*.

Ruby jumped and took her hand away from her mouth, shoving it in her pocket instead.

Hannah started to cry. She stood up and held her hands out to hug her daughter, but Ruby shook her head, not moving.

"I'm not…"

Hannah went to her and put her arms around Ruby's neck. Ruby didn't hug her back. Her eyes were hard, and her mind was calculating.

"I'm not giving up," she finished. "They can stop searching, but I won't."

"Ruby, Honey…" Hannah tried to control herself, but she couldn't stop trembling.

"Don't cry, Mom," Ruby said, finally patting her mom's back. "I'll find him."

Hannah shook her head, unable to answer. She let Ruby go, sniffing, walking toward the bathroom to find some tissue.

Ruby saw her mom's face, snotty and red and swollen. It terrified her more than the fog, more than the monsters inside them. She started running without really deciding that she was going to. She flew out the front door into the morning sun. The blue sky and the autumn breeze seemed to suggest that nothing bad was happening at all.

Ruby kept running, down the road and over the grassy field toward the old lighthouse. She wanted to cry but pushed it away. There was work to do.

Ivas and Tess were coming. They had a witch to find.

~

*I*vas woke throughout the night, thinking he heard the thundering footsteps of the giant, so it was surprising when he slept through Ruby leaving the cottage. By the time he woke again, it was late in the morning and Ruby had left a note.

*I*vas,

I had to sneak back home so as not to upset Mom. Let's meet at Beacon Point at noon. I want to meet the sea witch with you.

—R

. . .

*I*vas frowned at the letter. Were they meeting the witch today? Had that been agreed upon? He stood up, stiff and groggy, recalling the conversation from the night before. Blanc was awake and chipper as he stepped outside, and he envied her unending dog-energy.

Yes, the sea witch. It had been Ruby's idea to go see her. After all, she had provided the moonlight; maybe she had something that could help their quest. Ruby had argued further that she should join them because the witch might have something to get rid of her horns.

Ivas shook his head as he and Blanc went to the barn to release the sheep. He kept losing count of the sheep as they filed out. The counting made his eyelids heavy. He kicked himself for the stereotype. He would have never agreed to let Ruby go if he hadn't been half asleep.

Yeah, right.

Then again, maybe not. She had a will as fiery as her hair.

Beacon's Point at noon, that didn't leave much time for a nap. Ivas gave up counting the sheep and left Blanc to guard them. He went back inside and laid down on the couch, ready to rest his eyes for just a minute…

～

*T*wo hours later, he was woken by the sound of clatter from the kitchen. Tess was awake, making breakfast. No, lunch by now. Ivas looked at the clock and groaned.

"Ivas? Sorry, I tried to be quiet."

"No, no, I just… Were we supposed to meet Ruby?"

"Yes. Just relax, I doubt she'll be there on time either. We all needed sleep."

Ivas was happy to accept this excuse and settled back into

the couch, letting his brain come back to life slowly. Tess continued cooking and Ivas smelled sausage and potatoes. That was enough to give him strength to rise.

"Thank you," he said, sitting as Tess set out plates.

"You're welcome, though you look like you could sleep all day."

"I'm fine, really. Just been a rough couple of nights."

"What's been going on, Ivas? What's happened?"

"You're right about the wall of fog. Something is coming. Ruby and I… It's hard to explain, and a long story, but we received a warning about it."

"How?" Tess scooped out a spoonful of mashed potatoes for each plate. Ivas added a large slab of butter to his, allowing it to melt over the steaming mush. Tess set out a plate of sausages as well.

Ivas explained the events of the previous nights reluctantly, tired and not really believing his own words, but Tess seemed to accept it in stride, fueled by what she had witnessed the night before. As he recalled the bizarre events that had transpired, they became much more realistic in his own mind as a result, like a dream fading from memory that suddenly became sharp and clear again. Ivas felt his energy return as he finished the meal and the story. The urgency to act was apparent, and he went to the bathroom to clean himself and change clothes.

It was well past noon before they finally left the cottage. Ivas was torn about bringing Blanc along. He wanted her company, but at the end of all of this, the sheep were still his livelihood, so he left her on guard as he and Tess set off in Tess's old truck. The vehicle was one she had inherited from her father. It was prized for its terrain mobility and hated for its constant need of repair, which it usually didn't receive.

The truck clattered to life and chattered its complaints as

they drove away. Ivas pulled his cap down over his ears and wrapped his scarf around his chin.

"Sorry about the heater," Tess said.

"No complaints here. Better than my bike."

"This thing's about as good as a bike," Tess joked. They both knew she loved the car, if only for sentimental reasons. Ivas remembered taking many rides in the truck with Tess and her father when they were children, back when the radio worked and they could run the air conditioner on those rare hot days of summer.

"So, how do you know this witch?" Ivas asked.

"She's kind of a member of my family. My father's aunt by marriage. After her husband—my great uncle—passed away, she kind of entered a place of solitude. My great uncle worked on a barge and would be gone for long periods of time, so Great Aunt Marlene would spend her days on the beach collecting shells and little treasures the ocean gave her. Sometimes she would keep them, or sell them to tourists."

"You knew her pretty well?"

"Well, she's the only real family that lives nearby anymore, so we would always visit on her birthday, or stop by on Christmas Eve. I liked her a lot as a kid, but as I grew older, we didn't visit as much. Like I said, she became pretty solitary."

"But she's a witch...?"

"Practices witchcraft, yes. It's something she told me about when I was a kid. I asked her why she collected sea stuff, and she told me the sea was full of magic, and the things she collected were magical trinkets the sea gave to her. I didn't really think about it again until...all this fog stuff started happening."

Tess turned off the paved street onto a dirt road that led them uphill. Beacon Point was a historical landmark—the highest point in the area where an abandoned lighthouse sat. Tess parked her truck in the tourist parking lot and they made the short, uphill trek to the lighthouse. It stood beautiful but dark against the grey landscape of the overcast ocean. Since a new lighthouse had been built closer to the village, this one had stood vacant for many years—now just a historic location that acted as a weak draw for tourism.

"Does your aunt live far from here?"

"Just down the cliffside. I told Ruby about it; that's why she wanted to meet here."

Ivas looked around, trying to spot a flash of red hair among the green countryside. From Beacon's Point, he could see the entire rolling hills of the county. Ancient stone walls snaked between patches of farmland, smoke drifted from the chimneys of cottages that dotted the landscape, and several miles down the shoreline was the village.

"Ivas, look." Tess pointed to the horizon of the ocean. Ivas followed her finger but didn't have to search. On the horizon, he could see a plume of white. A wall was an appropriate name for it. The fog rose up from the ocean and touched the grey clouds above. Ivas shivered.

"That's it. That's why I went to Marlene. It scared the shit out of me, so I thought she would know something about it."

"Let's hope so."

"Ivas! Tess!"

They both jerked their heads like startled birds before realizing that the voice came from above. Ruby stood on the railing of the lighthouse, waving down at them. Ivas noted that she had the hood of her jacket drawn over her head.

"How did you get up there?" Ivas asked when Ruby came down. "I thought that place was locked up."

Ruby smirked. "My friends and I break in all the time. I mean, we don't hurt anything. We just like to go up top, look at the scenery, basic teenage mischief."

"At least we finally have some blackmail on you," Ivas joked.

"Marlene lives this way," Tess said. She led them down-hill along the cliffside. It didn't take long for Ivas to spot the cottage down below. It was close enough that Ivas wondered if it was the family home for the lighthouse keeper long ago. They went to the front door and Tess knocked.

It was answered by Marlene, a woman whose age was impossible to tell. She may have been forty or a hundred. She had long white hair tied into a loose bun on her head and wore long warm clothes. Ivas counted a shawl, cardigan, and sweater covering her skinny frame. She had a bright smile.

"Tess! So sweet of you to come by again so soon."

"Of course. Aunt Marlene, this is my best friend Ivas Sbarge, and *his* friend Ruby Mclaven."

"Hello, hello, come inside." Marlene moved out of the way and the three filed after her in an orderly fashion. The cottage was very small, but the space was well used, with cabinets and shelves piled up to the ceiling. They were filled with books, jars of seashells, boxes, vials, and other oddities. It might have had a cluttered, crazy-person vibe, but every-thing was clean and warm. A fireplace was burning, and Marlene put on some tea.

"Aunt Marlene, I wanted to thank you for the moonlight you gave me," Tess said, keeping her tone deep and serious. The three of them sat down on the sofa in Marlene's living room, a small space with a sliding glass window that looked out on the water and filled the room with light. Ruby pressed her fingers to her lips, studying everything with shy interest.

"You're welcome, sweetie. I hope it—"

"It worked."

Marlene looked at Tess with a raised eyebrow, then at Ivas and Ruby, who sat quietly.

"Oh, *good.*" Marlene smiled wickedly. "About time someone else noticed all this fog business. You've been inside it? You've seen the creatures?"

"Have *you?*" Ivas said, surprised by Marlene's frankness. She raised her eyebrows at him.

"That's a long story…"

Ruby stood up abruptly and removed her hood, revealing her horns. Marlene inhaled sharply.

"Here's our story: I went into the fog to find my dad. Ivas went in after me. We know something bad is coming, and soon. We've been warned about it multiple times."

Marlene nodded. "I know, I've heard it in the ocean. Every night the waves come to shore, whispering its name."

Ivas straightened up. "What name?"

"You're really a witch?"

"Auntie, are you doing your drama thing?"

Marlene silenced them with the arch of a very tall eyebrow. When she was certain that they were all listening, she continued. "Something *is* coming; I've known about it for a while. I've seen it in my tea leaves, heard the ocean whispering at night when the fog rolls in. It's taken villages before, and it'll take again."

"The story is true, then?" Ivas risked interrupting.

"To the best of my knowledge it has happened *many* times before. Over the course of hundreds of years, enough time for people to forget, strange enough that no one dares speak of it outside of fiction, the god comes for a sacrifice."

"The god?"

Marlene shrugged. "Too old for any living person to know its name or worship it anymore. It lives off the leftover superstition of the fog, the song the children sing, and now it comes for those who fear it."

"The village."

She nodded.

"But we know it's coming," Ruby said. "We can stop it."

"What can stop a god?" Marlene challenged, but her question was more curiosity than hopelessness.

"Your moonlight worked last night," Tess said. "What if we used something like that again? Something to drive...*it* away?"

"Yeah, do you have some more witchcraft you can use?" Ruby asked.

"Hmm, there is something," Marlene said thoughtfully, "but I'll need a lion's heart, a bat's wing, and the testicle of a shepherd."

It took a moment for the words to sink in. Just as Ivas's face started to burn, Marlene split into a bellowing laugh.

"Haha! Your face! I'm just fucking with you."

Ivas's face continued to burn red, stuck in embarrassment and bewilderment. Ruby smiled widely, and Tess shook her head.

Marlene chuckled to herself as she poured everyone tea. "Sorry, I just like to play on the stereotype. I know when people hear 'witch' they think pointy hats, devil deals, burn-them-at-the stake. That's why I always keep it quiet. I may practice witchcraft, but it's nothing so vulgar."

"Seriously, though, Aunt Marlene," Tess said, "do you have any more of this moonlight we can use?"

"I'm pretty sure it'll take more than moonlight if you really want to save yourselves from the fog," Marlene said. "I'll have to think about this one, consult the cards for advice."

"Have you always known about the fog?" Ivas asked.

"For a long time," Marlene said. "As a kid, of course, I had to sing the gathering song and pick the herbs. I didn't take it seriously until Henry and I moved here right next to the sea.

It's hard to ignore the things you hear at night, the shadows you see. After Henry died and I started practicing my witchcraft, that's when I really knew. The ocean started to tell me things, send me warnings."

Ruby perked up. "Were you visited by a messenger?"

"What do you mean? The postman?"

"No, this thing that lives in the fog, it brings letters from people that have died."

"I…I've never heard of such a thing," Marlene said. Ivas saw a spark of sadness in her eye, but she shook it away. "I'm sure if my Henry had something important to say, he would have told me."

"That's how I heard from my dad," Ruby said. "The Messenger brought me a letter from him, warning me to run. Ivas saw it too."

Marlene looked at Ivas for confirmation.

"It's true. I've seen the Messenger since I was a kid, and I saw it the night Ruby disappeared. That's how I knew to look for her in the fog."

"Really?" Marlene's eyebrow rose thoughtfully. She studied Ivas long enough that he broke eye contact to drink his tea, growing uncomfortable under her stare.

"It seems I have a lot to think about," Marlene said. "I need a walk."

"Want us to wait here?" Tess asked.

"I won't be long. Actually, would you accompany me, Mr. Sbarge? It's always nice to have the company of handsome young men. I could use your help."

"This isn't about my genitals, is it?"

Marlene beamed a bright, beautiful smile for an old witch. "I like a man with a sense of humor."

Marlene added yet more layers to herself, putting on a heavy coat with many pockets, a hat, then gloves, and a scarf.

Once she was sufficiently buried under many layers of wool she went to the door, and Ivas followed.

"Your aunt is amazing," Ruby told Tess as she drank from the teacup.

Tess smiled proudly. "I think so too."

~

"It's a relief to know someone has taken notice of the fog," Marlene told Ivas as they walked away from the cottage toward the sea. The hillside grass became sand under their boots.

"You said the ocean told you?"

"Starting to think I'm a crazy old lady, eh?" Marlene chuckled. "Do you know what witchcraft actually is, Mr. Sbarge?"

"I guess not. I'm guessing it's not like fairy tales?"

"No, it's not magic, it's not evil. It's just a way to worship nature, to use nature's energy for your bidding. I am in tune to the ocean, the high winds, and the storms. I could feel what the fog really was.

"My witchcraft was a great comfort after Henry passed away," Marlene said, her voice quiet in a way that resonated with Ivas's own loss-worn heart. "Being close to the ocean made me feel close to him. I feel the energy in the seashells I collect, and they give me strength." Marlene smirked. "This probably all sounds like the mad ramblings of an old woman to you."

"Not after what I saw," Ivas said.

"Why did you go into the fog, Mr. Sbarge? For the girl?"

"No." The "no" came immediately, but the explanation took a moment for him to put into words. "I just… The fog has taken from me before. When I was a teenager, it took my grandfather, and it almost took me."

"And you didn't want them to take another?"

"Not when there was something I could do."

Marlene nodded knowingly, then said, "Well, that was very stupid of you."

"Excuse me?"

Marlene raised what was becoming a trademark eyebrow at him. "Is guilt the only reason? You thought you could make up for your grandpa's death by saving her?"

"I... How is that stupid?"

"Feeling guilty is stupid. For *years* I was plagued with guilt about my Henry. Years! I didn't even do anything wrong. He died of pneumonia after a boat trip, peacefully in his bed. How is that my fault? But still I felt I must have done something wrong to draw the grim reaper to him. What good did it do me? Did Henry come back? Was he grateful for my sacrifice? No! He just stayed stubbornly dead. I wasn't making anything right. I was just making my own shortening life miserable."

"But...that's different. He died in bed. I actually made my grandpa come out into the fog with me. It *was* my fault."

"Oh? Then you've been tricking me! You're actually a monster from the fog disguised as a human!"

"That's not—"

"You didn't make that old man do anything. He was an adult, and he went into the fog of his own accord, and he gave in to the fog's influence and got himself killed."

"That's not fair!"

"The man is dead! Who cares what's fair for him? You're alive. Yours is the only fairness that matters now. And none of this is fair to you, this suffering you put yourself through."

"But...you couldn't..." Ivas tried to find the words to defend the things he had been telling himself for years.

My fault.

I deserve it.

I'm sorry.

I should have...

What if...

But grandpa wouldn't...

"The man is *dead*," Marlene said harshly. "He doesn't matter anymore. You matter."

Ivas was having trouble breathing. He wanted to scream at her, but his throat was swelling with the need to cry.

"Would you even still be here herding sheep if you didn't feel guilty? Or did you feel you owed it to him? Would you finally have asked out my niece if you thought you deserved to be happy?"

"Shut up!" Ivas hated himself for shouting those words because it made him sound like a teenager, and made it sound like she was completely right.

She's not...

Wasn't she?

He turned away before he could shout anything more, walking quickly away from her. Marlene didn't follow.

The sand made it hard for Ivas to make a quick escape. He concentrated on the harsh crash of the ocean to drown out his own chaotic thoughts. It was perfect brooding weather. The sky was overcast and the wind pushed his hair back away from his face when he looked out at the ocean where the fog was making its way to shore.

Then he stopped and looked back over his shoulder.

"Why are you telling me all this?"

"Because if you're going to go back into the fog you need to be strong, and guilt is a weakness. It's a lie the fog will use against you. Why did you go into the fog the very first time?"

"Because I was a stupid kid. I thought the fog would take me somewhere better. I wanted all the stories to be true, for there to be magic. So when the Messenger came to my window, I tried to follow him, and my grandpa tried to stop me."

That was when the tears broke loose and Ivas felt them roll down his cheeks, to his chin, down his neck and under his shirt. "It was always the fog, wasn't it?" he whispered. "They got in my head."

Marlene nodded, though Ivas had no idea how she heard him. "It's not stupid to look for magic in our darkest moments, Ivas."

Ivas felt his foot become wet and jumped back in surprise. The ocean slipped back, then rose again, rushing up to meet him. Ivas backed away, and when the water descended again, he saw something lying in the sand. Ivas bent down and scooped it up before the water could bury it in the sand. It was a beautiful yellow sphere, perfectly smooth and fit right in his palm. It was impossible to tell what it had once been, perhaps a piece of glass or a smoothed-down rare stone. It was the sort of thing Ivas would have loved as a kid. It felt full of magic.

A heavy gust of wind rolled off the water, stealing Marlene's hat and flying it out to sea. She watched it go.

"The ocean gives, but sometimes it asks for something in return. Can you hear it?" She stared as the cap hit the waves.

Ivas closed his eyes, concentrating on the wind.

"Even the ocean is worried. It's calling its name."

"What's its name?"

"It lost its name long ago. Now it's just The Dead God."

CHAPTER 10

THE WITCH DEALS THE CARDS

"The Dead God is called such because that was when his story really began," Marlene explained. She sat at the head of the table, shuffling a deck of tarot cards, with the eyes of the shepherd, the horned girl, and the sailor all on her, interrupting only with sips of tea.

"It is said that his last, dying breath came to earth as a cascade of evil fog full of the darkness of men. The story ended, and everyone forgot the most important part of stories that involve a god."

"What?" Ruby whispered.

Marlene smiled. "Gods always come back to life."

She handed the deck to Ivas. They were old and well-used. The tops were black with silver, archaic symbols.

"Each of you has entered the fog and come out alive. Shuffle the deck, take a card, and we will find the answer we seek."

Ivas gave the cards a brief overhand shuffle before taking the top card. Ruby took her time, expertly riffling the cards before taking her pick. Tess used a Corgi shuffle, taking her card after fanning the deck out in front of her. Marlene took the remaining cards and then the three, keeping them face down. She turned them over one by one. When she did, three illustrated suns smiled up at them.

"Huh," Marlene blinked in surprise. "There's only one sun card in that deck…"

"What does it mean?"

"Well, usually tarot is not so literal, but considering the power of moonlight, I'm guessing this means we need the sun."

"The sun? That's it?" Ivas asked incredulously.

"That's it?" Marlene taunted. "Oh yes, Ivas, it's that easy. I'll just make the sun come up in the middle of the night. Defying the laws of physics is trivial for a witch."

"I really can't tell if you're being serious."

"Half and half," Marlene admitted. "But I think that sunstone the ocean gave you should be of help. It's no coincidence."

"This?" Ivas pulled the gem out of his pocket. It was partially clear with a copper shine that caught the light. Marlene nodded.

"That's an ocean-smoothed sunstone, rare and perfect for sun-based magic. Obviously."

"What are you going to do?" Ruby asked.

"Catch the sun, I suppose."

"I want to help," Ruby said, jumping out of her chair. "I want to learn some witchcraft."

"It's getting close to dinner time, Ruby," Ivas pointed out. "Shouldn't you get back home?"

"He's right. I need a nap, and I need to do some research before anything else, but why don't you come back tomorrow? I would love your help."

Ruby nodded with warranty. "I'll tell Mom I'm meeting a friend for lunch."

"Always nice when your lie matches up with the truth,

eh?" Marlene smirked. She looked at the three smiling suns and shuffled them back into the deck. She dealt the cards face up one by one until the entire deck was revealed. Only one yellow sun card was present.

"Wow," Ruby gasped.

"I *saw* you put all three cards back in the deck," Ivas said.

"Are you tricking us?" Tess checked Marlene's many sleeves but found no cards.

"Remember how I told you that witchcraft wasn't really magic?" Marlene asked Ivas. "Well, sometimes magic is witchcraft."

Ruby found a clock sitting on the fireplace mantel and finally noticed the time. "Damn, you're right. Mom will be back from town soon. I'd better get going."

"I'll give you a ride," Tess volunteered. They all rose and Marlene saw them to the door, waving goodbye and insisting that they come back soon. Ivas left the sunstone with her for safekeeping.

"I'll have an answer for you in a couple of days."

On the way back uphill to the truck, Ivas held back. "You guys go ahead. Take Ruby home. I need to walk into town."

"You sure? I'll give you a lift."

"I'm fine, really. I need to think."

"I'll find you when I'm done."

Tess's truck puttered off into the countryside. Ivas turned the other way and followed the road to the village.

~

"I knew your dad," Tess said as she steered the truck toward Ruby's house. "He was a great sailor."

"Is," Ruby said gently.

Tess nodded. "I remember seeing you at the docks when you were little, but I haven't seen you there in a while."

"Yeah." Ruby felt a pang of guilt. "I get caught up in school and my friends like to hang out on the weekends. Dad always talked about teaching me how to sail, but...I don't know. I kind of lost interest."

"There's nothing wrong with that," Tess assured her. "What do you want to do?"

"I don't really know. The school counselor keeps asking everyone that, trying to help us figure out what to go to college for, but...I don't see why I have to decide right now."

"You certainly don't have to," Tess said. "Nothing wrong with just having some fun."

"You're, like, the first adult to say that." Ruby smiled. "Don't get me wrong, I have some ideas. I want to do something where I can work outside, but actually picking out a job is too much of a commitment."

The truck bumped along, but Ruby felt comfortable, like she was in a rocking chair. The truck smelled like old vinyl and the seats were torn, the floor rusting away. There was something comfortably rustic about it. "This truck is great."

Tess laughed. "It runs on sheer willpower. One of these days, it's going to just fall apart in the middle of the road."

"Nah, this is one of those cars where it gets so old it'll never die."

"It's been through so much I don't know what could stop it now," Tess agreed.

"You should teach me how to work on it, then I'll become a mechanic and my problem will be over."

"I totally will if you're serious."

"We'll see. I'm still having fun being a stupid teenager."

Tess smiled sincerely. "You're the least stupid teenager I've ever met."

They came to a rickety stop in front of Ruby's home.

Even in park, the truck continued to putter and shake. Ruby could feel the vibrations in her legs as she got out. Hannah stepped through the front door and waved to Tess.

"Hope she didn't put you to any trouble," Hannah said, walking up to the driver-side window.

"If she were trouble I would have made her walk her butt home," Tess teased, throwing a wink at Ruby.

"I appreciate it, Tess."

"Hey, no worries. See you later, Ruby!"

Ruby waved goodbye as Tess turned around and drove away, leaving a trail of foul-smelling, grey smoke. Hannah stood quietly at Ruby's side as they watched the truck move toward the hilltop.

"I'm sorry for running off like that," Ruby said as the vehicle disappeared over the hill. Her hand was back to her mouth, fingernails resting on her lips.

"I know this is hard for you," Hannah answered, placing a hand on her shoulder. "I think we need to talk about all of this, figure out what we need to do."

"Yeah… Okay."

"I'm going to make dinner. Why don't you wash up, then we'll talk. Okay?"

"Yeah." Ruby didn't *want* to talk. Figure out what they needed to do? What did that mean? What if her mom wanted to leave? Ruby seriously considered sneaking out again as she went to the bathroom. Her lips became dry as she continued to run her fingernails over them, no longer conscious that she was doing it.

She removed her hood to wash her face and was shocked by her reflection. The horns were still small enough to hide but had started to branch. Ruby's hands trembled, so she rested them on the faucet to catch her breath. She was running out of options. She couldn't wear a hat to the dinner table. She couldn't have whatever conversation her mom wanted to have. Ruby just wanted to rest.

She washed her face and hands, soothed by the warm water. She decided to fake ill, skip dinner, even though her stomach was empty and growling. When was the last time she had eaten?

Ruby leaned into the sink and made a loud moan, just enough for it to echo and get her mom's attention. She opened the bathroom door a crack and called down the hall. "Mom? I'm not feeling very good. I'm going to take a shower and lie down."

"Honey, you've been out all day. You need to eat."

Ruby agreed. The smell of food was tantalizing. Her mom was frying something and it made her stomach grumble.

"Okay, just let me shower," Ruby called back. She could at least wrap her hair up in a towel. That would buy some time.

Ruby turned on the shower and sat on the rim of the tub, letting the water run through her fingers until it became nice and warm. She threw off her clothes and stepped under the water. It felt glorious on her aching body. She shampooed her hair—odd with the horns in the way—and rinsed herself off.

Everything was fine. She would get some food, then go straight to bed. She and Hannah could talk tomorrow. Everything else could wait. She just needed some rest.

Ruby stayed in the shower until the water became cold. She thoroughly dried herself and got dressed again before concentrating on getting her hair dry, a difficult task with the protrusions on her head.

"Honey, are you throwing up?"

Ruby's head spun around at the sound of her mom's voice and terror clutched her stomach. The doorknob was turning. She hadn't locked it. Her towel fell from her suddenly limp hands as the door opened.

Hannah stared. Ruby screamed, more scared than her mom. Hannah jumped at the sound, but she didn't move, didn't take her eyes off her daughter's horns.

Ruby didn't think, she ran.

She almost knocked her mom over as she cannoned down the hallway. A chair fell as she tore through the kitchen. The door slammed shut behind her.

She heard Hannah calling her name.

But she didn't stop. It had gotten dark outside—how had it gotten dark so early? She kept running, getting swept up in the fog.

The fog was already there. She hadn't even realized…

~

*I*t was a short walk to the cobblestone streets, and Ivas was grateful to be in a populated area, away from the frightening isolation of his cottage. After what happened last night, he wasn't sure if he could spend another night out there. He considered the local inn as he passed by, and even stepped in to ask if they allowed dogs. Not that it mattered, he could always stay the night with Tess.

Would you have finally asked out my niece...

Ivas shook his head as if to physically dislodge the thought. In truth, he had never seriously considered Tess from a romantic standpoint. But then, he couldn't remember considering anyone that way. He tried to recall any crushes from his high school days or sneaking looks at magazines, enjoying women or men from television, but nothing was coming to mind.

He shook his head again. This was a terrible time to suddenly realize he might have some abnormal sexuality.

And with Tess, it didn't really matter. She was his friend, and that had always been more than enough.

"Ivas!" A heavy force suddenly struck Ivas's shoulder, knocking him forward. Ivas cried out and spun around. It was Jack, out of his sheriff uniform, with a twinkle in his eye that suggested some debauchery was at hand. There was some beer foam on his beard, and he had put his glasses away.

"Sorry if I startled you. I saw you walk by the pub and thought I'd say hello."

Ivas glanced over his shoulder. The pub Jack referred to was a favorite town watering hole. Tonight, it was full of people, humming with conversation, and glowing with warm firelight. It was very inviting.

"No, no, I was lost in my own thoughts," Ivas said. "How are you, Jack?"

Jack beamed. "Doing great, old chap. You were right about Ruby. She turned right up, safe and sound."

"Of course," Ivas said reassuringly. "That really got to you, huh, Jack?"

"Hmm?" Jack wasn't listening. He took Ivas by the arm and led him to the building. Ivas felt engulfed with voices and warmth as they stepped through the door. Jack pulled him up to the bar.

"A round for my friend, please! On me, Ivas."

"Very kind. How many rounds is this for you?"

Jack answered with a belly-shaking laugh, then gave Ivas a hug. "We're good friends, aren't we, Ivas? Since we were boys, you've been my best friend."

"Of course we are, Jack." Ivas felt butterflies from the compliment. Despite Jack's inebriated state, he knew it was sincere. "You and Tess are my best friends."

"Ah! Tess! Where is she? She needs to be here! We can't all… We can't drink together if we're not together."

"She might turn up soon."

"The three of us haven't hung out since… When was it?"

"We had tea at Cuppa a few weeks ago," Ivas reminded him, though that tea had been proceeded by several months of friendship absence that comes with the busy life of sailors, farmers, and lawmen.

"We must celebrate! Ruby's been returned and all is safe in the village." Jack sat down and looked at his drink. He was on the line of happy-drunk and sad-drunk. Sometimes it just took a swallow. "I'm a good sheriff, aren't I, Ivas?"

"You're not corrupt, you know everyone in town by name, and you take personal vendettas against any harm that comes to this place," Ivas said. "Even if you're not always the best sheriff, you're always the best man for the job."

Jack smiled, sobering slightly at the sentiment. "If we hadn't found Ruby…I don't know what I would have done, or what this town would have done. Every adult is the parent to every kid in a way. We'd all be heartbroken."

"But we did find her. You can't be too sensitive to these things, Sheriff. You'll break yourself."

Jack nodded. "Maybe being sheriff really wasn't the best job for me. I take it all so personally. When I find kids who graffiti the church, I know their parents. When someone robs a store, it turns out to be some chap I went to school with. It's easy to put strangers in cuffs and lock them up, but when it's people you know…"

Ivas rubbed Jack's back reassuringly. "It's all right, Jack. You can always move to the city, then you'll have plenty of strangers to lock up."

That was enough to get a smile, and Jack got back into the spirit of things. They enjoyed a couple of drinks together, and Ivas was beholden to the company.

Outside, the sky darkened and the fog started to roll in.

As if sensing the misty omen, the pub began to empty itself. Alcohol couldn't numb the ominous fear that years of superstition had instilled in the village. Everyone went home. Ivas sighed. He had been tempted by the escape from isolation, and now it was dark, his sheep were still out, and—after a scan of the many empty glasses in front of Jack—he had no ride home.

"I'm not *that* drunk," Jack said after listening to Ivas's dilemma. He then promptly laid his head down on the bar and started to snore.

"I'll drive your truck back up to my farm," Ivas said. "You'll just have to stay the night."

Jack grinned sleepily. "Will there be s'mores and fingernail painting?"

"There would be if you could hold a brush straight."

"Do it for me." Jack held out his hand as if for Ivas to kiss it. Instead, Ivas took Jack's arm and helped him out of his seat. Once on his feet, Jack was surprisingly steady and walked without aid. Ivas assumed he was much more tired than drunk.

Outside, the fog was crawling in, curling around their feet. The turquoise light of twilight was the only source of comfort, and it was quickly fleeting.

"Where's your car?" Ivas asked.

"Just over—" Jack interrupted himself. He was staring at the fog as it rose up around their feet up to their knees. Ivas grabbed an old-fashioned lantern that was hanging outside the pub and held it aloft. It was mainly for decoration, but Ivas knew they would need the light.

"It'll be okay. We just need to get to your car."

Jack nodded, but he wasn't moving.

"Jack, Ruby wasn't your fault. She's home safe."

"But what if it happens again?"

"That's the fog in your head. Come on." Ivas took Jack's

arm forcefully and made him walk. Jack took back control, leading him down the road to a public parking lot.

"I hate this fucking fog," Jack muttered. "Every night, it's been foggy. The sailors can't go out, everyone's scared. Every day, the kids are out in the fields singing that damn song."

As if in reproach to Jack's opinion of it, the fog thickened and rose up to their waists. By the light of the buildings, Ivas could see it billowing over the rooftops as it rose like a giant wave.

And in that wave he saw a familiar shadow.

"Car, Jack! Car!"

Startled by Ivas's insistence, Jack panicked and fumbled into his pocket, running for the parking lot. Ivas looked up at the sky where the figure of the giant stood in the cloak of fog. It was watching him with glowing eyes. The giant moved like a ghost, stepping lightly over the buildings. It placed its hand on a chimney for support without disturbing it. In two large strides, it was directly over them and reaching for Ivas.

Ivas held his lantern out, but the weak little candlelight did nothing to deflect the giant. "Get in the car and turn the lights on!" Ivas yelled.

He turned to run, but the giant's hand closed around him. Ivas heard Jack's muffled screams as his feet left the ground. He felt his stomach drop as the air rushed past him and the giant brought him to face height.

"Finally." The giant breathed with relief.

"Let go!"

"No, I'm never letting go of you again." The ground shuddered as the giant started walking away, stepping around buildings. Ivas felt nauseated, being held in the giant's hand.

"You can't keep me in the fog. I'm not afraid of you."

"I don't need you to be." The giant stroked Ivas's hair with one of its fingers, squeezing him tightly. Ivas felt like a mistreated child's toy.

"Why do you keep following me? Why are all you creatures obsessed with us?"

"You couldn't understand..." the giant whispered, and Ivas felt a twinge of sympathy. The giant almost sounded human.

"You have to let me go. Please, I'm begging you. If there's any part of you that remembers what it is to be human, then I am pleading with that part. My friends need me. My sheep are still out." Ivas scrambled for any reason to be released.

"I'm doing this to save you," the giant said. "You'll be safe with me. Something much worse than me is coming."

"You're talking about The Dead God? That's right, I know he's coming."

"He will leave everything to ashes. There will be nothing left. We must take what we can before he comes."

"No! You can't because...because I'm going to stop him."

Even in the dark, Ivas could practically feel the giant's appraising expression of doubt. "You, little shepherd?" As if to illustrate its point, the giant opened its hand so that Ivas sat small and helpless in its palm. Ivas glanced over the edge, wondering if he should risk the jump.

"Listen to me, little human, The Dead God consumes and destroys. He feels the little spark of belief you humans have for him. Yes, even your fear and superstition are enough to draw him. When he comes, the seas will flee, the light will die. Everything will decay under his touch. You will go mad at the sight of him. Your bones will crumble along with the stones of your houses. He is not a god of death, he is not an employee of Hades or Hell, he is simply...dead. And all will die with him."

"How? Why?"

"It takes a long time for a god to disappear when it dies.

Its ghost, its corpse, whatever you want to call it, will remain an echo of its divinity, dragging down with it anything it can reach."

"Does it even know it's dead?"

"Who can say? But that is not the point. The point is that now you know what The Dead God is. Is that what you want to face, shepherd?"

"No, I don't want to face it at all." Ivas stood up in the giant's palm. "But I can't let my village fall to something that's been dead for centuries."

"It will take more than your good intentions to stop The Dead God."

"I know. I'm going to capture the sun."

In the perfect timing that the universe takes pride in accomplishing, a beam of light suddenly flooded over Ivas. He cried out in pain, but so did the giant. They both fell, and Ivas tumbled from its grip, hitting the ground and rolling away. He lay still, hoping the giant would lose him, but the creature was fleeing the light, paling and becoming one with the fog.

"Good luck, shepherd."

Ivas looked up, shielding his eyes. He heard water lapping to his right. Under his feet, the ground was soft and gravely. He realized that the giant had taken him to the docks, where the timer for the automatic lights had kicked on.

Ivas laughed, shaking his head at the absurdity of the situation. Coincidence or not, Ivas had something on his side. He stood up and, feeling calm with the lights on, made his way back to the road. The dark village was the perfect setting for monsters, dimly lit and filled with the fog. Ivas shivered, but then hope appeared in the form of a pair of headlights and a blinking red cherry. The truck came to a stop and Jack jumped out.

"Ivas!"

Ivas ran forward and hugged his friend.

"Ivas, what was… The fog…it had you…"

"I got away. The fog lights came on at the docks and I could see."

"Thank God. You just disappeared. It was like something had grabbed you up. I can't believe you ended up on the other side of town."

"Jack, let's get in the car."

"Yes, come on, I'll drive you home."

Jack left the interior lights on as they drove. Unlike Tess's car, the heater worked fine, and Ivas blasted it on his hands. He was trembling.

"Jesus, now I understand why everyone gets so suspicious of the fog," Jack said. "I mean, I turned my back on you for a second and lost you, couldn't see at all. Luckily, I ran into the car and the alarm went off."

Ivas nodded. Jack seemed to be purposefully leaving out certain details of the experience, and Ivas let him. "It's amazing how paranormal it can seem, especially when you've been drinking."

Jack latched on to that thought. "Yes, yes, I had quite a few. Made me panic, see things."

"I got myself all turned around and lost."

"Happens to the best of us."

"Thank you for finding me, Jack."

"Hey, it's my job." Jack winked and floored the gas, zooming out of town limits toward Ivas's home.

The truck rumbled comfortably as they sped over the dirt road. The headlights only gave them a few feet of visibility, but Jack kept it fast in a hurry to get indoors.

This proved to be his error when a horned figure with flaming red hair suddenly appeared in front of them. Her eyes flashed yellow, and Ivas only had a brief moment to notice that she held some mangled creature in her clawed hand.

"Shit!" Jack screamed and hit the brakes. Loose dirt made the truck fish-tail and start to spin. Ruby glared at them and threw her arm out as the back of the pickup whipped around in a circle, coming on a full collision course.

Ivas closed his eyes until he felt the horrible *thump* as the back of the car hit something and came to a stop. He quickly opened his door, searching for Ruby.

We hit her. She's hurt...

Ruby stood next to the car, her arm buried in a dent where she had forced the truck to stop. Ruby was very much unhurt. She walked toward him and Ivas noticed that she was now considerably taller than him. She grabbed the scruff of his coat and pulled him out of the car.

"Ruby, stop! Calm down!" Ivas struggled, but the once petite fifteen-year-old girl man-handled him without any dilemma. "What are you doing?"

Ruby didn't answer. They walked through the dark with Ivas held under her arm like a misbehaving toddler. Ivas heard Jack calling for him, but the headlights of his car were already lost.

"Put me down right now!" Ivas mustered up the deep, frightening voice he had inherited from his grandfather, and at this, Ruby finally hesitated.

"You need to stay close. It's not safe," she said.

She didn't put him down, but the answer at least assured Ivas that she wasn't completely fog-mad. She carried him directly to his cottage, where all the lights were burning bright. Ivas didn't hear the sheep crying, and Blanc was inside, tail wagging as if there was nothing strange about an eight-foot-tall horned girl carrying her master underarm.

Ruby finally sat Ivas down inside and shut the door, locking it.

"What in the hell—?"

"Mom saw my horns," Ruby said. Tears started to fall, and Ivas watched her visibly shrink back to normal size, like a flower closing in on itself. Her eyes returned to their comforting chocolate brown, but the claws and horns stayed.

"Oh, Ruby."

"I didn't know what to do! She walked in on me in the bathroom while I was drying my hair and saw them! I ran away and came here. I even put the sheep away, but when the fog came, I got worried and impatient…"

"You went into the fog?"

"I just… Yes, I went into the fog," she snapped. "And you know what? Nothing touched me."

"But I saw you holding something…"

Ruby smirked. "One thing *tried* to touch me."

"You put a dent in Jack's truck."

"I'm not a monster!"

"I didn't say that!"

"Then what are you saying?"

"I'm worried about you! I just want you to be okay."

Ruby lowered her gaze. "I'm not sure if I'm okay. In the daytime, it's not so bad, but when the fog comes in, it's hard to think."

"It's okay. You can stay here for now. As for your mom…I don't know."

"I don't know either. She probably thinks I'm a freak."

"She doesn't—"

"It's fine. I can handle this. We'll go to Marlene's in the morning and figure something out."

"You can't just hide from your mom."

Ruby gave him an impatient look. "I can't go home and explain these." She pointed at the horns, which had grown bigger since Ivas had seen them last.

"Well…you can…at least call her."

Ruby deflated. "What do I even say?"

"Just let her know you're safe. Go on, use my phone. Just let her know you're with a friend."

With great reluctance, Ruby went into the living room where the landline was. Ivas stayed in the kitchen to give her privacy and realized he was starving. Luckily there was still leftover bangers and mash from Tess's lunch.

Someone tried opening the door, but finding it locked started banging on it violently. Ivas gasped, remembering Jack, and quickly opened it. The sheriff stumbled inside, sweaty and pale.

"Ivas, thank God. Why did you run off like that? I did circles around my truck. I thought you got lost again."

"No, I'm fine. I'm sorry, Jack, it's just that…" Ivas thought quickly. Blanc appeared and jumped onto Jack's knees, demanding attention.

"It was Blanc! She was the thing in the road. I had to chase after her."

Jack's eyes glazed over as he stared down at Blanc, his brain fighting an internal battle between what his eyes saw and what he wanted to see.

"Man, I must have really been drinking," he finally whispered to himself. "I thought Blanc looked like a… Never mind. Just the fog playing tricks on me."

"That's right," Ivas said.

Jack sighed. "I'm completely beat, Ivas. This has been more than enough scares for the night. I'm going home and sleeping 'til noon."

"You and me both, Jack."

Ivas held the door open. Jack had left his truck running with all the lights on. It was parked right beside the porch.

"You, me, and Tess, we do need to hang out," Jack said.

"We do. When the fog finally clears up, let's have a night out together, all three of us."

Jack smiled and nodded.

"Drive safe."

The door snapped shut and the phone clicked as Ruby hung up. They both met in the kitchen.

"Was that your friend?" Ruby asked sheepishly.

"Mmhmm, just making sure I was okay. What did you tell your mom?"

Ruby shrugged. "I told her I was safe. She kept demanding to know what was going on, so I just hung up."

Ivas sighed, shaking his head. "This is a right fine mess."

"It's pretty big. I'd rather go into the fog than explain this to Mom."

"Which you have."

"Which I did," Ruby agreed. "But it's going to be okay! Tomorrow we go to Marlene's and we figure this out."

"Yeah, right," Ivas mumbled to himself. He went through the kitchen, absentmindedly going through the cabinets and fridge looking for food. He seemed to keep forgetting that he was looking for food, however, and made two more circles before Ruby spoke up.

"Are you okay?"

"No."

"Oh… I'm sorry." Ruby was fifteen and she had never seen an adult in mental anguish before, or at least never heard one admit it. She stood there uselessly dumbfounded.

"I envy my friend. Tonight, he saw me kidnapped not only by you—all eight feet and horned head of you—but the giant from the fog, and he was able to shut it all away. He gave himself an explanation and is going home to sleep soundly in his bed. Ignorance really is bliss."

"Yeah, until The Dead God comes and swallows him up," Ruby said. She didn't like how Ivas was talking and was growing angry with him. "Ignorance is what will lead everyone to their doom. But we're not ignorant, we know, and we can do something."

"Can we?" Ivas asked. His question had the same effect deflated balloons and falling streamers have on a birthday party. Ivas sank to the floor. "*I* can't."

Sensing his woe, Blanc came to his side and licked his cheek. Ivas didn't acknowledge her.

"But, Ivas, you've done so much already. You just said you walked away from the giant this very evening."

"That was dumb luck."

"Dad used to say there's no such thing as dumb luck."

"Okay, fine, you want me to say it? I don't *want* to do it. I don't want to fight a bloody god! I don't want to deal with things that belong strictly in horror novels! I'm a fucking shepherd and *I don't want to!*"

The silence was heavy with the tension that followed. Ruby looked at her shoes and Ivas kept his eyes locked on his hands, face burning red.

"You don't have to do anything tonight, Ivas," Ruby finally whispered. She was terrifyingly aware that she was fifteen and knew nothing of the fragility of the human mind and that her words would mean nothing to a man who had lived much longer than her and lost so much more. "You don't even have to do anything tomorrow. The sheep are put away, the fireplace is lit, so, tonight, right now, there's nothing you have to do."

Ivas didn't answer.

"Well, I lied. There is one thing you have to do."

"What?"

"Stand up and go to your bed. But after that, you don't even have to move." Ruby stepped forward and offered her hands. Blanc wagged her tail, sensing that the climax of the silent tension had passed.

"See? Blanc believes in you."

Ivas sighed and took Ruby's hands, letting her help him up.

"I bet she'll keep you company in your room."

"Blanc would sleep under the covers with me if I let her."

Ruby laughed, and the sound made Ivas's shoulders slump in relaxation. Ruby shut the door to the bedroom so that Ivas could change. Shedding his clothes was like shedding the day, and he found that he at least had the energy to take a shower.

Ruby heard the water running, so she went to the kitchen. It took some scrounging, but she managed to find some nonperishable food items that would make a decent dinner, including some pasta noodles in the back of a cabinet, and a can of tomato paste.

When Ivas stepped out of the shower there was a plate of spaghetti waiting for him on his bedside table. Ruby had used leftover sausage from the lunch Tess had made in place of meatballs. Ivas put on pajamas, then took his plate out to the kitchen. Ruby was eating hers there.

"Why don't you eat in bed?" she asked.

"I'm not feeling well, but I'm not going to be rude," Ivas said. He joined her at the table. Blanc watched them both eagerly, and Ivas noted her begging demeanor as a sign that Ruby had already snuck her a sausage or two.

"I'd…like to apologize for…" Ivas began.

"For what? Being human?"

"For being a weak-willed human."

"You're not weak-willed, otherwise you would have done what your friend had done. You would never have gone into the fog after me. After all that, I think you've earned a breakdown or two."

"So, what's your excuse? Have you been secretly crying in the bathroom this whole time?"

"No, no crying, not even nightmares," Ruby said. She pointed at the things protruding from her head. "It's the horns."

"What about them?"

Ruby shrugged. "They…they're my shield. I don't know how else to put it."

Ivas stared at them, for the first time really studying them, having always averted his eyes before. He raised his hand as if to touch them. "May I?"

She nodded and leaned her head forward. Ivas ran his fingers over the cartilage, solid and real. He touched the base where the horns met flesh, even gave them a little tug to reassure himself.

"Sorry, I just…"

"It's okay. I get caught up in them too." Ruby lifted her head again. She felt oddly proud of her horns.

"But you're not scared about having them?"

"Not really. They make me feel…strong."

"You're walking a fine line, Ruby."

"I'm *not* going to become one of those fog monsters," she said pointedly.

"You seemed pretty close tonight. You scared the shit out of me."

"But I didn't hurt you. I know it's dangerous, but Marlene is going to help me."

Ivas nodded. He couldn't scold her for something that was out of her control. "You're right. I'm sorry. We've been through so much together, but I don't know anything about you."

"Are you asking?"

"Yes."

She shrugged in that way teenagers do when they're asked personal questions. "I don't know. I go to school. I have lots of friends. Or I did. I haven't really seen any of them since Dad died. Mom let me stay home from school."

"What do you like to do?"

"I don't know. I play lacrosse at school and croquet with my family."

Ruby paused as if to let him interject, but Ivas remained silent. In doing so, Ruby's gaze drifted away, her eyes seeing some past memory, one where her family was whole and everything was happy.

"Dad always kicked my butt at croquet," she said quietly, handling the memory with care. It was a happy one, but full of pain. "He never took it easy on me. Mom would hold back and let me win, but Dad would always knock my ball really far away and tease me. It was always this silly thing with us —he would knock my ball too far, so I would hit his, and we wouldn't even be playing anymore, just chasing each other around with mallets."

Then the tears came, as they would always come when she thought of him. "I think he wanted me to learn how to laugh in the face of failure."

She took a moment to sniff and wipe her cheeks. Ivas watched her, respectfully silent.

"I can still see him so clearly," she said, voice cracking. "He had this jacket that was torn, but he wouldn't get a new one. And I can see his smile. I still remember how his laugh sounds—he always laughed at stupid things like puns and old cartoons."

Her voice broke, and tears were falling too hard to speak, so she put her head on the table to cry. She pressed her thumb up against her bottom lip. Ivas continued to watch her, finally starting to understand. This was why she was so desperate for the fog and adventure—even if it meant danger and deformity. At the end of the day, when all was quiet, there was nothing to take her mind off her grief. That was what the horns really were.

Ivas took her hand away from her mouth and squeezed it tight. Ruby squeezed back.

"I know it's hard, but I'm right here. It's okay."

She cried until she became too tired to continue. It seemed that all the turmoil had finally caught up with her. This time, Ivas helped *her* to bed, and it felt good to be of use to someone. On the couch, Ruby fell asleep right away. Blanc joined her, and the two cuddled against each other. Ruby buried her face in Blanc's white fur.

Ivas sat by the fireplace, watching over them until he was sure they were both fast asleep. When the fire started to die, he added another log, then went to his own bed. He slipped under the covers and entered a death-like sleep, blissfully devoid of dreams.

CHAPTER 11

THE WITCH AND THE HORNED GIRL
CHASE THE SUN AND THE SHEPHERD
GETS A LETTER

While the night left tears and exhaustion, the sun brought renewed energy and things seemed a bit more manageable. Ivas and Ruby woke naturally from an uninterrupted sleep, both happy to see the sky free of clouds and the fog gone. Ruby wanted to join Ivas in his morning sheep-tending rituals. Ivas tried not to rush the chores; he felt that he had been neglecting the sheep the past few days. After opening the barn door, Ivas went from sheep to sheep, checking their wool for parasites and their faces for signs of illness. The sheep responded irritably and moved their affection to Ruby instead.

"Do they have names?" Ruby asked. She followed Ivas as he worked. The Valis Blacknose were curious about the new human and followed after her, sniffing at her hands. Ruby squealed when the bellwether started to nibble at her shirt. The bell jingled merrily.

"I just call them the color of their tags."

"So Blue, Yellow, Green...?"

"Yep."

"That's so boring. I thought 'Blanc' was bad..."

"I'm not good with names," Ivas defended himself. He pointed at the one lamb of the group. "That one kind of has a name. I've started calling her Little Lost."

"That's a good name," Ruby said. She cooed over the baby sheep, lifting her up for a cuddle. The mother, Pink, watched unconcerned.

Ivas dumped the dirty water out of the water trough and carried fresh buckets from the pump. Ruby helped as well. She struggled a little at first, splashing water over her legs, but when Ivas tried to help, she huffed and raced past him with a steady hold. She deposited the water without any more spills. She proudly ran back to the pump for a refill. Ivas was happy for the help since it cut down on the number of trips he had to take. Once the trough was full, Ivas walked back to the barn.

"When do you shear them? You harvest the wool, right?" Ruby asked.

"Right, I shear them in the spring, although they could use some crutching soon." Ivas noticed that—due to the wet weather—the wool around their bellies and rears was getting soiled. He would need to trim them.

In the barn, he and Ruby hauled out a couple of bales of hay for the sheep to eat, as well as a salt brick. Usually the pasture offered enough grass, but Ivas provided some hay every few weeks as well. As they worked, Blanc enjoyed a leisurely day, rolling in the grass and chasing squirrels.

Once the food was out, the sheep forgot their investigation of Ruby and went to enjoy their treat. Ruby ran her hands over their wool and touched their curved horns.

"They're so cute," she said, "and their wool is so curly!" She was inspecting Red, lifting the locks of wool from the front of his face to see his eyes.

Ivas nodded. "They're Valis Blacknose sheep."

"I love them."

Red started tasting Ruby's pants. The girl teased her with a gentle, "Boo!" and the sheep startled, dancing away and bleating playfully. Noticing the game, the other sheep approached her as well. Ruby turned her back as if she didn't notice, then spun around with another, "Boo!" The sheep fled. Blanc joined in the game, running circles around Ruby, waiting for the order to gather the sheep.

"Does Blanc know herding commands?"

"Of course," Ivas pursed his lips and whistled sharply, catching Blanc's attention. "Away to me, Blanc."

Blanc jumped into work mode and started circling the sheep, gathering them up in a group. The sheep bleated in protest and tried to scatter, but Blanc barked a few warnings and kept circling them until they were in a tight group.

"That'll do!" Ivas shouted. Blanc ran to his side and took a seat, grinning proudly.

"She's so smart," Ruby said with awe.

"It's in her blood," Ivas said, rubbing Blanc's ears. "My grandfather bred her mother—his dog—with another Berger Blanc Suisse, who was an award-winning sheepdog right out of Switzerland. Grandpa must have called in a lot of favors to get that done, all just so I could have a puppy of my own. There was a litter of five. Granddad sold them all except for Blanc. He taught me how to train her."

"Wow, so you guys have been together since the beginning."

"Just about. When I was about your age, Granddad said I either needed to work to make money for school or I needed to start learning how to be a shepherd because that was the only thing he could teach me. I opted to be a shepherd, so he got me Blanc."

"Why didn't you want to go to school?" Ruby asked, confused as to why someone wouldn't take the opportunity to leave the little village.

"You have to understand, I had lost my mom and dad. The idea of leaving the only family I had to fend for myself scared the hell out of me. University seemed so expensive and out of reach at the time. Being a shepherd was safer and easier."

"Do you regret it?"

Ivas shrugged. "There are some days where I wonder, but I don't regret it. Regret is kind of useless in the end. I'm happy. I have a house. I have Blanc."

"That's goo-gah!" Ruby jumped in surprise when a pair of silky lips started kissing her hand. During their conversation, Red had snuck up behind to further investigate Ruby.

"She doesn't have any treats for you, Red. Shoo!" Ivas clapped his hands, and Red hopped away, startled by the loud noise. The other sheep looked up curiously.

"Let's get back inside before they surround us. These mischievous bastards have stolen my lunch on occasion."

Ruby laughed all the way back to the house. Once inside, she volunteered to make breakfast. Ivas didn't argue since he was in need of a shower. He stayed under the spray of warm water long after the soap was all washed away, enjoying the soothing waters. By the time he stepped out, the smell of scrambled eggs was strong in the air. He dressed in fresh clothes and returned to the kitchen.

Ruby placed a pile of eggs in front of him. She was already halfway through hers, applying a fresh sprinkle of hot sauce to the yellow and white pile.

"You're welcomed to have a shower, but I might have used up all the hot water."

"I'm fine," Ruby said, chewing and swallowing quickly to answer him. She was wearing the same clothes from yesterday—a knitted sweater with jeans and boots, good clothes that would last a couple of nights without a wash. Her hair was tied up in a messy bun to hide its dirty state. It blended well with her horns. Ivas wished he had a tooth-brush or deodorant to offer her, but he had been unprepared for a sleepover.

"Marlene might be able to lend you some toiletries," he said.

"Good call," Ruby nodded.

Ivas added some salt to his eggs and made conversation between bites. "So…how about you? What do you want to be when you grow up?"

Ruby smiled at the cliché question. "Well, I *want* to be an explorer, like an archeologist, or maybe a nature photographer. Or even a park ranger—like for a big park, you know? Anything that will get me outside… Maybe a zoologist. I was reading this story about a park ranger and how he had to go searching for missing people in the park he worked for because it was so big. I would love to do stuff like that. Not look for missing people, of course, but just getting to walk around outside all day would be the best. Mom has to work in an office and she hates it, so I promised myself I would never get stuck at a desk job."

Ivas smiled as Ruby rattled on, nodding and making appropriate sounds since there was no room to get a word in. He was happy to just listen. It made her seem like a normal girl. He even forgot about the horns and the fog for a little bit. His stomach twisted a little, unaccustomed to having so much company over a long period of time. He liked having someone to eat with and talk to and didn't realize how much he had really missed it.

"…Mom is the receptionist at the medical office in town and is always complaining about how boring it is. But Dad always had stories going out on the boat. Like, yeah, it's hard work and you have to get up early, but at least it's an adventure every day, and that's what I want too. Not actually sail… Maybe, I don't know, I really can't decide. I might have to go to school in another country, but I don't really mind. I want to see the whole world anyway."

"You should," Ivas agreed. "I know I'm just a hermit, but traveling is one thing I regret not doing more of."

"You probably can't leave the sheep for too long, huh?" Ruby scrapped up the last of her eggs and hot sauce, tilting the plate over her mouth so she could catch each morsel.

"No, a day trip at the most. Any longer and I have to find a babysitter, and no one likes taking care of sheep."

"I could do it," Ruby said. "You could go on trips and I could watch the sheep. You'd have to do it now, though, because I'm going to have to leave for university in a few years."

Ivas laughed. "Well, you certainly proved yourself this morning."

"See? You should totally do it. Where would you go?"

Ivas considered the question seriously even though he would never put such a responsibility on one so young. "I'd go to a big city and take up the luxury, eat out, stay at a fancy hotel, get a massage. Just take a real vacation." Ivas always heard stories about people taking trips full of museums, tours, and kid's entertainment, and it always sounded very stressful. He imagined himself having a weekend with beach-sitting, fruity drinks, and the best restaurants he could find.

"That does sound nice. You should totally do it, man. I will watch your farm. Maybe you'll meet a pretty lady." Ruby grinned teasingly. Her cheeks reddened at the thought of matchmaking a man twice her age. "Oooor, you could take Tess with you."

Ivas smiled. "Tess deserves *much* better than me."

To Ruby's surprise, he actually sounded sincere, not sad or rueful.

"Oh, I figured you guys…" Ruby trailed off, not sure how to finish.

Ivas smiled. "I'm really not a romance person."

"You guys just seemed like good friends."

"We are," Ivas said calmly. "The best of friends."

Ivas ate the rest of his eggs and took the plates away. "Speaking of Tess, we should probably get going. Marlene is expecting us."

Ivas left the plates in the sink for later and grabbed a backpack from the closet. He started packing food into the bag, foreseeing a long day ahead.

"We'll have to walk to Marlene's house. It might take a while. You up for the walk?"

"Of course. I walk to town all the time."

"Off we go then."

With lunch slung over his shoulder, Ivas led the way to the road. Blanc followed after them, and this time Ivas let her come along. He felt uneasy leaving the sheep unattended, but he was tired of being without his greatest comfort in his rapidly estranging life.

The three of them walked down the road and Ivas felt almost normal, like they were just friends taking a picnic into the countryside. The sun was warm and the wind was still, so it wasn't too cold. The autumn leaves were falling rapidly. Winter would come strong and suddenly as it always did.

Eventually, Ivas led them off the road and through the pastures—a shortcut to the old lighthouse. The terrain became a little uneasy, slowing their walk. Ruby sighed. Even after the big breakfast, she was already becoming hungry again.

"What did you pack to eat?" she asked.

Ivas handed her the bag. "Nothing special. Help yourself."

Ruby dug through the backpack, producing some slices of bread and a hunk of cheese. A couple of water bottles rested at the bottom. Ruby ate them without complaint. The bread was filling and the cheese was flavorful. She shared some of it with Blanc, who had shifted her loyalty slightly to the person who shared her food. Once she was satisfied, Ruby washed it down with water. Ivas ate the remaining bread and cheese.

With renewed energy, their pace quickened. The landscape was a lush green against the fiery trees. Ahead, Ruby could see the blue line of the horizon as they neared the sea. After an hour, the lighthouse appeared, and they angled their course, making a straight line for Marlene's cottage. The sea greeted them with its gentle chant, and the cottage waited like something out of a fairy tale.

Marlene answered immediately and invited them inside. Ivas noted that she had cleaned the house up. Her jars were dusted and tea was already waiting.

"Where's Tess?" Marlene asked.

"I think she'll meet us here later. She went home last night and I didn't think to call her," Ivas said.

"Well, no matter. The three of us can get to work."

"Do you have a plan?" Ruby asked. They took a seat at the table and Ivas gulped down his tea, tired from the walk.

"I wouldn't really call it a plan, but it's a place to start," Marlene said. "You'll find even well laid out plans turn into spontaneity."

Marlene set out an assortment of items on the table, showing them to Ruby before packing them into a leather satchel. The first thing was the sunstone Ivas had found yesterday.

"I'm not overly familiar with gem-based magic, but from what I understand, you can charge it with the energy of the sun."

Next into the bag went a small wooden bowl and a glass vial. "For charging water, which we know for sure works."

Then a small notebook. "Full of spells."

Once the bag was packed, Marlene nodded and scanned her kitchen for anything she might have forgotten. "I hope one of these things works. I still don't understand how that moonlight water I gave Tess did what it did."

"We all saw it," Ruby said. "This great illumination that drove away all the monsters."

Marlene nodded. "That's what Tess told me. The water I gave her was some I had left out in the moonlight, but it was to make her feel better, really. Moon water doesn't burst into actual moonlight."

"It's the fog," Ivas said. "Look what it did to Ruby. There's something about them that brings out the...magic in everything."

"There is much power in a god, even a dead one," Marlene agreed. "It brings out the monsters and everything else."

She held up her bag. "But better safe than sorry. Come on, you two."

Ivas involuntarily let out a groan as he stood up, his body complaining about more physical exercise.

"Not you, shepherd," Marlene said. From her pocket, she pulled out another vial, this one filled with swirling white that looked just like she had captured a bit of fog. "Today, yours is an emotional journey."

Marlene threw the vial down and the glass shattered. The room immediately filled up with fog, blinding Ivas, who cried out and shielded his face.

"You crazy witch, what are you doing?"

"Summoning the demons you must face." Marlene's voice sounded far away, as if echoing over a great chasm.

"Don't leave me here!" Ivas cried. "Ruby!"

There was no answer, and Ivas was all alone. Taking a few steps forward, it became apparent that he wasn't in the house. There were no obstacles in his way. He felt about for the table, or the kitchen cabinet, but the space was empty. He told himself to stay calm, to take deep breaths, but as usual, he didn't listen to himself and instead began to hyperventilate and panic.

Can't do this...

He went to his hands and knees, trying to catch his breath.

Can't take anymore...

Ivas couldn't see. The fog filled his lungs, blinded him, slipped up his nose and into his brain. He thought he would build an immunity to it, but each time the fog came, it seemed to only get worse.

No more, no more...

He heard a sound, like fabric flapping in the wind, and realized that the fog was retreating. He looked up and saw the Messenger standing over him, bringing a bubble of fresh air with it.

"Stay away from me," Ivas gasped. "I don't need you."

The Messenger remained ever silent and invisible under its hood. It raised one of its spiny legs and reached into its leather bag, bringing out a scroll tied with a green ribbon.

"No!" Ivas screamed at it. "I don't want that!"

He turned to run away, but upon turning only saw the fog waiting for him. In the corner of his eye, he saw some mad creature waiting for him. Blobs of grey filled his eyes and his ears started to ring. Dizzy, Ivas fell forward, unable to move. In his panic, he had caused a fainting spell.

He felt something wrap around his body and lift him up, pressing him against something warm. Ivas didn't fight back. In fact, he felt oddly comforted, but that could be because he couldn't see or hear.

The Messenger wrapped Ivas tightly in its arms and carried him away.

~

"You just put some of the fog in a bottle?"

Ruby half-followed Marlene out the door, being pulled along by the old woman once the fog appeared. Marlene had quickly taken them both outside and shut the door. Blanc greeted them, having been sitting outside patiently.

"Why did you do that? Ivas is really sensitive. What if the monsters come?"

"This is something he has to do," was all Marlene would say on the matter. She knew it was dangerous, and trying to explain herself would only sound like excuses, so she didn't bother.

"But what will happen to him?"

"Hopefully, he'll stop running."

"Now, *wait* a second." Ruby stopped walking and crossed her arms. In that stance, with her horns, Marlene found herself listening very carefully.

"You said so yourself, you don't know what you're doing. You had no right to do that to him. You can't just throw someone into a pit of whatever they're afraid of."

Marlene didn't answer, just stared, appalled that she was being reprimanded by a teenager.

"What you did is not okay. It isn't some magical tough love bullshit, it's cruel." Ruby returned to the cottage and opened the door. Fog rolled out around her feet, dispersing in the midmorning sun. When it cleared, the cottage was empty. Blanc entered the house, sniffing at the floor. She whimpered with confusion, smelling Ivas but not seeing him. She looked at Ruby for answers.

"He's gone," Ruby said through gritted teeth.

Marlene hesitated. She might be able to shrug off the anger of Ruby, but one couldn't deny the wisdom of animals. Blanc whined, trying to catch the scent. Marlene sighed. "You're right. I shouldn't have done that." She let the words sink in and waited for Ruby's shoulders to relax before continuing. "Messing with the fog isn't smart, but I promise, I wouldn't have done it if I thought it would put Ivas in danger. It's just… Ivas has been putting himself through so much for so long, I knew that if he stopped running and turned to face what's really been scaring him, then he would see that it was really nothing to be scared of at all."

Ruby turned, anger slowly disappearing. "You're sure he'll be all right?"

Marlene wasn't, but she nodded anyway.

"Nothing I can do for him now in any case," Ruby muttered. "We might as well get to work. I know he'll find his way back."

Marlene nodded and turned, leading the way away from the cottage and down the beach. Ruby had to coax Blanc out of the cottage before she would follow.

Marlene's mind became occupied with Ruby's accusations. Marlene had never claimed to be a kind woman—she knew the reputation of witches. But she wondered if her isolation had caused her to lose a connection to people in general. After all, casting a man into the fog was not a reputable form of therapy.

She realized that Ruby had said something.

"What was that? Sorry, my mind was wandering."

"Where are we going?"

"Oh, yes, there's an alcove just down the beach. It gets perfect afternoon sunlight. Just the place we need. I picnic there often."

The beach was much more friendly in the sunlight.

Coarse sand crunched under their shoes and ocean water lapped up gently without any fuss. The alcove Marlene spoke of was a beautiful space of beach that retreated into a hollow area of smooth, climbable rocks. Ruby admired the location. Even at high tide, it made the perfect beach spot. Blanc forgot her woes and became enamored with beach fun. She played a game of tag with the fluctuating shoreline, barking and running through the sand.

Marlene went to her favorite rock, which rose just below waist height and had a fairly flat top. She placed the sunstone on top, as well as her bowl, which she filled with a bottle of water. There was still half left, which she offered to Ruby, who drank it down.

Marlene put her hands over the two objects and chanted a short spell under her breath. Ruby didn't hear, only catching a few rhyming words.

Ruby found a rock to sit on and settled herself, feeling warm between the sun and the sun-warmed stones. The waves made a lullaby of sounds. Marlene sat next to Ruby on another rock.

"The water and the stone will 'charge,' so to speak, with the sun's energy. Hopefully to our advantage."

"This place is beautiful," Ruby commented.

Marlene nodded. "It was my favorite place to go after Henry died. It's where I found magic in the ocean."

"Where it would give you gifts?" Ruby asked.

"Mmhmm. I thought it was nature's way of comforting me. Pretty sea glass, empty shells, old coins. They all had stories to tell, long journeys to share." Marlene snorted in her throat. "I've never told anyone this, except Tess. I fear people would think I'm mad."

"I think it's nice that you can find magic in things like that," Ruby said.

Marlene looked at Ruby's horns. "You got a taste of the real stuff."

"What, these?" Ruby grabbed one of her horns, squeezing it. "These aren't magic. These are…all the pain in me, coming out."

Marlene frowned. "I assumed you had just gotten lost in the fog. I didn't even think to ask—"

"I didn't get lost; I went in. I was looking for my dad."

"The sailor who disappeared."

Ruby sighed. "News travels everywhere in a small village."

"The ocean told me."

Ruby froze, clutching her horn. "What did it tell you?"

"Well, it doesn't actually *tell* me anything. I just hear things. The cries of a frightened man, lost at sea. The sound of an empty boat, floating with no captain. And the warning, the sailor screaming his warning, to run…"

They both heard voices echo down the beach. Marlene stood up and peered around the rocks, spotting two boys walking their way.

"There are some kids coming. Cover your horns," Marlene hissed.

Ruby quickly put her hood over her head, trying to remember how to behave like a person who had nothing to hide. Marlene went back to her own seat, becoming very interested in her nails as the boys approached.

Ruby recognized them from her school. They were the same age as her, but the three were not sociable. They recognized Ruby as well, and their conversation ceased.

"Whoa, Ruby!" They stared at her as if she were a celebrity. Ruby realized that she had probably been the biggest source of gossip in their tiny school.

One of the boys, Luther, noticed Marlene as well. "Dude,

is that the witch?" he whispered to his friend, but not quietly enough.

"What are you doing out here?" the second boy, Brian, asked.

Ruby, full of spite and sarcasm, raised her eyebrow. "On the beach? On the first sunny day in, like, a week?"

"Someone said they had to lock you in your house because you went crazy," Luther said. There was no malice behind his comment, only the lack of tack that comes from the inexperience of youth. Still, Ruby narrowed her eyes.

"Just taking a break from the riffraff," she said.

Brian stared at Marlene, eyes practically shining with the possible gossip of seeing the runaway hanging out with the witch. This would make him popular for days. "What's that stuff over there? You guys doing some weird curse?"

"It's a rock, Brian, maybe you've heard of them."

Now there was malice in all three. Ruby was so accustomed to defending herself against boys that she safely assumed the worse of any that came her way, and they were not used to being challenged.

"She wasn't locked up, Luth," Brian said. "Sean said he saw her with that crazy shepherd guy, Sbarge. They've been hanging out, sneaking up to the lighthouse."

Luther laughed. He made a circle with his fingers and slipped his index finger into the hole suggestively, snickering. Brian upped the suggestion by shoving his whole fist through the hole. They both cackled.

Cheeks burning red, Ruby slipped off the rock, crossing her arms. "Well, aren't you two just a pair of weak, wrinkly testicles. Fuck off."

"Careful, Brian, her witch friend will put a curse on you," Luther said.

Marlene, for her part, ignored useless drama, putting as much space between her and the hormone-fueled catastrophe as possible. But she noticed two lumps forming under Ruby's hood, and her heart started to pound.

"No," Ruby growled. "I don't need a curse. I'll pick up that rock and use it to smash your skulls in."

She gritted her teeth and winced, aware of the pain in her head as her horns grew. They pushed the hood off her head. The two boys' mouths dropped in fear. Luther screamed. Ruby frightened herself by how much she enjoyed their looks of terror.

"Fuck, man, what is that?"

"You fucking freak!"

Brian reached into his pocket and pulled out a handful of greenery—a clove of small wild garlic and some holly leaves. They both ran down the beach, Brian holding the leaves aloft like a protective symbol. Ruby started to run after them, her mind filling up with images of what she could do to them. Hold their heads under the ocean until they knew what it was to fear death. Kick sand in their eyes. Impale them with her horns. Make them hurt as much as she hurt…

Marlene grabbed her arm and held her back. Ruby didn't fight, but stared after the boys, breathing heavily. Marlene gently led Ruby back to the rocks and sat her down. She rubbed Ruby's hands until the girl's eyes stopped glowing yellow and her breathing steadied.

Blanc, whose many dog senses included the ability to know emotional need, came up to Ruby and placed her head in her lap. Ruby ran her fingers through Blanc's white fur, focusing on the warmth and the softness until she calmed. Blanc wagged her tail.

"You know," Marlene said quietly, "when Henry died, I was so filled with…hate. I was furious with the world and all the people of this stupid little town. There I was in the worst pain of my life and everyone else was just going about their days like nothing had happened. Like the whole world hadn't gone dark and shattered like a window, cutting me all the way. They came to the funeral, they cried and patted my hand and said, 'There, there.' And then they moved on while I still grieved, crying every night, hurting and missing him every day. I felt worse than alone. I felt abandoned."

Ruby stared at her feet, fists clenched. She was holding back tears, but when she spoke, her voice cracked and they fell. "Those stupid fuckers. They don't understand anything. I hope they lose everything. I hope they lose their parents and are attacked by monsters, and all the world does is turn their backs on them. Then they'll know how it feels."

"Ruby…"

"It hurts! They don't understand! My dad…" Ruby had to stop for a moment to sob. Marlene reached into her pocket and handed her a handkerchief. Blanc licked her knee.

"They're all so fucking clueless," Ruby said once she regained her voice. "They're just so goddamn stupid! I hope bad things happen to them. That they'll be all alone too. That *they're* the ones that will go crazy."

"Ruby, they're just boys. Of course they don't know how you feel. Don't waste so much energy hating them. They're not worth it."

"I hate *everyone*."

"I know." Marlene patted Ruby's knee and took back her handkerchief, which was now soaked with tears and mucus. "You just let it out, honey. It's part of the grief. Just don't forget that the important people understand, and they won't leave you alone. Your mom, me, Ivas, we're all here for you."

Ruby nodded, wiping away the more gentle tears that came. "Thank you."

Marlene nodded. "Here, let me get us a snack."

Ruby let herself slip off the rock to sit in the sand where she put her arms around Blanc.

Marlene went to her bag and with her back turned, she

secretly held the handkerchief over the sun-soaked bowl of water. She had to squeeze very tightly, and only got a drop, but she managed to coax one of Ruby's tears out of the fabric and it fell into the bowl.

~

When Ivas woke up, the Messenger immediately set him down and waited for the shepherd to fully come to consciousness.

Ivas tried to figure out where he was by the kind of ground he laid on, but it was just grass. He sat up and looked at the Messenger, who regarded him expressionlessly.

"What do you want?" Ivas asked weakly.

The Messenger offered Ivas the letter again. The paper was old and discolored, the ribbon frayed. Ivas shook his head.

"The dead should just stay dead and leave me alone," he spat. "I don't want their letter."

The Messenger heaved a deep sigh, like the wind echoing over a mountain top. It sounded more than slightly annoyed. It placed the letter in Ivas's lap.

Ivas fought the urge to crumple it up and throw it away. "You've been following me all this time," he said. "Is it really that important?"

At this, the Messenger nodded and patted its bag of letters. They were all important.

Ivas took the ribbon between his fingers and pulled it, unrolling the scroll quickly. He found that it wasn't just one letter, but several all wrapped together. He looked at the words but didn't read them. At the bottom, he saw that it was signed by a person he didn't know. Not recognizing the name, Ivas frowned and went back to the beginning, actually reading the letter.

Dear Nicholas,
There's something coming, on the water, in the ocean. It has taken
me. It has taken all of us. I tried to get away, but I got lost in the
fog and it trapped me here. Leave the village. Please run.

Ivas went to the next one.

Mary and Carol,
I think I must be dead. Yes, I am dead. But I am lost. Please, help
me. Leave a light, hang some garlic, anything that might help me
get out of this hellish fog. There is something here. It's coming for
me. Please help.

Then the next.

I have no one to write this to, but please, anybody, I am lost, and
more are lost here with me. I can hear them screaming, moaning,
wanting to be found. If anyone can find us, I'm begging you, please
do. We're in the fog.

There were others, but they were all much the same. The dead asking for help. Some warning their loved ones to run, all talking about the fog, or the thing in the fog that kept them there. Ivas shuddered and pushed the letters away.

"Why were you trying to bring all of these to me? Why not take them to Nicholas, and Mary or Carol, or whoever the hell they're for? I…I thought you were trying to bring me a letter from Grandpa, or Mom, or Dad. I don't know any of these people."

The Messenger pointed at Ivas with one of its spider legs.

"But why? I was just a kid. I couldn't…" Ivas stopped. Yes, he had been just a kid, the same age as Ruby, in fact. He had sung the Gathering Song and had nightmares about what was in the fog. Ivas shook his head and actually laughed a little. "You wanted me to do exactly what Ruby is doing now. You wanted me to save them." He held up the letters, the cries for help.

The Messenger nodded.

But why give a child a job suited for an adult? Ivas was just the example of why not, as was Jack. At their age, their minds learned how to protect themselves. Not Ruby. With her horns, she had practically embraced the fog.

"You gave me the chance to stop all this years ago. Now, the monsters are at our doorstep and Ruby is…" Ivas sighed. "I'm a fucking coward."

The Messenger shook its head and placed one of its legs on Ivas's shoulders. Ivas realized that he couldn't have been the first, or the last. The Messenger must have gone to several children who hid or ran just as Ivas did. Ruby was just the first one to open the door. The first who had something to go into the fog for.

"Well, I won't run this time," Ivas said somberly. There wasn't a shred of victory or determination in his tone, only a sense of duty. "God or no, the dead should stay dead."

The Messenger didn't answer. The letters it had given Ivas were slowly crumbling, falling into ashes and sitting in a still pile.

Ivas stood up, wondering how he was going to find his way out of the fog, when he heard the comfortingly familiar sound of a sheep bleat. He turned his head and saw the lamb Little Lost appear in the bubble he shared with the Messenger. He had left the sheep unattended; had she escaped again? Was she even real? Ivas knelt down and ran his hands over her wool. She felt real. As he petted her, he found that her wool was coming off, tangling up into strands of fabric in his fingers. Ivas kept rubbing, taking off her wool and coming up with fabric magically created in his palms. Little Lost bleated as Ivas tugged and pulled, unraveling the coat.

He would have released her, but the strings and cloth were entangling him, binding his hands and arms. Ivas pulled himself away, leaving Little Lost naked, as if she had been freshly shaved. He stumbled and fell onto his back, completely bound by the wool. Except that now it wasn't wool at all. Ivas was wrapped in a serape, not his grandfather's, but a brand new one, one Ivas had made himself.

He put the serape around his shoulders, feeling warm and comforted by it. The garment was still sheep-wool white. Ivas found his pocketknife and cut one of his fingers. A drop of his blood fell to the serape and spread through the fabric rapidly, spiderwebbing across the pattern of the thread, dying it a beautiful royal red. Ivas closed his eyes and breathed deep. It felt important, like a piece of his past and his present. Like a piece of *him*, not his grandfather. Even with the comfort of the serape on his shoulders, Ivas also felt oddly vulnerable, as if he was wearing a piece of his very soul on the outside of his body. A piece of soul he never had before.

When Ivas opened his eyes, the fog was gone, as was the Messenger and Little Lost, but the serape was still very real and wrapped around his body. He was standing on a cliffside, overlooking the sea. Peering down, Ivas saw two figures and a white dog sitting in an alcove. He smiled and called to them.

Marlene and Ruby looked up, seeing a man clad in red looking down at them. They couldn't clearly make out his face but knew there was only one person it could be. Blanc barked happily and ran up the beach to meet him.

THE HORNED GIRL SHOWS HER CLAWS

Marlene wrapped the sunstone in a piece of black velvet and gave it to Ivas. She put the water in a vial, which she corked and tied with a leather string. She gave this to Ruby.

"Wear it around your neck. It'll be a light to guide you through the fog."

The day was waning, and the three had grown quite tired. They walked back to Marlene's cottage with a trudge to their step, emotional exhaustion weighing just as heavy on their minds as the physical. Not wanting to walk all the way back home, Ivas asked Marlene to call Tess once they got back.

While Marlene was on the phone, he and Ruby sank into her couch together, both noting the change in the other.

"Your horns are longer."

"Where'd you get that robe?"

"It's a serape."

"Where'd you get it?"

"I...got it in the fog."

"It looks good on you."

Marlene came into the living room with a tin of cookies and sat down as well. "I called Tess. She'll be on her way shortly. She's a bit cross with you, shepherd. Said she's tried calling you all day. Tried calling me as well, but I'm an old lady; I can't be blamed for my shortcomings."

Marlene sighed as she sank into an armchair. "Speaking of which, you'll have to wait on tea. I need a breather."

"Just rest, Marlene. I'll get it," Ivas said. He heaved himself out of the couch, regretting his decision to volunteer. Too late now, he went to the kitchen and put water on to boil.

"How's your head?" Marlene asked Ruby.

"It hurts."

"Want something for the pain?"

"What do you have? Some magic herb thing?" Ruby teased.

"Honey, I'm an old woman. I've got the *good* stuff." Marlene opened the drawer of her side table and pulled out a pill bottle. She tossed it to Ruby. "That should clear you right up."

A few minutes later, the kettle whistled, cups clinked, and Ivas carried in the tray of tea. Ruby swallowed her pill with her cup while the others quietly sipped, taking in the moment of relaxation, which was promptly destroyed by a screaming woman pounding on the door.

"Ruby? Are you in there?"

"Mrs. Mclaven, calm down. Marlene Burlock, are you home? This is the police."

Ivas recognized the panicked voice of Ruby's mother, Hannah, followed by the ever-straining voice of Sheriff Jack. Ruby jerked upright, dropping her tea.

"Crap, those boys must have told…"

The door flew open, revealing Hannah, looking even more distraught than Ivas had seen her last time. Her eyes were wild with panic before they found Ruby.

"Ruby, baby…" She choked back a sob.

"Ivas?" Jack stared at them in confusion.

In the few seconds of the door being opened, Ivas realized that these two weren't alone. Several feet away from the house, a small crowd had gathered. Upon returning to the village, the boys, Luther and Brian, had caused quite a drama in reporting to their parents that they had been attacked by a witch and a devil girl. When it was reported to Jack—and, incidentally, Ruby's mom, who was in the station reporting her daughter missing for the second time—the boy's parents, their friends, and some people who had overheard, decided to take a walk down the beach at the same time Sheriff Jack went to Marlene's to investigate. They agreed that it was for everyone's safety to see for themselves what was going on. After all, rumors like that can be dangerous in such a superstitious town.

"Shit." Ivas got to his feet and pulled Ruby with him, making sure she was hidden behind him. "Close the door!"

Jack did so.

"Good. Now, Blanc, *guard*." Ivas emphasized the stress in his voice, and Blanc immediately went between him and Jack, growling, ears laid back. Ivas never trained her to attack. The growl command was for warning off predators.

"Ivas, what are you doing?" Jack asked, appalled.

"You brought the fucking mob here. You're not touching her."

"Give me my daughter!" Hannah shouted. Blanc barked at her, egged by the sudden noise. Hannah flinched and backed away.

"Mom, I told you I'm fine! Stop freaking out!"

"You need to come home!"

"Yeah? You want to take home this?" Ruby stepped out from behind Ivas, showing off her horns. Hannah gasped and looked away.

"That's what I thought. How about you just parade me outside in front of all these people? If you can't even look at me, then fuck off."

"That's enough." Jack stepped forward, pushing Hannah back. "Ivas, we're friends here. Call Blanc off."

Ivas hesitated, fuming over the crowd that waited outside. But Jack was right, they were boyhood friends, and Hannah was Ruby's mother. "Blanc, that'll do."

Blanc immediately relaxed and went to Ivas's side, sitting next to him dutifully.

"Look," Jack said, "I'm sorry I let this happen. I had no idea that…Ruby…" Jack fumbled for the words, and Ivas realized he was avoiding looking at Ruby's head.

"It doesn't matter! She's here. We found her. Ruby, I just want to take you home."

That's when Ruby ran.

She darted behind Marlene, through a door in the living room that Ivas had not noticed before. He quickly followed her. The door led to a small sunroom that had a sliding glass door leading outside. Ruby ran through this, toward the ocean, through the back of the house. She wouldn't have gotten away, of course. Hannah would have caught her or Jack would have gotten in his truck. But another car came to her rescue.

Ivas recognized Tess's truck as it rumbled up next to Ruby, who was still running. Slowing down, Tess drove the car to Ruby's side, and the girl clamored into the passenger seat. Tess floored the gas and sped away as fast as she could.

Hannah was outside, screaming after them. Jack turned to run to the front of the house where his car was parked, but Ivas intentionally got in his way and Jack barreled into him, sending them both sprawling to the floor.

"Goddamn it, Ivas," Jack panted. "What the hell is going on?"

"She's just scared, Jack," Ivas said, helping him to his feet. "What did you expect with the sheriff and a mob of people at the door?"

Jack looked shamefully down at his feet. "I tried to make them go away, but, for God's sake, I never actually expected her to have…those…"

"She needs a doctor," Hannah said. She came back inside, flustered, but deadly calm. "That's all. It's just a condition, some weird skin growth. I'll take her to the doctor and she'll be fine. What I want to know—" Her eyes locked on Ivas. "—is why she was here with you."

Everything fell silent as Hannah and Jack stared at Ivas, both waiting for an explanation. There was a sudden clink of china, which—though a small, innocent sound—made everyone jump.

Marlene set down her empty teacup. Ivas had forgotten she was there. "Well, this is my home, which you people entered quite rudely. As for Ruby, she and Ivas came here seeking my help for that…growth of hers. All you silly people seem to be under the impression that I'm a witch and that I can simply snap my fingers and magic things away."

As she talked, Ivas's own mind formed a compatible lie and he added, "That's right. Ruby came to my house yesterday after she ran away. I was the first neighbor she found, and…well, frankly, I didn't cause a panic at the sight of her, so she stayed with me. This morning, I suggested we visit Marlene. I thought she could help since there were rumors she was a witch."

Marlene scoffed. "Of all the nonsense."

"I can't believe this." Hannah clutched her hair, trying to catch her breath.

"Just calm down, everything is okay. Ivas, was that Tess's truck I saw?" Jack asked.

"Maybe…yes." Ivas gave up lying about that. "Marlene is Tess's great aunt. She was coming over."

"Alright, right now, we need to find Ruby. She's safe with Tess, Mrs. Mclaven," Jack said. "She just got scared. Once things calm down, I'm sure Tess will bring her back home. In the meantime, I'll put out a search."

"No," Hannah said, sighing deeply. "Don't search. We'll just scare her away again, and I don't want the town seeing her."

"I won't advertise it, but I'll keep an eye out for her," Jack said. "And, Ivas…you're just lucky I trust you. You're my friend, but I really should question you."

"About what? That's all there is to it."

Jack narrowed his eyes. "Ivas, there's a reason everyone is so scared right now. Ruby isn't the only person to go missing these past few days. Mr. Morganstern disappeared last night, and I just got a report that the Robertsons' son Geoffrey hasn't been home since the night before last. They all stayed out too late in the fog."

Ivas felt himself grow cold, could practically feel the blood leaving his face. "I hadn't heard…"

"So, you can see why Hannah is so upset and why everyone is so nervous." Jack sighed and rubbed his brow. "Just go home. I need to clean this up. Mrs. Mclaven, why don't you come with me? I'll give you a ride home. I bet Ruby will be back any time."

Hannah nodded, looking very tired, and allowed Jack to escort her outside. Ivas stayed behind, not wanting any of the townspeople to see him. He heard Jack shout something at everybody.

"Thanks for that," Ivas said to Marlene.

"You owe me one. I'm an old woman, I don't need this messy drama in my own home." Marlene sat up and gathered up the dishes. "So, you know where they went?"

"Yeah, I think I have an idea."

~

Ivas wasn't interested in more walking, but his destination was on the way home. He walked from Marlene's house to the main road, following that further inland to the forest. Blanc followed happily by his side. When he reached the treeline, he saw Tess's car parked next to the natural trail that led to Floborough Deep. He followed the path into the woods where he found Tess and Ruby sitting at the ruined stairway. Ruby was surprisingly melancholy, leaning against Tess, who had an arm around her shoulder. Blanc went to the two girls, offering assistance.

"Are you okay?" Ivas asked.

Ruby shook her head, horns bumping against Tess's shoulder. "Mom probably hates me."

"No, she doesn't. I assure you, she just wants you to be safe."

"What am I going to do? I can't go home. Mom will want me to go to the doctor, and if anyone in this town saw me..."

"You can hide out with me until we figure this out," Tess said. "Speaking of which, *have* we figured this out?"

"Well, Marlene gave us the magic stuff," Ivas said. "And if we're going to do something, we need to act. I...have it from a good source that whatever is coming is almost here."

"That's obvious by the fog on the water," Tess said. "Every day, that wall gets closer."

"Then...isn't that it?" Ruby asked. "The wall of fog, we have to go there."

Neither Tess nor Ivas answered at first, both knowing she was right and scrambling for an excuse to say she was wrong.

"I definitely don't want to go into the fog on a boat."

"No, but now that you mention it, we could hide on my boat," Tess said. "The docks are pretty deserted. We can keep Ruby there until we figure things out."

Ivas nodded. "That would work. We'll have to be careful, though. Jack is on the lookout for your car."

"We'll have to risk it," Tess said. "Rain's coming anyway. The fog will roll in early."

Ivas frowned and looked up. She was right. Their beautiful, sunny morning had turned cloudy fast. The wind was high, pushing more clouds in, darkening the world.

"Let's head back."

They returned to Tess's truck, huddling close to each other for warmth. As the clouds gathered, the temperature began to drop and Ivas found himself finally wishing that the heater in Tess's old truck worked. He was incredibly tired but unable to relax with all the shivering. They even let Blanc sit upfront for extra body heat.

Tess stayed on the side roads leading into town. Ruby stayed low, slouched down in her seat, hugging the ever-reassuring Blanc. Ivas kept a lookout for Jack.

The side roads turned out to be a poor choice. As they drove, Ivas spotted several figures walking ahead of them. It was a group of men and women, all walking in a straight line. Most were in the grass, looking down, but some were walking in the road, forcing Tess to slow down.

"Shit, what are they doing?"

"It's a search party," Ivas said, recognizing the formation. "They must be looking for one of those missing people."

"Damn. I heard they were searching for Geoffrey today. I completely forgot," Tess said. "What do we do?"

The two men in the road noticed their car and were approaching them. A couple of search dogs poked their heads up and barked.

"I...I don't—" Ivas couldn't think; he was starting to

panic. Blanc sat up, growling quietly at the sound of other dogs.

Tess honked her horn. "Move! I need through!" she shouted at the man approaching her window.

The second man had circled the other side and immediately saw Ruby.

He grabbed Ivas's door and yanked it open. "My god, those boys were telling the truth! She's here!"

Ivas spun onto his side and threw a kick at the man. By now, the other man had seen Ruby too and started shouting.

Tess hit the gas, but only made it three feet. The rest of the search party heard the commotion and stepped into the road, blocking her getaway.

"Shit!" Tess put it into reverse to back away, but the man Ivas tried to kick off had grabbed his ankle in defense and inadvertently caused Ivas to fall out of the truck as Tess backed up.

The wind was knocked out of Ivas's lungs as he hit the ground. He heard the crunch of tires as Tess stopped the truck. He tried to call for her to keep driving but couldn't catch his breath.

Ruby jumped out of the truck and tried to run for it but was grabbed by another man. "Jesus, fuck," the man whispered, staring in horror at her horns. "She's been possessed!"

"Get off me!" Ruby's voice came out as a growl, which she realized did not help her case. She tried to calm herself down, but the panic and the fear were heavy in the air.

"Let go of her! She's not possessed!" Tess jumped out of the truck as well and laid a heavy punch on the arm of the man holding Ruby.

The small act of violence was all it took to tip the scales. The search party saw the attack and immediately swarmed on the three fugitives. Ivas felt himself pinned down and watched as, outnumbered, Tess and Ruby were grabbed as well.

The man holding him pulled out a walkie-talkie. "Johnny, we're on county road two-two-four. Bring your truck over here right now."

"*Did you find him?*" Johnny asked from the other end.

"No, not the kid. But there's some kind of monster."

"No, she's not," Ivas grunted, getting his wind back.

"Martha, head to the nearest house. Call for Jack!"

Ruby pulled against her captors. She could feel their hot, overwhelming breath on her head, their too-big hands making bruises on her arms. They were panicky, stupid creatures taking up too much room. She remembered Brian and Luther, and that urge to cause harm returned. All she wanted was to push their faces into the dirt, hard enough that the gravel would embed itself in their skin. She wanted to punch them in the face and cause their teeth to fall out. She wanted—

"Shit!" One of the men screamed and jumped away from her. On Ruby's hand, black claws had replaced her fingernails. She glared at her other captor with yellow eyes. With her free arm, she rammed her elbow into his stomach, making him double over in pain. The one who had flinched away tried to grab her again. Ruby grabbed ahold of his jacket and flung him off his feet with a single throw. He hit the ground and stared at her. Ruby felt herself swell with pride. He was afraid of her, a little girl. It felt *good*.

"Let them go," she ordered the others, not holding back her deep monster-voice.

"Ruby, stop!" Ivas called. "Don't become this thing. Stay you!"

"This *is* me," she snapped at him. "This is my strength, my power. I'm the one making things right. I'm the one saving you."

A second car came barreling down the gravel road—Johnny, Ivas assumed. It came to a stop behind Ruby and a young man stepped out, bewildered.

"Johnny, be careful! She's dangerous!" the one who took the elbow to the stomach warned.

Johnny reached back into his car and came back out with a pistol. Ruby froze. Everyone else lunged.

Someone grabbed Ruby from behind, followed by two more. Someone else went to Johnny's truck and pulled a coil of rope out of the back seat. Soon, a pile of people was on top of Ruby, pinning her down while the rope was tied. Ruby screamed with a ferocious animal cry that gave Ivas goose-bumps. She threw her hands about, cutting with her claws. Blanc was snarling and barking, but in the chaos, she was too confused to make an attack.

Johnny remained in place with his pistol aimed. He was just a kid, only a few years older than Ruby, and Ivas didn't trust the frightened look in his eyes. The gun was already cocked.

The crowd backed away, some nursing wounds. Ruby lay on the ground, arms and legs tied haphazardly but tight. She thrashed against her binds and her yellow eyes locked with Johnny's, mad and wild. Johnny screamed.

Ivas heard a gunshot and started screaming too.

Tess fell to her knees, fainting.

The crowd turned to the source of the shot and saw the sheriff standing on top of his car, gun pointed in the air. Ivas looked back at Johnny, who dropped his gun and put his hands in the air. Ruby stopped struggling, but her breath was heavy and angry. She was okay.

Ivas whimpered, crying with relief.

Everyone shrank from the look on Jack's face. His dark eyes narrowed on every one of them, taking names and faces. He jumped off the car and stepped forward.

"Look at yourselves, panicky fucking animals. You're no better than the sheep Ivas keeps— *Get off of him, Mitchel.*"

The man holding Ivas down immediately backed away. Ivas pushed himself up.

"Look at her, Sheriff! You know she went into the fog. Something got ahold of her!" Mitchel said.

Jack ignored him and walked over to Johnny, snatching his gun off the ground. "Johnny, were you about to shoot this fifteen-year-old girl?"

Johnny's skin turned ash grey. "N-no!"

"Then why did you have a gun pointed at her?"

"She…she was…"

"What? What was she doing? Did she have a weapon?"

Johnny couldn't answer.

"Go sit in my car, son. You're under arrest."

"But look at her!"

Jack did, and even he couldn't suppress the shudder that went through his body. "I am the sheriff. This is my job. You're just a mob."

Ivas went to Ruby and started untying her, working against the strange, panic-tied knots. When she was free, he picked her up and held her close. "It's okay, you're safe."

Ruby's breathing steadied and she rested her head against his shoulder. He felt her horn brush against his cheek.

"Am I a monster?" she whispered.

Ivas knew Ruby was unpredictable, but he didn't expect her own self-doubt.

Jack stepped forward. "You're both coming with me," he said.

Ivas held Ruby close. "It's going to be okay," he whispered.

They didn't leave right away. Johnny refused to ride in the same car as Ruby, and Tess had woken up, dizzy and disoriented. Jack radioed for his deputy to meet them. Ivas and Ruby were put into Jack's police car. Tess and Johnny were put in the deputy car; Tess was being taken to the local health clinic. While they waited, Jack reprimanded the crowd and sent them away.

"That was good work, Sheriff," Ivas said sincerely.

Jack sighed, a deep, very tired sigh. "This wouldn't have happened if you had just told me where she was," he snapped.

"You saw her last night," Ivas said. "I told you it was Blanc that ran in front of the car, but it was Ruby. How could I expect you to handle this situation?"

Jack gritted his teeth. "I guess neither of us trusts each other."

They rode the rest of the way in silence.

~

*B*lanc sat next to Tess's truck for a while, trying to figure out what to do. When the gun had gone off, she had immediately taken cover under the vehicle and waited until all the shouting was gone. But by that time, Ivas had been gone too.

Now she sat alone, using her dog-logic to find the best course of action. Go back home and wait for Ivas? What if he was in trouble? Should she track him down? Eventually, she decided she didn't want to be alone either way and decided to go to the one person who could understand.

Blanc followed the trail back up the road. This time, she didn't allow herself to get distracted by little things. She was on a mission—Ivas needed her.

She reached the main road with little difficulty, and from there it was easy to find her destination. She just followed the scent of the ocean. Blanc found Marlene's cottage and scratched at the door. Marlene answered and raised an eyebrow.

"Oh, you're Ivas's dog. I never did catch your name."

Blanc wagged her tail at the friendly voice.

"I take it Ivas is in a spot of trouble? Well, you better come in." Marlene stepped aside so Blanc could enter. "Let's see if I have a treat I can whip up for you."

~

The sheriff's station wasn't often used, so everything was clean and in good shape when they arrived. The jail cells were down the hall from Jack's office, out of sight, but open enough for Jack to hear anything going on. Ivas and Johnny were put into two different cells. Ruby was taken to the other side of the jail where she could have privacy.

"Wait, Jack, wait." Ivas reached through the bars of his cell and grabbed Ruby's arm. She let him pull her close. Her horns bumped against the bars, making them clang. Johnny whimpered at the sound.

"You're not a monster," Ivas whispered. "Everything you've done has been to save us all. That's who you are. Don't forget that."

Ruby pulled her ear away to look at him. Her chocolate eyes softened and she smiled.

Jack took her away—no handcuffs were used for any of them—and out of sight.

"Are you hurt?" he asked. Ruby noticed that he stared at the ground, the wall, anything but her.

"No, I'm not hurt."

"I'm going to call your mom. You can go home with her."

"I'd really rather you didn't."

Jack sighed and opened the cell facing his office. It was

the only one at the front of the building, meant for those who posed a risk to themselves. Jack rarely used it, but he didn't want Ruby to have to sit with the two other men.

"Since you're a runaway, I have to lock you up," he explained.

"Please don't call Mom, Sheriff. Not tonight."

"I have to tell her."

"I don't want to go home, not yet. Mom will try and take me away to a hospital or something and that's not what I need."

"How do you know what you need?"

Ruby narrowed her eyes. "Because it *was* the fog, Sheriff. A doctor can't help me. Besides…" She tried to appeal to his sheriff way of thinking. "What if the village comes after me again? I'm safer here."

Jack rubbed his eyebrows. "I don't have a choice, Ruby. You're a minor. I can't even question you without your mom here. Just sit tight. I'll hold off on calling her until I finish the paperwork, okay?"

Ruby sat on the cot in the cell and Jack locked the door. Ruby found that after the adrenaline rush of being attacked, she was actually very tired. She lay down on the thin mattress, closed her eyes, and let her body relax.

Jack was glad to see her be compliant. In the back of his mind—the evolved part that had learned to fear things with horns and claws over thousands of years of survival—he kept expecting her to fight back. But Ruby remained calmly and logically human, despite what his eyes were seeing.

He sat at his desk and pulled out the processing paper-work but was having trouble concentrating. He stared at the paper and tried to fill in the first block—the names of those in jail—but realized he wasn't holding a pen. He grabbed one, and in doing so his eyes snuck another glance at Ruby. At first, he just saw the awkward, pubescent body of a teenager, the unique red hair, and relaxed posture. Her hands were resting on her stomach, the hands with curved black claws. Her fingertips were tinted black too. From her pretty red hair protruded the horns. Jack noticed that other branches were growing from them, similar to antlers, but ugly and tangled, like thorns.

She had said so herself—the fog had done this to her. Jack was covered in goosebumps, fists clenched. He suddenly found himself understanding why Johnny had pointed a gun at her.

The snap of the door opening frightened him out of his thoughts. Jack stood up to block whoever was coming in. He recognized Mitchel, the man who had pinned down Ivas, and who was also Johnny's father.

Mitchel's eyes locked on Ruby, and Jack quickly got between them.

"Mitchel, let's talk outside."

Mitchel had come in ready to oppose any of Jack's opinions, but this one he agreed to. They stepped outside where Martha, Mitchel's wife, was waiting in the car. Other witnesses from the search party were there as well.

"I don't want any trouble from you people," Jack warned.

"They just want to know what's going on," Mitchel said, "and I want Johnny."

"Mitch— Mr. Carter, Johnny was in possession of an illegal firearm, threatening another person. If you want to post bail, that's fine, but I have to do this by the books."

"Yeah? What do the books say about handling *her*?"

The others murmured in agreement.

"She's my responsibility. I am handling it."

"You got her locked up?"

"Yes." Jack gritted his teeth.

"What about the fog?" someone else asked.

"What about it?"

No one answered, but the tension was high. They were scared, the ghost stories manifesting before their eyes. People were disappearing, and now there was a horned girl. Jack didn't blame them, but he also knew that mass fear was more dangerous than the fog.

"Look, everything is all right." Jack tried to sound confident. "I know things have become complicated, but as long as we keep our heads, we'll get through it. Stay home after dark, hang up your talismans, don't go anywhere alone. Mr. Carter, I'm confiscating Johnny's gun, but…he can go home. Just let me finish the paperwork."

Mitchel's expression softened. "No bail?"

"No. Johnny's a good kid; no need to put a black mark on his record." This was true, but Jack knew Mitchel was really just afraid of Johnny being locked up in the same place as Ruby, and letting him go would cool the crowd.

"I appreciate that, Sheriff."

"Just wait out here, I'll have him out in fifteen minutes. The rest of you should head back home. It'll be dark soon."

Those words were enough to get the restless crowd to start moving, though reluctantly. The sky was a dark grey, and thunder rumbled in the distance. Everyone knew that the rain would only bring the fog sooner. Mitchel went back to his car to sit with Martha. Jack returned inside.

Ruby was lying on her side, staring as he came in. He shuddered. She looked too calm, as if she knew exactly what was going on, and Jack didn't trust that. Neither spoke, and Jack went quickly to his desk, keeping his eyes averted.

~

*R*uby watched Jack return to his desk. She had never really felt impressed by an adult before, but Jack was earning her admiration. She liked how confident and stoic he was, dealing with the mob that had attacked her.

She touched her horns absently, letting her mind wander as the silence sank in. She tried to embody Jack's calmness, to not be angry at the townspeople, at the bars closing her in. Jack hadn't shown any fear or anger—he had been in *control*.

That's what she needed.

Ruby took deep breaths, biding her time. Jack would let her out soon, or Hannah would come and get her. Then she could plan her next move. Try as she might, the silence kept pushing her mind toward the past, wandering through memories instead of thinking of a plan. It was hard to ignore them when everything became quiet. For a month now, Ruby had been able to avoid it. She had music, distractions, the fog…

Now there was nothing, and she found herself in the summertime, only four months ago. Ruby was just out of school and had decided that she didn't want to spend her three months of freedom fishing with her dad like she usually did. She hated getting up early, and she hated the smell.

Her dad, unable to completely hide his disappointment, said that it was okay, but she couldn't spend her summer slacking. She had to get a job or go to summer school. Ruby suggested going to stay with her aunt in the city for a while. Her parents had balked at the idea before remembering that she was fifteen and it wasn't entirely out of the question.

Dad had acted odd about it, clamming up and becoming uncharacteristically quiet. He kept asking Hannah what she thought. "Do you think it would be okay? Would your sister mind? Should we? Do you think she's old enough?" He kept wanting someone else's opinion. Their insecurity was more frustrating to Ruby than if they had just said no. She spent days trying to convince them to just let her go. Her mom eventually warmed up to the idea after talking to her sister about the details, but Dad continued to be vague and unsure.

Ruby tried not to whine, but phrases like "I'm almost sixteen" and "I can't stay in this town forever" kept entering her arguments, making her feel like she really wasn't old enough to go on this trip by herself. After all, a real adult didn't have to argue this much.

Then one day, Dad came back from a fishing trip, took a nap, and when he woke up, he packed a bunch of food and told Ruby to put on some sailing clothes. He wanted to take her out on the boat.

"Why? What are we doing?" Ruby asked, confused.

"Just hanging out, having some fun. Is that okay?"

"Yeah, sure." Ruby was surprised. Just her and Dad on a spontaneous boat trip?

Ruby remembered that day. It was warm enough that she actually got to wear a new dress she had been saving, along with sandals. She braided her hair against the sea wind and put on a light cardigan. The sky was a perfect blue, no clouds at all. The countryside practically glowed with the fresh summertime green. It was dazzling and hard to look at, so she brought sunglasses as well. Her dad had also dressed casually and carried their food in a picnic basket.

They drove down to the docks. The fishermen were gone, but other people were enjoying the weather by playing on the beach or taking their boats out. They waved to friends, but Dad didn't stop to chat like he normally did. They went straight to the boat and cast off.

Dad's boat was a trawler called *Fair Hannah*, but he wasn't shy about its recreational use. The wind was strong enough that Ruby didn't mind the fish smell. In fact, she was very much used to it by now, having accepted many fishy hugs from her dad.

Dad let her steer the boat, and they left the little crescent-shaped bay, heading out to sea, away from the other sailors. Both Ruby and her dad valued privacy, and they left the shore far behind. Once they were satisfied, Dad let the boat drift, and they sat on the deck to eat the picnic together, drinking wine, eating cheese and bread.

Dad kept prompting Ruby to tell him stories, about boys she had crushes on, what subjects she liked in school, what she wanted to do this summer.

"Gross, Dad, no boy is worth crushing over in this town," Ruby said, rolling her eyes at the idea of all the pimple-clad, awkward, and rude boys that made up her school. "I like science class, actually. Chemistry was awesome, so next semester I'm taking physics." This was true. Ruby genuinely enjoyed the math and formulas that went into science. Ironic, considering she hated general math. "I just want to go on an adventure this summer. It's not like I want to leave you and Mom behind. I just… It seems like we always just go up to Balliecroy for vacation and I just wanted to see something new."

"That's good," her dad said. "You should always be looking for something bigger and better. Go out and see the world. I just… I guess I was ignoring how much you were growing up. How soon you'll be going out into that big wide world."

Ruby's stomach tightened, scared of the implication of leaving her family, of going off someplace and forgetting about Loch Lamond. "But, I mean, I'm not going to *leave* leave. I'll always come back."

Her dad smiled. "Well, I sure am glad to hear that."

He stared at her for a moment and shook his head. Then he took her in his arms and hugged her tight. Ruby hugged back. He tucked her head beneath his chin, and Ruby felt the scratch of his whiskers.

Ruby's eyes filled with tears. She still remembered the

scratch of his beard. His smell. How tight and big his arms were around her.

"You're the perfect size, right here," he said. "You fit right under my chin."

Ruby had laughed. Now, her tears rolled.

They ate the rest of their food and watched the sun go down. Neither was in a hurry to go back. They watched the blazing sun soften into a lavender twilight, then lay down on the deck to watch the stars.

So far from the village, swaying in the rocking arms of the sea, their view was unhindered. As the night deepened, Ruby was able to make out a strand of clustered stars—a piece of the milky way.

"Did you know that our DNA makes a spiral, just like the milky way?" she whispered. Her dad looked at her and smiled.

"You're so much smarter than I ever was."

"It's because we're made of star stuff. We're spinning with the rest of the universe."

"Hmm."

"Are you upset that I don't want to be a sailor?"

"Not at all. I want you to do whatever you want. But I'll miss you. I just wanted to spend some time together."

"Okay."

"What *do* you want to do?"

"I want…to figure out what I want," Ruby said honestly. "To experience everything until I find what I love."

"Some people spend their whole lives trying to do that," her dad said. "It'll be your greatest journey. Speaking of which, we'd better head back."

They both stood up. Ruby felt sleepy from the rocking of the ship, but Dad insisted that she drive them home.

"In the summer sky, do you remember which stars to follow to get home?"

Ruby studied the constellations until she found the three stars that connected Aquila, Lyra, and Cygnus in the summer triangle. From there, she was able to find Pegasus and turned the boat northeast. Dad confirmed it with his compass.

"Well done."

"See? I pay attention," Ruby bragged.

"Well, sailing is still always an option."

Once they got close to the bay, Dad took over and steered *Fair Hannah* back to the dock. Ruby wasn't sure what time it was, but she was exhausted, dozing off in the car as they drove back home. Her dad had to wake her once they arrived.

He opened the passenger door and shook her shoulder. "Come on, Pumpkin. We're home."

"Will you carry me?" Ruby asked sleepily. "Like when I was little?"

He laughed at that. "You're too big for me to carry you anymore. Ah, hell." He set down the picnic basket. "One last time."

He picked her up and rested her head on his shoulder. Ruby put her arms and legs around him, giggling as he managed to get her out of the car and toddle toward the house.

"I love you," she whispered.

"I love you, too."

"Today was a lot of fun. Thank you."

"You're welcome."

Ruby wiped her face on her sleeve, taking deep breaths, trying not to cry. She pushed the rest of her thoughts away because they all wanted to think of Dad and she was far too tired. Ruby sat up and stared at the bars of her cell, rubbing a horn, concentrating on what needed to be done.

❧

*D*own the hall, Ivas sat on his cot with his back against the wall. Johnny had been curled into a ball since Jack shut the door and was gradually raising his head, cheeks streaked with tears.

"I wasn't gonna shoot her," he finally whimpered. "I-I would never…"

Ivas didn't answer, partly because he didn't believe him. He knew that in that moment of panic and fear, people would do things they would "never" do. But it was hard to be angry. After all, Ivas had been just as scared.

"No one got hurt, that's all that matters," Ivas finally said.

"Y-you're with her? I mean, you were helping her…"

"Yes, I am helping her, because she needs help."

Johnny lowered his eyes shamefully. "I'm sorry."

"I'm not the one you tried to shoot."

"What happened to her?"

"She…she's not dangerous." Ivas tried to think of a way to explain. It was important that Johnny went back to society not spreading more fear. "The fog…put a curse on her."

Johnny nodded. Curses made sense. Ruby wasn't at fault —the fog was to blame. "I heard what happened to her dad. It's awful."

"She's been very brave, but she's just a little girl, scared like the rest of us."

Johnny sat up, coming out of his ball. "Well, at least she's with the sheriff now. He can find a way to break the curse."

"I hope so."

On cue, Jack came down the hall holding a ring of keys. He went to Johnny's cell and unlocked the door. "Your parents are waiting outside. I'm keeping your gun. There might be some community service in your future, but for now just go home."

Johnny's face was cleansed with relief. He eagerly left the cell.

"Jack," Ivas called, "is Tess okay?"

Jack kicked himself. He had forgotten to follow up with Tess. He made a mental note.

"She's fine. I need to follow up with the clinic, but I'll let you know."

Jack and Johnny continued down the hall. When they reached the office, Johnny saw Ruby and flinched. He wanted to run out the door but made himself stop. Jack gave him credit. Johnny's eyes were locked on the floor, but he managed to blurt out an "I'm sorry" before leaving. Ruby opened her eyes and looked in his direction before going back to her rest.

Jack remained at the door for a moment, making sure Johnny and his family drove away. He went to his desk and picked up his radio.

"Gavin, come in. Do you read me? Over."

Gavin was one of the few people that hadn't been born and raised in the village. He had taken the job as Jack's deputy after graduating school in the city a couple of hours away. He came looking for a quiet life of law enforcement where he could have a vegetable farm on the side and marry a farmer's daughter. He was successful in two out of three of these goals so far.

"I read you. What's up, Jack?" Gavin answered through the radio.

"Thanks for dropping off Johnny for me. Are you still at the clinic? And you forgot to say over. Over."

"Yeah, I'm still here. The doctor said it was just a fainting spell, but I guess it hit her pretty hard. She was really upset. *Over.*"

Jack frowned. Having known Tess since childhood, he

found it odd that she would still be in shock. She was a sailor first and foremost, and she knew how to keep her cool.

"Are you in the room with her, Gavin? Over."

"No, I'm in the lobby."

"Go check on her real quick. Over."

"Gottcha. Over."

The line went quiet, and Jack waited. He realized that Ruby was watching him. He turned in his chair.

"Uh, Jack." The radio came back to life. "The girl is gone. She slipped out the window."

Jack sighed, that was the Tess he knew. "Is that all?"

"Yeah."

"You didn't say 'over.'"

"*Over.*"

"Okay, get in the car and run a perimeter. See if you can find her and bring her in for questioning. Umm…" Jack rubbed his brow.

"I'm already in the car. I'll search the town. Over."

"Gavin, I didn't say 'over.' That means I'm not done talking. Over."

"Sorry. Over."

"If you see anyone out on the streets, send them home. I'm issuing an unofficial curfew. We don't need any more disappearances. If you don't find her by nightfall, come back to the station. Over."

"Jack, you're not scared of the fog like these other guys, are you? I've never known you to be suspicious. Over."

"That's an order. Over."

"Yeah, yeah. Over and out."

The radio clicked silent.

"Sheriff, is Tess okay?" Ruby asked from the cell. Jack didn't turn around.

"Oh yeah. She's on the run. Can't imagine why, though. I don't know why all my friends refuse to just trust me and tell me what's going on." Jack got to his feet and stormed down the hall to Ivas's cell.

"Did you hear that?" Jack asked.

Ivas nodded.

"Care to tell me where she might have gone? Without lying this time?"

"I don't know, Jack. She probably just didn't want to be arrested and went home."

Jack sighed. "I don't want to arrest anybody, but… Goddamn it, Ivas, what the hell is going on?"

"Is this how you interrogate all your prisoners?"

"No, this is how I ask my friend to help me."

Ivas looked at his hands, feeling the first flickers of guilt. "I'm sorry, Jack. We are friends, and I do trust you. I just…I saw how torn up you were and I didn't want to pull you into something that even I didn't believe was happening."

"What *is* happening?"

"The fog."

Jack's anger flared. "Enough about the fucking fog. I'm tired of hearing that old ghost story. I just saw a mob of people almost kill Ruby because they thought she was a monster from the fog. It's not the fog—it's mass hysteria."

"Then how do you explain Ruby?"

Jack shook his head. The longer he went without looking at Ruby, the easier it was to put the horns off as a growth or disorder. It wasn't supernatural, of that he was certain, and allowing himself to think so didn't make him any better than the panicky rubes from earlier.

"Ruby needs help from a doctor, not a fucking witch." Jack looked at Ivas with disappointment. "I'm beginning to see why you really didn't come to me. You're as crazy as the others. This is all just mass hysteria, and when it's over, you'll all realize how idiotic you were being. Now, I'm going to call Mrs. Mclaven, and you can just spend the night in there."

Ivas didn't answer. He stared at his hands, hurt by Jack's words, wondering somewhere in the back of his head if it was true. Maybe he was crazy. He listened to the click of Jack's shoes as he left. When everything was silent again, he stood on top of his cot to look outside the small window attached to his cell. It was big enough only to let in a little sunlight. Jack had been insistent on the windows during the jail's remodeling, stating that—as a small jail that would only house locals—vitamin D was important.

Ivas was grateful for it now. Even though he could only make out some overgrown grass, he could tell it was starting to drizzle, and the fog was already rolling in. Thunder rumbled in the distance.

There's no lightning in the fog.

CHAPTER 13

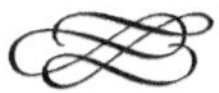

THE SAILOR FIGHTS BACK

From her warm cottage, Marlene and Blanc both raised their heads at the sound of the thunder. Marlene's face turned white. She stood up and opened her ocean-facing window. She closed her eyes and listened to the sound the ocean made. It wasn't crashing, wasn't writhing under the wind. It was rhythmic, swaying and rising over and over. It sounded like footprints.

"Oh boy." Marlene shut the window. "He's here."

Blanc whimpered.

"I know. We'll do something, just…" Marlene turned her head, and in the corner of her eye she saw the lighthouse uphill from her home, sitting empty and unlocked.

"Come on, puppy dog. Maybe some light will help us out."

Gavin drove his patrol car through the village, stopping every pedestrian—there weren't many— to send them home and ask if they had seen Tess.

One shopkeeper said he had seen a woman sneaking down an alleyway toward the docks. Gavin went that way.

The docks were eerie with the oncoming rain. Boats creaked on the water, and the fog rose to knee height. Gavin walked over to the offices where the dock supervisor was locking up.

"Good evening."

"Evening, Officer. Anything I can help you with?"

"I'm looking for someone. Have you seen Tess Burlock in this vicinity?"

The dock supervisor looked uneasy. Gavin didn't blame him. The sailors and fishermen were like a family. It was unfair of Gavin to ask him to betray any of them.

"I assure you she's not in trouble. I just need to ask her some questions about an incident earlier this afternoon."

The supervisor seemed unsure, but he nodded toward one of the boats. "That's her boat there. *If* she's around, that's where she'll be."

"I appreciate it," Gavin said. He walked down the dock to the *Ocean Scorn* and regarded it. It was a large catboat—its single sail packed and tied to the boom. It came with a motor and had lodging below deck. Though well taken care of, the boat was older and worn out.

Gavin considered his options concerning his restrictions against entering property that wasn't his own. In the end, he decided that stepping on board would be alright as long as he didn't open any doors.

"Ms. Burlock?" he called, hopping onto the boat. "This is Officer Harkness. I need you to come on out."

There was no answer. The boat creaked softly as a wave bumped against it, making the fog heave and roll over the deck, caressing Gavin's shoes. Gavin felt himself shiver as a raindrop hit the back of his neck.

There was a small pair of doors in the middle of the boat,

leading below deck. Gavin tried to open them, but they were locked. "Ms. Burlock, I know you're here. Let's make this easy on both of us. I just have some questions for you."

The rain sprinkled down on him, coaxing the fog up higher. It slipped up around his legs and arms. Gavin could taste the moisture in the air as he breathed.

And he knew Tess was down there. She had run away, which meant she was hiding something. He had driven around this entire town looking for her and he wasn't about to walk away just because she didn't answer the door.

He stepped toward the small door and pounded on it. "Open up! This is your last warning!"

After a moment, he heard a scuffle from behind the door. He raised his boot and planted it next to the doorknob, splintering the door open. There was a cry from the other side and he saw Tess retreat into the boat. There wasn't any place to hide, however. Below deck, there was just a triangle-shaped room with two lounge beds that doubled as storage. Tess grabbed the doors and tried to shut them in his face, but he grabbed the handle and yanked it out of her grasp. Tess stumbled back in surprise. Gavin stepped in after her, the fog rolling in behind him.

Gavin felt taller as he stepped into the room—he had to stoop to enter. Tess cowered under him, falling back onto the cot behind her. Gavin felt himself filling up the entire room. There was no way out, and she was lying there, defenseless, all his...

Tess stared up at Gavin in horror. He had grown to a startling height, filling up the small room. The fog followed in after him, flowing off his back like a cloak. He reached forward and pinned her down to the cot, gripping her upper arms. Tess didn't see human eyes staring down at her. They were black, full of hunger.

"He knows what you're up to," Gavin said, his voice

rumbling, a growl haunting his words. "Your sunshine won't save you. He's coming. This world belongs to him…"

Gavin leaned forward. He inhaled deeply, taking in her scent, eyes rolling back with pleasure. Tess felt his breath hit her, startling her as he exhaled. Not satisfied with her smell, Gavin dipped down and ran his tongue over her neck.

"And *you* belong to me."

He was close enough now for Tess to make her move. She raised her hand, clutching a long fishing hook, and rammed it into Gavin's cheek. The deputy hissed in pain and released Tess's arm to remove the hook. This was enough for Tess to get her bearings. She drove her fist into Gavin's windpipe, then elbowed his ribs to shove him aside so she could dive through the door.

Tess ran through the broken door, shoes slipping over the floor as she ran, panicked, outside onto the deck. She heard Gavin close in behind her. She ran across the deck of the boat and jumped over the loading plank onto the dock. The long jump made her collapse to her knees, and as she scrambled back to her feet, Gavin overtook her.

His fist met her back, making Tess fall to her stomach. She lay there, trying to regain the breath that had been knocked out of her lungs. Gavin grabbed the collar of her dress and started dragging her across the dock.

Tess fought back, slapping at his arm and kicking her legs. She tried to call for help, but her voice refused to work until her body regained oxygen. Gavin ignored her struggles and took her to his police car. Tess noticed Gavin's surprising lack of effort as he lifted her up and placed her in the back seat. The fishhook was still stuck in his cheek, and blood had made a heavy red line from the wound down his neck. He seemed not to care.

Tess kicked at his face, planting her toes in a good upward strike on his chin. Gavin's head snapped back, and the momentum sent him stumbling. Tess sat up to go after him, but Gavin managed to fumble the door shut before she could make it. She was trapped.

Gavin tapped on the glass and grinned triumphantly at her. From the front seat, the radio chattered with white noise and Jack's voice came through. "Gavin, do you read me? Over."

"Jack!" Tess screamed and grabbed the cage that separated her from the front. "Jack, help me!"

Gavin opened the door and snatched the radio. He shut the door, blocking out Tess's cries. Scared and trapped, Tess felt hopelessness fall over her. She huddled in the back seat, hugging her knees. Outside, Gavin smiled evilly at the radio and gave Tess an equally unnerving wink. He said something to the radio, then clicked it off.

Gavin opened the driver's side door and slipped in. "Two birds with one stone," he said, giving Tess a taunting smile.

"Officer Harkness…Gavin," Tess said gently. "The fog is in your head."

"And my heart," Gavin agreed, "whispering all my deepest desires. I'll put them in you too." He licked his lips. "See what you desire."

Tess drew away and hid her head in her knees. Gavin laughed and stepped on the gas.

~

*I*vas stared out his window, watching the fog roll in and the shadows deepen as rain began to fall. That was when he suddenly remembered.

"Jack? Jack!"

"What?" Jack's voice was tired and irritated.

"Jack, my sheep are still outside."

"They'll be fine, Ivas."

"Jack, please. I know things don't make sense, but those sheep are all I have, and I don't know where Blanc is…" His stomach panged briefly with worry. "Please, it'll take fifteen minutes."

He heard a chair squeak and Jack walked back down the hall to give Ivas an annoyed look. "I don't know anything about sheep."

"It's fine. Just open the barn door. In this weather, they'll go right in."

Jack sighed. It was a simple request, and no matter how he felt about Ivas, they were still friends. "Alright, fine."

"Thank you, Jack."

"Yeah."

Jack went back to his desk. Truth be told, he was happy to have a reason to leave. It would be good to drive, get away from Ruby and clear his head. He picked up his radio.

"Gavin, it's Jack. Do you read me? Over."

There was silence for a moment. Jack wondered if Gavin was still searching for Tess, then he answered.

"I read you, Jack. Over."

"I have to run an errand. Any luck finding Tess? Over."

"Oh, yes. I have her right here. Over."

Goosebumps rose over Jack's arm for some reason, but he ignored it. "Great, excellent. Come on back to the station, then, and keep watch until I get back. Over."

"You got it, Jack. Take your time. Over and out."

Jack hooked the radio to his belt and went to the door. He felt Ruby's eyes on him and quickly left without a word.

Once they were alone, Ivas breathed a sigh of relief. "Hey, Ruby, can you hear me?"

His voice echoed clearly down the hall. "Yeah," Ruby called.

"How are you doing?"

"I'm okay. It's weird being in jail."

Ivas laughed. "This is my first time too."

"We're outlaws," Ruby said. "After twenty minutes, I don't think I can go back to the outside world."

Ivas chuckled. Ruby's untainted humor gave him strength. "Since Jack is gone, we need to plan our next move."

"My next move is avoiding Mom killing me."

"Good plan. While you do that, I think that Tess and I should take the boat out during the day and do some recon, get a closer look at the fog."

"But what should I do about Mom? What if she tries to lock me away?" This time the humor yielded to genuine worry.

"I'm not going to let that happen," Ivas promised.

Ruby remained bored on her cot, head hanging off the edge and her feet planted on the wall. "I like the idea of just sailing away. It would be cool to live on a boat."

"You'll have to ask Tess about it. She's been a sailor since she was a kid. We used to go out with her dad all the time."

"Does she do any fishing?"

"She does some fishing, gives tours and rides, even a few rescue missions. Whatever needs to be done."

"I loved going out on the boat with my dad. He would let me drive it once in a while, but I kind of fell out of the sailing thing."

Ivas hesitated, choking on a series of words that either sounded too casual or too insensitive. "I bet Tess would teach you."

"Yeah," Ruby whispered. "Maybe someday."

The door suddenly slammed open, and Ivas heard Ruby cry out.

"What? What's wrong?" Ivas yelled. He pressed his face against the bars in a vain attempt to see.

Ruby saw Gavin come in from her upside-down position.

She quickly spun right-side-up, eyes wide. As someone with her own souvenir from the fog, she recognized the effects right away. Gavin was large—unnaturally tall with haunting eyes. His cheek still bled from where the fishhook had been. She noticed that his shoulders were oddly pointed under his shirt. He smiled at her without any trace of the humor or sincerity that is supposed to come with a smile.

"There you are."

Ruby glared at him and stretched her fingers, showing off her claws.

"Ruby? What's happening?" Ivas called.

Gavin looked down the hall with a raised eyebrow. "That your little shepherd friend?"

"Don't worry about him," Ruby hissed. "Open this door so I can rip you to shreds." Ruby was ready to finally fulfill the need for carnage in her heart.

Gavin approached her cell, looking down at her through the bars. He smirked. "There will be something ripped to shreds." He swiftly reached between the bars, snatching her blouse and ripping it off her shoulder. Ruby withdrew, face burning red. She pressed the fabric back into place, trying to hide the bra it revealed.

Gavin laughed happily at her embarrassment. "Come here, little one," he whispered, unlocking the door. Ruby backed away, baring her teeth.

"Ruby?" Ivas grabbed the bars of his cage, shaking the door.

"It's the deputy!" Ruby yelled. "He's being controlled by the fog."

"You make this hard for me and I'll take care of him first," Gavin warned. "I'll drag him out here so you can watch."

Anger snapped inside and Ruby attacked, slashing her claws toward Gavin's face. He grabbed her wrists and slammed her against the cage. Ruby cried out in pain and swung her leg to kick him instead. Gavin reached into his pocket and pulled out a taser.

"Ivas!"

He heard Ruby scream, followed by a shriek of pain. He smelled something burning in the air.

"Ruby!"

Gavin scooped Ruby off the ground as she blacked out from the taser's voltage. He ran his eyes over her body, balanced between youthful clarity and budding adulthood. But there would be time to enjoy it later. He didn't want to be bothered by Jack suddenly returning. He wanted privacy, to take his time. His grip tightened with anticipation, and he carried Ruby outside to his car where a terrified Tess still waited.

Silence fell over the police station, and Ivas started to scream.

CHAPTER 14

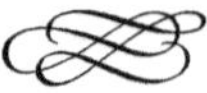

THE SHEPHERD MAKES A DEAL

Ivas started screaming Ruby's name, hoping that she would answer, having defeated whatever villain had entered the jail. But there was no answer, and when Ivas exhausted himself, the jail remained tauntingly silent.

His mind began to race with worry and solutions. He could wait for Jack…but when would Jack return? And how would he be able to find Ruby? Ivas needed to act now, but his cell was strong and unyielding. He stood on his cot to look outside the tiny window, seeking any possible escape. He picked up his blanket, wrapped it around his arm, and slammed his arm against the glass. Pain shot from his knuckles to his elbow, but there was enough adrenaline to cope with the pain. Ivas hit the glass again, this time making a nice spider-web crack. A third strike shattered the glass, and it tinkled down like a magical rainfall. Ivas used the blanket to knock away remaining shards, then stuck his head out the window.

"Hello?" he called. "Is anyone out there? Please help!"

Ivas reached his arms through the window, searching the

grass for…anything. The fog crept in over his arms and down his back, slipping into the cell, dissipating in the warm room.

Ivas spotted a light on the horizon, shining on the ground like a flashlight. "Is someone there?"

"I'm here, shepherd."

Ivas recognized the voice and the pale blue light that fell over him. The giant laid down so that it could peer into Ivas's cell. Ivas didn't break contact with its glowing eyes.

"I need help."

"You said you wanted to face The Dead God, little shepherd. It would be kinder for me to leave you in there."

"Something from the fog took someone from me. I have to find her."

The giant laughed, it sounded like thunder in the dark. "You're always looking for someone in the fog, aren't you?"

"It seems that way."

"The fog is thick tonight. The Dead God is upon us, and we who live in his dying breath are restless for company. I'll take you with me and you'll be safe."

"No, I have to find her."

"I'll help you find your horned girl," the giant agreed, "but I need something in return."

"I'd rather not give up my fear again."

"No, not your fear." The giant reached through the window, fingers flowing through it as easily as the fog. Ivas felt them wrap around his body. "Close your eyes," the giant ordered.

Ivas did so, feeling himself drawn into the fog as they wrapped themselves around him and pulled him through. He felt small and stretched thin, and when he opened his eyes, his body seemed to snap back into place and he was lying in the giant's palm outside the jail.

"I want your serape."

Ivas ran his hand over the fabric self-consciously. "I made this."

"Hence it's value."

Ivas knew it was only a piece of clothing, but he was struck by a strong instinct that he shouldn't give it up.

"Your horned girl is waiting, shepherd," the giant warned. "I can take you to her."

"You know where she is?" Ivas asked warily.

"Yes, I can see a great deal in this fog." He blinked his shining blue eyes to make the point.

After one last hesitation, Ivas sighed and pulled the serape over his head. "Alright, take me to her."

The giant took the serape in its free hand and hid it away. Ivas felt lighter and colder without it, almost lonely, but Ruby was more important. He sat down in the giant's palm, steadying himself as the giant carried him over the landscape in long, quick strides. In a few steps, they were out of town. Ivas followed the giant's gaze and saw that they were heading toward the Bastille Overlook—a hillside by the beach that offered a beautiful view of the ocean, just uphill from town. It was a favorite spot among romantics.

The giant stopped at the bottom of the hill and lowered his voice. "I see your quarry."

Ivas strained to seek out shapes or shadows in the fog but could see nothing.

"A man has them, his mind is warped by the fog. It has stolen his restraint…"

Ivas's heart skipped a beat. "'Them?'"

"There is another. She has short hair."

"Tess." Ivas anxiously went to the giant's fingertips. "Put me down, hurry."

"The fog will try to separate you from them," the giant warned, placing Ivas on the ground. Ivas hit the earth and reached into his pocket.

"I have my own weapon," he said. He touched the velvet lump within in his pocket. He could feel the heat of the sunstone even through the fabric. Ivas pulled it out and clutched it tight.

"Which way?"

"Directly forward, straight uphill."

"Thank you." Ivas started running and the giant was immediately swallowed up. The fog was so thick, Ivas might have been anywhere in the world. He might have been running off a cliffside, but he trusted the giant to keep his word and held the stone tightly.

He could feel the fog trying to change his direction, to confuse him and turn his legs, but Ivas kept a straight path following the hill. It wasn't long before he heard a woman scream and a taunting voice floating through the fog.

❧

Tess fought back as Gavin dragged her out of the car, but her fight was limited as Gavin had placed her in handcuffs. The metal bit into her wrists and lower back as Gavin tossed her to the ground. Ruby was in the back seat, groggy and in pain.

"She won't be any fun for a while," Gavin said, turning to Tess.

Tess raised her feet up to meet Gavin's midsection as he tried to lay on top of her. He pushed her barrier aside, forcing her onto her stomach instead. He pressed himself onto her back, lips brushing her ear as he licked her neck and ran his hands down her sides, brushing over her breasts and down the curve of her waist, then coming to a rest at her hips, which he clutched. He rolled her over again, hands holding down her shoulders, hips resting on her pelvis, effectively binding her with his own body.

"Why don't you take these handcuffs off and make it a fair fight?" Tess spat.

"I'm not interested in a fair fight." Gavin smiled. "I like you right here." He slid one of his hands down her chest and grabbed her breast. Tess winced at his tight grip. Gavin savored the expression, then reached down into her blouse, massaging his hand over her.

Tess screamed, fighting against the other arm that still held her down. She whipped her head up, snapping her jaw in an attempt to bite him. Gavin laughed.

"Yes, I like you right here." He squeezed his thighs against her more tightly for emphasis.

That was when the sun rose.

Tess was certain it was the sunrise, it was so bright, hitting Gavin in the face like a punch. He winced and screamed, covering his eyes. Tess looked up and saw a great beacon floating toward her. Under it, she saw a shadow of a man holding it aloft…

Ivas ran straight to Gavin—now able to see his surroundings perfectly—and slammed the sunstone into his face. Gavin pitched backward, crying out. The rock came down again, this time drawing blood.

"Ivas!" Tess's cry made him stop his barrage. Ivas looked at her—disheveled and handcuffed—and felt his stomach tighten with sorrow and anger. He grabbed the keys from Gavin, who flinched away, and quickly unlocked her.

"I'm sorry, I just—"

"Shut up," Tess snapped. She took the sunstone from Ivas. It shined beautifully in her hand. Her teeth clenched, eyes dark. "That fucker's mine."

Ivas sat back, speechless, as Tess advanced on Gavin. The deputy tried to back away, but Tess landed an impressive blow on his jaw. Blood flew. Gavin started to sob.

No one spoke as Tess proceeded to slam the rock into

Gavin's body. First into his stomach until he coughed blood, then she began driving it into his groin, receiving howls and screeches from Gavin. Ivas had to look away.

Eventually, mercifully, Gavin's body allowed him to blackout from the pain.

Tess stood up, cold and hard as the rock in her hand. Its light was already starting to dim. Ivas watched her, having no idea what would comfort her. Tess met his gaze and the coldness melted away into tears. She dropped the rock and ran to him. Ivas opened his arms and held her tight so that she wouldn't feel him tremble.

"I'm so sorry," he whimpered. "I should have gotten here sooner."

"No," Tess gasped. "You made it just in time."

Ivas sagged with relief. "Tess…Tessie…"

Tess choked briefly on a laugh at the familiar nickname that Ivas hadn't used since they were kids.

"Lock Tess Monster," he whispered.

She sniffed and giggled through the tears.

"The bravest of us all."

"And smartest," Tess said.

"And strongest." Ivas kept her in his arms as he led her to the police car. The sunstone offered a campfire glow from the grass. In the car, Ruby had come to, holding her side where Gavin had tased her. She looked at them with heavy eyes.

"Ivas…how did you get out?"

"Got a lift from an acquaintance," Ivas said shortly. "I know you two have been through a lot, but the Messenger told me that The Dead God is upon us. He's coming tonight. We either need to think of a plan or run, right now."

Ivas looked pointedly at the driver's seat. It would be easy for the three of them to drive away at that moment and never look back.

"My boat is at the dock," Tess said. "Just downhill. Let's get to it and head that thing off before it reaches shore."

Ruby nodded in agreement.

"I used the sunstone on Gavin," Ivas said, worried.

Ruby reached into her shirt and pulled out the vial of sun water. "I've still got this."

"Alright, then."

Ivas found the car keys on the unconscious Gavin and took the wheel. Ruby and Tess both huddled in the passenger seat together, neither wanting to face the bars of the back again. Kicking up dirt, Ivas drove the car downhill, ignoring the roads and driving straight to the docks.

When they arrived, everyone jumped out and Tess led the way to her boat. the *Ocean Scorn* waited for them silently. Tess went to the till and started the motor, not bothering to put up the sails. From the controls, she also turned on all the spotlights, making the vessel glow. She set the speed control, then went below deck to the storage room. She came back with lifejackets and flashlights.

"Put these on," she ordered. Ivas and Ruby did so. Tess made sure the straps were secure, then handed them each a flashlight. She returned to the till and made sure they were steered safely out of the docks. It was almost impossible to tell because of the fog, however, even with the spotlights.

"We'll head toward Knocktopher Island and get our bearings," Tess announced. "I don't want to go any farther from there. We'll get lost in the fog."

Ivas was smiling at her. Tess was her best on a boat, in her element. She could drive them to Knocktopher Island with her eyes closed. Here she knew how to operate and keep everyone safe. She was in charge.

Knocktopher Island was about a quarter-mile away from land—a small circle of earth that had no use other than as a landmark. As kids, they often boated there for picnics. It was close enough that you were supposed to be able to see the lights from town, but in the fog it was impossible.

Ruby took one of the seats next to the controls and sat quietly. Tess stayed at the steering wheel, concentrating on the mission. Ivas went to Ruby's side.

"Are you hurt?" He hadn't taken the chance to check on her.

"My side hurts," she said, indicating where the taser had struck. Ivas squeezed her shoulder.

"I'm sorry."

Ruby smiled at him. "Don't be. You found us. You stopped him. How did you get out of the jail?"

"I asked for help from someone in the fog."

Ruby frowned incredulously. "I can't imagine anything from the fog helping us."

Ivas nodded in agreement. "There was a price to pay, but it was small compared to you two."

Ruby's face collapsed in worry, "A price? What did you do?"

"Just a piece of clothing. My serape."

"But…you made that. It felt important."

"I doesn't matter," Ivas said. "I don't know what's going to happen here. Do you want to go below deck? There are cots down there, so you can rest."

Ruby seemed like she wanted to take the offer, but she firmly shook her head. "I'll just stay. I'll feel better if I'm up here."

Ivas understood and didn't press the matter. Silence fell over the boat as they approached the island. When Tess spotted the tree line in the spotlight, she cut the speed and put the boat into reverse so that the change in momentum would bring it to a halt. When they were close enough to the island for shallow water, she pulled a lever on the controls that dropped the anchor. Ivas heard the chain mechanism clatter as the anchor was released.

Ruby started to shiver and winced from an unseen pain. Ivas grabbed her shoulder.

"What's wrong? Do you feel sick?"

"I feel *him*," she gasped. "He's here."

"Where? How do we find him?"

Ivas looked up into the fog, heart pounding. Tess hit a switch, making one of the spotlights point straight ahead. They stared into the fog.

"You won't. He's been waiting for us," Ruby said.

As the boat stilled, Ivas finally noticed something strange about the water. It was hitting the boat in a pattern, rising and falling. From the fog, he could hear something—a soft pounding that whispered from the darkness. Then he finally realized...

"Footsteps."

The Dead God appeared then, its dark form pushing the fog away to make a terrifying clearing that revealed the monster. It stood agonizingly tall, taller than the giant. Seawater fell like rain from its body.

It's body...

The Dead God was true to his name—a skeleton covered in mummified flesh, kept intact by the salted water. The smell was still there, but not of rot. Ivas had dealt with dead sheep before and knew what rot smelled like. This was something else, something that entered the nostrils and reminded his soul just how short and fragile it all really was. How nothing mattered. Its eyes were clouded white, but it saw them nonetheless. It looked down at their boat and Ivas wondered what he had been thinking. How three little humans could put themselves in the most vulnerable vehicle imaginable and place themselves right in his path.

Should have run...

They should have run away.

Must run...

He should have gotten into that police car and drove until the engine gave out.

Tess sank to her knees to hold him, and Ivas realized he was already on the floor, his legs having given out.

But Ruby stood.

Ivas stared at her in terror, but he was unable to speak or rise. Tess let out a sob next to him and lowered her face.

Ruby walked across the deck, letting her lifejacket fall off her shoulders along with her cardigan. The Dead God exhaled, releasing a fresh gust of wind and fog that hit the boat, making it rock. Her cardigan floated away.

Ruby didn't react to it. She stepped up to the bow of the ship and stared up at the god. In her heart, she felt the promise of fifteen years—that there was truth in fairy tales, that death was something that happened to those that deserved it. Something deeper and wiser spoke to her, but in Ruby's eyes, there was no room for wisdom. This god had taken something from her and was coming for more. Though she was small, she still stood between him and the only thing that mattered.

Her horns began to grow rapidly, and she ignored the pain. Thorns and tendrils of cartilage grew forth, getting tangled in strands of her orange hair. Her claws grew strong and taunt. She felt fangs in her mouth and the blackness in her eyes.

Finally, there was nothing in her heart more scary than what she was becoming. The anxieties, the guilt, the sadness all bowed and hid from her. There was no room in her heart for them, not with the fog filling up every nook and cranny of her being.

Ruby felt the boat tilting under her weight, so she

stepped off. The water came up to her knees, and the stars seemed closer.

Ivas marveled at Ruby, who now stood at eye level with the god, naked and glorious. The Dead God stared at her, surprised but unimpressed.

"You may have changed your shape, but you are still one mere human."

Its voice sent a fresh wave of panic through Ivas. Ruby only stepped closer.

"There's nothing 'mere' about me."

The Dead God stepped forward.

Ruby didn't let him make another move. She snarled like a wolf and slammed her foot forward, marking her territory.

The force of her stomp made the boat pitch, sending Ivas and Tess sliding over the deck. They both screamed as they hit the rails.

The Dead God noticed their peril and used it to his advantage. Instead of attacking Ruby, he turned to the boat, bending down and slashing his hand through the water. A wave rose from the gesture, rising high, threatening to capsize the *Ocean Scorn*. Ruby jumped in its way, letting the wave hit her chest and force her back. Ruby spun around quickly, risking having her back to the god, and scooped Ivas and Tess off the boat deck. Ivas was pressed against Tess as Ruby bound them with her fingers, then she set them down on Knocktopher Island.

The Dead God took his chance and laid a hard blow onto Ruby's back. Ruby screamed, and her mouth instantly filled with water as The Dead God pushed her head below the surface.

Ivas felt himself sitting on the wet soil of the island, watching the battle of gods before him.

What do I do?

He remained frozen.

The light...

The one thought, simple and vague, stood out amongst the chaos of his head. Ivas turned to Tess.

"The sunlight. The vial."

Tess looked at him and sanity glinted in her petrified eyes. "Ruby had it…"

Ivas looked at the boat, bobbing in the thrashing water. In the light, he could see Ruby's abandoned shoes and clothes sitting on the deck.

"It's there. It all fell off."

Tess swallowed and stared at her boat. It was the one thing she knew. It grounded her, and she started to think again.

"We have to get back there. Come on." Tess stood up, pulling Ivas with her. Ivas was still in shock but let her lead him along to the shore.

"Don't let go of my hand, just keep swimming," Tess said. "We have to get to the boat."

Ivas nodded and allowed himself to be pulled into the water. Strong waves splashed up against them as they stepped in. A wave grabbed them and pulled them out to sea. The lifejackets kept them above water, but Ivas started to panic and thrash.

"Stay calm!" Tess screamed. "Hang on to me!"

Ivas looked at Tess. Her strong arms fought against the water and her eyes locked on the boat as she swam them forward. Ivas got himself under control and started kicking his legs.

Ruby pressed her hands to the bottom of the sea and pushed up with all her might, breaking the water and pulling in a long breath. The Dead God placed his weight on her, and Ruby let him. She curled her legs under her body, and slipped herself forward, causing the god to fall from his own weight.

The two of them came back to their feet and Ruby swung her head, threatening The Dead God with her horns. He swiped at her skull with his claws, and Ruby knocked his hands away with her horns.

It felt good to finally use them. She felt the strength of the impact vibrate through her body and stepped forward for more, thrusting the horns at the god's midsection. One of the points made contact, and Ruby heard the thunder-like crack as one of his exposed bones broke.

"I traveled through the stars to get here," Ruby said. "I am the product of every human who conquered this terrible world. You are from the frightened imagination of a child. You're a shadow under the bed. You are nothing."

"*You are flesh,*" The Dead God answered. He grabbed Ruby's horns in his clawed hands and started to bend them. Ruby fought against him, raking her claws over the tops of his hands.

Ivas's and Tess's swim had been slow moving, but when the two giants changed position, it gave them a better advantage. Ivas was able to let go of Tess and swim beside her. They made it to the side ladder, and Ivas helped Tess up. She climbed to the deck with Ivas behind her, and they collapsed next to each other, exhausted.

Ivas wanted to sleep, but seeing The Dead God take hold of Ruby's horns sent a shock of adrenaline through him. He and Tess came to all fours so as not to fall on the rocking boat and started searching the deck for the vial of sun water. They found Ruby's clothes at the head of the ship—shoes, socks, and pants abandoned. Her shirt had fallen a few feet away. Ivas grabbed it and ran his hands through the fabric until they felt something hard and small. He held out the vial triumphantly.

"I found it!"

"We have to use it!"

Ivas nodded and started to uncork the bottle, but looking up, he felt that the vial would be inadequate. The god was so tall, would the light even reach him? Ivas's eyes wandered from the giant to the long mast of the sailboat.

"We need to go higher," he said, nodding his head pointedly. Tess looked at the mast.

"It's way too dangerous with the ship rocking—"

"Then I need you to do what you can to steady it. I have to get higher. We can't risk a wave hitting and putting out the light."

"Okay. I'll get the rigging to hoist you up."

"No time. I'll climb it myself." Ivas put the vial around his neck.

"Ivas!"

Ivas ignored her and went to the mast. He grabbed the ropes that ran along its body and planted his feet on the pole. One hand at a time, he started to climb his way up before Tess could stop him.

Tess sighed in frustration, but she felt more sure of herself as she went to work.

"Come on, girl, we can do this," she whispered to the vessel. She went to the wheel, turning a light to point at the mast so Ivas could see. He had reached the boom and was slowly making his way up. Tess was glad to see that he was taking it slowly, turning his body against the tilt of the ship so that he got more support from the ropes. Tess gripped the wheel and didn't let go.

Above them, Ruby slammed her fists into The Dead God's arms, trying to break free of the grip he had on her horns. He whipped her head from side to side to dissuade her struggles. He placed a knee on her head and pushed against her horns.

Ruby screamed in pain. The cry sounded the way lightning looked—breaking across the sky, vibrating into Tess and Ivas's hearts. The sound that followed made Ivas black-out. A tremendous cracking filled the air, mingling with Ruby's screams until there was a mighty snap and her horns broke—the same spot where Ivas had broken them.

Never...

Ivas's legs gave out, and his hands slipped from the rope.

Never again...

Ivas fell through the air and hit the deck of the ship, slipping from consciousness.

Never take her horns away...

The Dead God held up Ruby's broken horns. The girl fell back in pain and dismay, sobbing as The Dead God flaunted the horns over her head.

"Flesh," he spat.

He dropped the horns into the water and raised his fist for a killing blow.

~

Rain and wind harrowed the uphill journey Marlene and Blanc made. Marlene wrapped herself up against the strong winds, fighting gravity as she and Blanc made the slow trek up the hillside to the light-house on top of Beacon Point.

"Not making it easy for us, eh?" Marlene scoffed.

Blanc seemed unbothered by the weather and took things slow for Marlene's sake.

"Could have brought my walking stick, I suppose," Marlene said. She hadn't thought of it before they left. Her thighs and calves ached from the effort, and part of her wanted to crawl on all fours.

"No matter!" she said loudly and positively. "One little hill isn't going to stop me." She remembered then that light-houses had stairs and sighed.

"Give me a hand here, shepherd dog." Marlene grabbed hold of Blanc's collar and allowed the dog to propel her forward. Blanc happily obliged.

When they reached the lighthouse, Marlene found the door lock already broken and for once she was grateful for rule-breaking teenagers. But just the once.

She let Blanc and herself inside and sat down on the stairs to catch her breath. She looked up to the top of the spiraling staircase and felt that it was a long way up.

"Well, I suppose time is of the essence," Marlene grunted, coming back to her feet. She felt annoyed that her leisurely beach walks that she took every day had not kept her in better shape. The stairs at least offered an easier climb without the unhelpful weather and she came to the top much more quickly.

Once there, she entered the small glass room where the lightbulb cast its guiding beam, or at least it once had. The bulb was dead. It was still in the socket, but no one had cared enough to keep it maintained. The windows were dirty, and Marlene doubted there were any spare bulbs.

It was going to take some magic to bring this place back to life.

Marlene considered her options. There was no spell that could bring a light bulb back to life. But then again, it wasn't supposed to make rocks glow either. From the oversized pockets of her coat, Marlene pulled out her notebook of witchcraft notes. It was a simple school notebook, the cover curling and faded. Inside was a mess of notes organized only by date. Most of them were simple, like *Found a perfect spiral shell today.* Others were spells she had made up, little rhymes that fit certain situations. One of her favorites was a line she chanted whenever she started to hurt from missing Henry. *Heart be still, the pain will pass, look ahead, leave the past in the past.*

It wasn't exactly Shakespeare. In fact, she was pretty sure it was cheating to rhyme pass with past, but it seemed to help. Marlene flipped through the pages until she reached the period of time where she had learned about sigils. She had discovered these magical symbols in a book from Old Popper's shop. They were for things like inner strength and making important decisions. She had none that would fix a broken light bulb.

But that didn't mean she couldn't draw one. The book had said it was okay to make up your own. Marlene pulled her marker free of the notebook's wire spiral and experimented with different pictures, using images like flames, light beams, and functional light bulbs. Eventually, she came up with one that felt right.

Marlene took her marker to the light bulb and drew her sigil on the glass of the bulb, concentrating on her intent. When the sigil was complete, she stepped back, staring at the bulb expectantly, then realized that nothing was happening.

"What do you think, shepherd dog?" Marlene asked.

Blanc wagged her tail helpfully.

"Yes, it does feel a bit silly," Marlene agreed. She was feeling slightly embarrassed at herself for attempting to do real magic. Was her rock and water spell even working out in the fog…?

Oh yes, the fog.

Marlene thought quickly. She could open the door downstairs, but it would take too long for the fog to rise. She studied the windows that surrounded her. They didn't open, but…

Well, what was one more broken rule?

Marlene took another long journey down the stairs to the main floor. The lighthouse was stubbornly empty, but just outside, she found a perfectly sized rock. Her joints complained as she went upstairs again.

"Okay, don't tell anyone, yeah?" she said to Blanc. The dog hung her tongue in response.

"Sorry to whoever cares about this lighthouse," Marlene said, then threw the rock through the window with a satisfying shatter. The fog entered like thick soup, pouring through the broken window and into the tiny room. Blanc growled in the back of her throat.

Marlene nodded with satisfaction, but the light still wasn't coming on. With a frustrated grunt, she gave the bulb a firm tap, and the light that followed almost blinded her.

Marlene went to her hands and feet, feeling her way back to the stairs. She felt Blanc's soft body next to her, and the two of them found the stairs, away from the light. Marlene blinked and rubbed her eyes, coaxing sight back into her retinas. Once the photopia faded, she looked up at the beam of light, the first the lighthouse had produced in years.

"We did pretty good, eh?" Marlene said to Blanc. She received a lick on the cheek in answer. "Just hope it helps."

CHAPTER 15

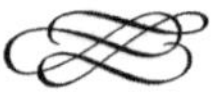

THE SHEPHERD FALLS

*I*vas opened his eyes and grabbed the rope. His head rushed in protest as he lifted himself up, but he ignored it. Half-blind, back groaning, Ivas heaved himself up the mast, running purely on adrenaline and the knowledge that if he failed, Ruby would die. His feet skidded, but he never lost momentum, relying on upper body strength to propel him upward.

The Dead God brought his fist down. Ruby raised her arms in self-defense. The blow knocked her back down again, and The Dead God planted his foot on her stomach.

Ivas reached the masthead and planted his forearms on the top. He swayed back and forth recklessly as he got his bearings. Putting all of his weight on his legs, Ivas pulled out the vial and held it aloft.

The Dead God spread his claws to drive into Ruby's face once she was pinned. Only her upper body was still above water. She looked up and finally tasted her own bitter mortality, like acid in the back of her throat.

Ivas popped the cork off the vial and a dazzling light came forth. Unlike the moonlight, it was warm and golden and made the fog evaporate around it. The Dead God moved away from it, hiding his face. His rotting corpse singed under the touch of the rays.

It wasn't like looking into the sun, though. Ivas could feel a magic in it, a passion hitting his face and filling him up.

Ruby felt it too. She stared into the light with longing. In it, she felt every bit of pain and joy, of loss and gratitude, all the strange emotions that had plagued her since her father disappeared tangled up in the light and touching her skin, filling her up, driving away the fog.

It was clearly hurting The Dead God, but it wasn't having the same effect as the moonlight had on the monsters. It didn't send him running. The Dead God reacted angrily, trying to shield his eyes as he thrashed and threw his arm out, sending up a tall wave of water.

The wave struck the boat hard. Tess pushed her body against the wheel but ended up hanging onto it for dear life. Ivas was not so lucky. The pole slipped easily from his fingers and he was thrown from the ship.

Ivas fell and fell. It seemed he might fall forever. When he hit the water, he wished he had. Now, he was sinking and sinking, the breath having been pushed from his lungs from the impact. Everything was blissfully silent down there, and Ivas experienced a brief moment of pleasantness before the pain of no breath hit his chest and the pressure of the water pressed against his head.

He kicked his legs in an attempt to swim but had no energy to do so. All would have become the pitch blackness of the ocean if it weren't for the vial he still clutched in his hands. Its sunshine still glowed in the watery depths. Droplets of sunlight floated out of the vial and drifted around him like fireflies, keeping the shadows away.

When he couldn't take it anymore, Ivas inhaled, filling himself up with sunshine.

A hand reached through the water and found him there, grabbing him up and dragging him out. A painful hiss met him when Ivas broke through the water. He still glowed, wet with the sun-filled water. He felt that he should be gasping for air now, but it no longer seemed necessary. He was lying in the palm of The Dead God, who glared down at him.

"You should be mine. None die in my fog and escape me."

A shining drop of water ran down Ivas's cheek. It tasted like a Sunday morning walk through the shimmering moors. It tasted the way blooming flowers looked.

The Dead God's hand was trembling with the effort to hold the sun-soaked shepherd. *"Your witchcraft will not save you. No amount of sun will keep me from your soul or those that reside here. I will swallow all that I must to come to power again. I will be a dead, forgotten god no longer..."*

His mouth opened wide and Ivas was lifted up.

Then he was falling, falling, again.

The darkness inside The Dead God brought back the same feeling of hopelessness that Ivas had felt when he had no fear. It ate at him, pulling into it all that Ivas called Ivas. Reaching for his thoughts and memories, dreams and philosophies. And yet Ivas was shining, and in the absolute darkness, he shined even more brightly.

~

"Ivas!" Ruby saw The Dead God fish him out of the water and swallow him whole. Sobbing with pain and despair, she tried to stand. Ivas was dead... Her shepherd friend, the man who had followed her into the fog.

"You monster! Give him back!" Ruby struggled to her knees, and as she worked for balance, one of her hands found her broken horn in the water.

The Dead God didn't answer. He stepped back toward

her—back in control now that the light was gone—and grabbed her hair. His free hand rose high, claws outstretched, ready to drive themselves into her face.

A terrible pain ripped through his body and The Dead God floundered, releasing Ruby and grabbing his stomach in confusion.

"How can you be without a soul?"

Ruby felt something warm touch her face gently, like the gentle stroke of a lover's finger. She looked up at the struggling god. Tendrils of light shined from The Dead God's stomach, through the holes in his flesh and between his ribs, shining on her face.

"Where is it?" The Dead God clawed at his stomach, as if searching for something. *"There's nothing, just the…"*

"Sun." Strengthened from the touch of the rays, Ruby stood up, holding her broken horn. Seawater cascaded off her body as she rose to full height again. She grabbed The Dead God's arm and pulled it away. He tried to stop her with his free hand, but she didn't give him a chance.

Ruby drove the horn into The Dead God's stomach, right to the source of the sunlight. The Dead God's body cracked from the force, ribs breaking and falling away. Even his arm snapped under Ruby's grip.

With The Dead God screaming and collapsing before her, Ruby withdrew her horn and reached into the sun-filled hole it left. She withdrew her hand from The Dead God's wound, holding Ivas's limp body in her palm.

Holding Ivas gently in one hand, she started to rip the god apart with the other. She used her horn to shatter his skull, tossing the pieces out into the water. When The Dead God was headless, she moved to his torso, tearing his ribs away. She might have worked on him for hours, but she heard a voice calling.

"Ivas!" Tess was screaming from the deck of the ship, waving up at Ruby.

Ruby blinked in surprise and looked down at Ivas. He was motionless, not even a rise in his chest. With a frightened gasp, she brought him to Tess and laid him down on the sailboat.

"Ivas! Oh my god, Ivas!" Tess pressed her fingers to his throat. When she felt nothing, she put her ear to his mouth. No breath came. She pressed her mouth to his, pinching his nose shut and tilting his head back, exhaling deeply. Ruby looked down on them, fingers pressed against her mouth. She reached down to touch him, then withdrew. Her size was no help here.

Tess counted under her breath as she pressed her palms into his ribs, forcing his heart to beat.

Ivas watched the chaos unfold around him. He could hear and see Tess but couldn't respond to her. He felt oddly certain that he was dead, or should be, so why was he still here? He felt oddly in between, with no place to go.

Behind Tess, he saw a shadow appear in the fog. He wanted to warn her, but he couldn't speak. Then he heard the sound of ghostly bells and saw the figure's odd frame. The Messenger stepped forward, creating a gap in the fog. Tess noticed the change and looked over her shoulder. With a squeal of fright, she spun around, holding Ivas's head protectively.

But the Messenger ignored her and looked down at Ivas. It reached into its bag and pulled out his red serape, the one Ivas had exchanged for help from the giant. Ivas frowned in confusion. The garment unfolded and floated over Ivas's body as if knowing exactly what to do. It hugged against him, keeping away the cold and soaking up the still-glimmering sun water from his body.

As the warmth sank in, Ivas suddenly wanted to breathe

—could breathe. He sucked in a gulp of air and was rewarded with a painful chain of coughing. He rolled over, hacking up seawater and sucking in rattling breaths that almost hurt too much to be worth it. He felt Tess's strong hand on his back, rubbing and patting, encouraging him to keep breathing.

He did so, and after several minutes was able to breathe with relative ease. He tried to speak, and his voice croaked with effort.

"It's okay, Ivas. We're right here. Everything's all right," Tess said.

Ivas stared at her and started to tremble. Tess suppressed the shaking with a hug that pinned his arms down and filled him with warmth. Ivas buried his face into her shoulder.

The Messenger shifted its strange spider legs, tapping against the aluminum of the boat for their attention. When Ivas looked up, the Messenger handed him a simple piece of paper with a note scrawled across it. One last message to deliver.

I kept it safe for you.

The chicken scratch of loops and scribbles that followed were illegible to all but Ivas, who recognized the mark as his grandfather's signature. Ivas looked at the Messenger in awe, looking for a sign that the message was real. The Messenger, of course, gave no indication. Instead, it turned away, having completed its job, and let the fog fall back behind it like a curtain.

"What does it mean?" Tess whispered.

"The serape," Ivas rasped, clutching the garment in his fist. "He kept it safe for me… It was him all along…" He was unsure how to explain further, lacking any words that made sense. Perhaps sense would come later.

Over Tess's shoulder, he saw the grey remains of The Dead God floating in the water around Ruby's giant legs. He stared at the body parts, fully expecting it to rise up again. His breath came in quick, panicked gasps, and he started to shake again. Tess gripped him firmly.

"It's okay. I've got you."

Ivas allowed himself to be held. The note from his grandfather crumpled in his hand. He heaved a painful, salty sob.

"Hey," Tess whispered, lifting his head. She smiled at him in surprise. "Your tears are glowing."

Ivas caught one with his finger and looked at it. The droplet shined like a distant star. Even Ruby could see it from her height.

As if in answer to its glow, a beam of light appeared through the fog, hovering steadily in the distance. Ruby saw it and gasped.

"The lighthouse…"

"What?" Tess turned her head in surprise, then glanced at the compass she kept on her belt. "It can't be. The lighthouse should be east of here."

"It's the abandoned one," Ruby said. "It's Marlene. She's showing us the way home."

Ruby stood up to her full magnificent height and lifted the sailboat up with her. It might as well have been a toy in her arms. Ivas and Tess held on to each other, jolted by the sudden change in altitude, but Ruby was gentle, cradling the boat tightly as she carried them toward the light, back to shore.

Ruby plucked Ivas and Tess out of the boat and set them on the cliffside next to the lighthouse. Ivas pressed himself against the earth gratefully, running his face over the grass. He smiled. Ruby set the boat down in the water.

"I can take it back to the docks for you," she said.

"No, no." Tess shook her head, exhausted. "Just leave it there."

Ruby stood at eye level to them. She was soaking wet,

blood running down her face, bruises appearing over her body, but she couldn't stop smiling. Her eyes sparkled.

Ivas was suddenly hit by a wall of white fur. He winced in pain, but Blanc's happy licks were too wonderful to stop. He put his arms around the dog and held her tight.

"I knew you'd find me."

"Oh, she's a smart one, to be sure," Marlene said. She stepped through the lighthouse door and sat down in the grass next to them, appearing to have had a busy night herself.

"Aunt Marlene, how did you get the light to work?" Tess marveled. "That light hasn't come on in twenty years."

Marlene shrugged. "Magic." She raised an eyebrow at Ruby and smirked. "They really do grow up so fast. You going to come down and join us?"

Ruby swallowed, suddenly—unbelievably—unsure of herself. She looked over her shoulder, toward the ocean.

"Ain't nothing for you out there, little one," Marlene said gently, choosing her words carefully to remind Ruby of her true size.

"It calls to me," Ruby whispered.

"What? The fog?"

She nodded.

"Ruby." Ivas considered using his "grandfather" voice, but spoke gently instead. He stood up, telling Blanc to stay, and walked to the edge of the cliff so that he could meet Ruby's chocolate eyes. She pressed her large fingertips into the earth, peering at him shyly, like a child peeking over a blanket.

"It's hard to let go," she whispered.

Ivas nodded.

"It's hard to go back to being small with no horns."

"Well, you do what you need to," Ivas said. "What you

think is right. But…" Ivas hesitated, then looked up. Ruby followed his gaze.

Even though it was the middle of the night, the fog was starting to clear and revealed a rare sight—a clear sky full of stars. Ruby's breath caught and Tess gasped.

"It's actually going away," Tess murmured, afraid that if she said it too loudly, the fog would return.

A giant tear swelled up in Ruby's eye and she wiped it away. She rested her head in the grass next to Ivas. "Do you think my dad is okay?"

"Is that why you're scared?" Ivas asked. "Afraid the job isn't done?"

"I thought…I might see him," Ruby said. "One last time and know he was safe. I thought I could save him and bring him back."

Ivas placed his hand on her cheek. Ruby closed her eyes and sighed. Above them, the beam of light from the lighthouse faded as the fog drifted away. And when Ruby opened her eyes again, she found that she was lying in the grass, now the height of a normal fifteen-year-old girl. Ivas sat at her side, now annoyingly taller. The shepherd took off his serape and wrapped it around her.

"This seems important," she said. "You probably shouldn't give it away."

"It's all right," Ivas said. "The fog is disappearing. I think things are going back to normal."

Ruby looked at the ocean where the fog was retreating, drifting away into clouds and water droplets. She felt a soft longing in her heart and quickly looked away, putting her forehead on Ivas's shoulder.

He leaned forward and whispered in her ear, "Your father is safe because you set him free. You saved all of us, and you saved all of them." He motioned to the fog. "You were the one that saw that the monsters were only human."

He gently touched the stubs of broken horn on her head and sighed. "I'm so sorry, Ruby. I should never have taken your horns away."

"You didn't," Ruby said. "They grew back."

"And you'll always have them," Ivas said. "You always did."

He put an arm around her and they climbed to their feet. Tess came to the other side to keep them balanced. Ruby felt completely weak now and let the two half-carry her. Marlene motioned for everyone to follow her, and they made their way down the hill back to the cottage where the path was clear, and Blanc ran ahead like a guiding specter.

CHAPTER 16

THE SHEPHERD TELLS A STORY

In Marlene's cottage, Ruby was given a bath to remove the salt and grime from her body. Purple bruises blossomed across her skin, and her entire body ached. Tess and Marlene helped her, scrubbing and soaping what Ruby was too tired to reach. Ivas and Blanc sat in front of the fireplace, drying off. Ivas felt his mind wander into the ether. He tried to stay focused, tried to remember what happened out in the fog, but out of mercy, his brain only relayed bits and pieces, as if they were memories of a bad dream. Ivas sighed in frustration, wondering if, someday, he would forget the night entirely.

Blanc placed her head in his lap reassuringly and he scratched her ears. "What the hell, Blanc?"

She wagged her tail so that it thumped against the floor.

The girls returned then, Ruby wearing a dress borrowed from Marlene. It was too big and hung off her like a blanket. The last of her horns had started chipping off in the bath, and she was starting to look more normal. Everyone sat down and Marlene made tea. The warm liquid brought much-needed comfort, and soon everyone started finding their voice.

"I'm supposed to be in jail."

"Mom's going to kill me."

"That deputy is still out there."

"Where did I put the sugar?" Marlene hunted through the cabinets until she found it and returned to her seat. "What'd you say?"

"We're trying to figure out what to do when the sun rises."

"Oh?"

"Things were a bit of a mess yesterday." Tess shuddered. "God, was that only yesterday?"

"Seriously, guys, my mom will send me to the insane asylum if I go back," Ruby said.

Ivas kicked the coffee table, upsetting the tea, and all eyes went to him. "No, she's not, because you're going to volunteer for it. Tomorrow, you are going home and telling your mom that you want to see a therapist because you are in trauma over your dad and what happened here tonight. Because you are, in fact, a normal fucking girl and you need to mourn your father properly, get help, and move on with your life."

Ruby stared at him, words flying through her head but none coming to her mouth. Two tears suddenly sprang up out of nowhere and fell across her freckled cheeks. She lowered her eyes and sank back into the couch.

"As for Gavin, he was a human in the grip of the fog. If he remembers what happened, he's going to torture himself for the rest of his life. You do what you need to do to feel safe, Tess."

The sailor nodded.

Ivas sighed. "Blanc and I are leaving."

Tess gasped in surprise. "What?"

"I don't know. I'm going to be away for a while. I'm going to Switzerland." The words came as the ideas did, and Ivas slowly pieced together his plan. "I'd like to breed some more sheepdogs, maybe. I might just visit and come back. I don't know for sure. I just know I want to be away, even if it's just a little bit."

"I guess that's understandable," Tess said, "as long as you write."

Ivas smiled. "Of course I will, Tess."

Ruby fell asleep on the couch, but the others didn't feel like sleeping. Marlene stepped away for a nap, and Tess and Ivas went outside to sit on the back porch where they talked. The hours passed by steadily as they went on and on, talking about Ivas's options. He said he wanted to hike the mountains and find a breeder so he could get a mate for Blanc. Tess said she would find some way to help the farm while he was gone. Ivas told her to give the sheep to Archibald Portman, a shepherd who worked on the other side of town. Ivas would compensate him later.

When they grew tired talking about the future, they reminisced about the past, comparing childhood memories, arguing about what really happened that time Ivas fell off Tess's father's boat, how mad Jack was going to be when he found out Ivas was leaving, and how they hoped they would never hear children sing the gathering song again.

When dawn came, casting pretty colors over the horizon, Marlene joined them with fresh tea. She took a walk down to the beach as she did every morning to fill her lungs with that fresh morning air and listen to what the ocean had to say.

Today, it was calm and full of melodies. It even had a present for her.

Ruby woke up and went outside as well, sleepily drinking

tea and nodding when Ivas and Tess volunteered to take her home. Marlene returned to them, holding something in her hands.

"The sea gave me something to give to you," she told Ruby. The witch held out her hands, and there was one of Ruby's broken horns, shrunken down to a normal size. Ruby took it eagerly, astonished that it was there.

"That horn is full of power. Keep it safe. It will remind you of the strength you have."

Ruby nodded and pressed it to her heart, seeming at ease.

And so, with the new day beginning, the five of them parted ways, with Ruby returning home, Tess taking her boat back to the dock, and Ivas getting ready to pack.

~

It was obvious that Hannah had not slept for the past two nights in which her daughter had been absent, and it broke Ruby's heart to see her mother sitting at the kitchen table with a cup of coffee. A broken woman who, for a moment, had lost the only things in her life worth having. Her eyes were bloodshot, and her hands were shaking. Ruby took it all in, forcing herself not to look away. Because she had caused it and needed to always remember.

When she stepped through the door, Ruby broke too. Hannah looked up at her, speechless, chest heaving with the need to sob even though her body had gone dry. Ruby cried instead, giant tears pouring down her cheeks in a sticky mess.

"Mommy," she gasped.

Hannah went to her daughter.

"I miss my dad!" Ruby screamed. Hannah held her. "I miss my dad. I want my dad..."

Ruby cried and cried because now there was nothing to

fight, no horns to make her scary, just an emptiness that nothing could fill. There was nothing left to do but mourn.

But it was okay because her mom was there holding her so tight. She didn't ask any questions, didn't scream or accuse, because everything was already forgiven.

So, she cried, and they held each other tight.

~

*I*vas had forgotten about Jack, and the last thing he expected was the sheriff to be in his home that morning.

Ivas and Blanc came back to the cottage, where the sheep were safely locked away. Ivas opened the barn door and let them out. He then went to the house and upon opening the door, found Jack inside waiting for him.

The two blinked at each other, both slightly surprised.

"Gavin let you out?" Jack asked. Ivas didn't answer, realizing that Jack had been in his house all night.

"Sorry I never came back. It's…weird being out here all by yourself. You see things, hear things. I didn't want to go back outside when it got dark, so I figured I'd just stay."

"That's alright, Jack," Ivas said gently.

His friend looked him in the eye. "I'm sorry I arrested you, Ivas."

"Don't apologize. You were doing your job. A job your good at, by the way."

Jack smirked.

"If it wasn't for you, who knows what could have happened to Ruby. When everyone else was going crazy, you kept your head."

Jack's smirk turned into a grateful smile. He rose and poured two cups of coffee, handing one to Ivas. "Yesterday *was* pretty crazy."

"You have no idea."

"Do you think we'll be able to laugh about this later?"

"I would like nothing more," Ivas said. He brightened with a sudden idea. "In fact, let's make it as soon as possible. Let's you, me, and Tess go out tonight."

Some life came back to Jack's eyes. "Yeah?"

"Yes, five o'clock at Cuppa. It'll be my going-away party."

Jack's eyebrows rose. "Come again?"

"I've decided to go on a trip. Don't know when I'll be back, just looking for some adventure, you know?"

Instead of heartache, Jack's smile widened. "That's wonderful, Ivas. Good for you. Time to get away from this one-horse town and see some of the world. Where you going?"

"Switzerland, for starters. Figure I'll show Blanc where she came from."

Blanc wagged her tail, hearing her name.

"Hmm, that's beautiful country. Well, I'll let you get to packing then. I need to get back to the station."

"Actually, would you mind giving me a ride to town?" Ivas asked. "There are some things I need to get. A suitcase for one."

Jack laughed heartily. It was a laugh that suited his flannel shirt and bushy beard. "Sure, buddy, hop in."

They drove to town with rising spirits, the events of yesterday seeming to fade into unspoken forgiveness and a willingness to move forward to more positive memories. Jack dropped Ivas off at a general store where he could pick up some basic necessities.

"Five o'clock, no excuses."

"No worries. I have a feeling it's going to be a clear night," Ivas said.

In the store, he found a suitcase that was small enough to carry around but big enough for all his things. He bought travel-sized everything and some portable snacks and threw it all in the bag. After his shopping was complete, Ivas made his way down to the docks where he found the *Ocean Scorn* sitting back in its proper place. Tess and Marlene were there as well, and they looked like they were going on a trip.

"What are you doing?" Ivas asked.

"Ivas!" Tess hopped off the boat and hit the dock hard. She was dressed for sailing, and Marlene was wrapped in a life jacket. "We're on a mission! Want to come?"

Tess noticed the way Ivas's face paled as he looked at the boat and the prospect of going back out to sea. She corrected herself quickly. "Sorry, I didn't think… No, I told Marlene about what happened last night and she wants me to take her to the place where the god was killed so she can exorcise it or something."

"Are you worried it might come back?" Ivas asked nervously.

"Gods are hard to kill," Marlene said from the sailboat, "but I'm going to make sure this one stays dead." She held up a bag full of plants, matches, and spells that guaranteed a proper cleansing.

"Marlene said that with the fog gone, everyone's superstition should go away as well, with time anyway, and that will kill the god for good."

Ivas nodded. Tess noticed his suitcase.

"You're leaving already?"

"No, just shopping. I'm glad I caught you, though. Jack and I want to meet at Cuppa tonight at five. We want you there, all three of us."

"Yeah, that sounds great! It's been a while since all three of us hung out."

"Good. Don't be late, and be careful out there."

Tess grinned. "Not to worry. The wind is good and I've got a sea witch on board."

"And the best sailor in the country," Ivas added. He leaned forward and hugged her tightly. "I'm serious. You kept us alive last night."

"I made the ocean my bitch," Tess agreed. "Get out of here before I start crying. Marlene and I have work to do."

The witch waved to Ivas. "Have a blessed journey, shepherd. You carry the sunlight in you."

Ivas smiled at her. He stepped toward the boat and reached up to take her hand. Marlene bowed down and squeezed his in kind. "Thank you, Marlene, but you're the one who caught it."

Marlene nodded. "It was certainly nice to do some real magic."

Ivas bid them farewell and slowly walked away, looking over his shoulder until the *Ocean Scorn* left the dock. Ivas watched in admiration as Tess operated the vessel by herself, raising the sail and setting out into the blue horizon. When he could no longer see them, Ivas turned away and started walking down the street back into town. He considered getting another ride from Jack, but it was a beautiful day and shouldn't be wasted.

As he walked up the cobblestone street, a door to one of the buildings suddenly popped open ahead of him and a familiar face peered out with a wicked smile. Old Popper greeted Ivas as if he had been expecting him.

"Oi, Mr. Sbarge, I was hoping I would catch you again."

"Good to see you, Mr. Poppermill."

Old Popper grinned. "So then, you ready to pay up? Remember, you owe me a story."

Ivas laughed, remembering his deal.

"Sure thing. I think I have a story you're really going to enjoy."

Old Popper rubbed his hands together eagerly. Ivas followed him inside, where sunshine flowed into the living

room and he was wrapped in the smell of tea and aging
books.

EPILOGUE

*R*uby stood on the top of the lighthouse, staring out at the sea. The sun was high, but the wind had become icy in the winter months. She was padded down in mittens, a scarf, and a hat. Her nose was numb and runny as the wind hit her face, but she didn't leave her perch, too eager for the arrival of Ivas.

She pulled a handheld telescope out of her pocket as she spotted a vessel on the horizon. The instrument had been a Christmas present from her mom. It was a beautiful tool that folded out and back together with a satisfying click. Ruby raised it to her eye and searched the sea until she found the boat. Sure enough, it was the *Ocean Scorn*.

Tess had gotten a phone call from Ivas saying that he was in another port town just down the shore from Loch Lamond. Instead of letting him make the final leg of the journey by himself, Tess had taken her boat up to meet him and bring him home.

He had sent a couple of letters since his departure, and Tess shared them with Ruby whenever they saw each other in town. Ivas had arrived in Switzerland and found a dog breeder there. They had worked out a deal to split Blanc's litter and sell the puppies once they were old enough. This meant that Ivas had to stay in the country for a prolonged period of time. He stayed on a farm with a couple who had been friends with his grandfather and worked for them in exchange for room and board.

In his letters, he described the beautiful mountains and all the things he saw. He said that Blanc was pregnant and doing well. Then that the puppies had been born and were all healthy. They would sell for a good price. He was learning a lot from his shepherd friends and was thinking of investing in some more animals once he got back.

Ruby collapsed her telescope and ran down the spiral stairs of the old lighthouse, thankfully getting out of the high wind.

Marlene was seated on the last step down below, waiting for her. She was wrapped up in several layers of coats and drank cocoa out of a thermos. She looked up as Ruby reached the bottom of the stairs and smiled. "Spot them?"

"Yep! They'll dock in just a little bit!"

"Good, good." Marlene nodded. "I cast a little spell to aid their journey. Will you walk me back to my house?" She grabbed the stair rail and pulled herself up.

"You don't want to come meet them?" Ruby asked.

"It's too cold to walk into town," Marlene said. "They'll come visit when they're ready. But thank you for bringing me along with you today. I've worried about you."

"Why?" Ruby asked. She took Marlene's arm and they left the lighthouse, steadily making their way downhill.

"Because I know what it's like to be in your kind of pain," Marlene said, patting her hand.

Ruby didn't know how to answer. She was better, yes, but she wasn't sure what that meant. She still hurt, still missed her dad. There wasn't a day that went by that she didn't think about him. But she had been seeing a doctor in the city who told her that this was all normal, that grief lasted a long time.

Sometimes, Ruby felt that grief never really ended.

But it was getting easier. The nightmares had stopped. She'd had nightmares for weeks after facing The Dead God. Now, she was at least able to sleep through the night.

They made it back to Marlene's house and the old woman squeezed Ruby's arm. "Come visit me if you ever need to talk," she said.

"I will," Ruby promised. "I think I'll come even if I don't need to talk."

Marlene chuckled. "Sweet girl. Go on, go meet those hooligans."

~

"How was Switzerland?" Tess asked, gloved hands gripping the steering wheel of her boat. The motor pushed them across the icy waters toward home. Ivas sat nearby, wrapped in a large coat. He had a small piece of surprise cargo hidden beneath it. Blanc hunkered down at his feet. Even she was trying to avoid the cold.

"Beautiful," he said. "Every day, I woke up and saw the mountains."

"Sounds wonderful," Tess said, envious.

"I learned a lot too. A surprising amount. I thought I knew everything about sheep and farming, but the family I stayed with had a lot of insight."

"I saw in your letter that you wanted to expand your farm a bit."

Ivas nodded. "I do. I think I'll build a chicken coup. In Switzerland, the farm I worked for had goats that they used for milk and cheese, so I've been thinking about that as well."

"You'll be set," Tess said. "You'll be able to sell a lot more to the local markets."

Ivas nodded in agreement. "How about you? How was your holiday?"

"Really nice. I stayed with my parents. Dad and I worked on the truck a little bit and finally got the heater fixed, but that's about it."

"Why didn't you just pick me up in the truck?" Ivas asked, pulling his coat tighter. His extra passenger stirred.

"Because every time I fix one thing something else breaks." Tess's teeth chattered.

"How's Jack been?"

"A complete doofus," Tess said, a little less kindly than she meant. "I told you about Gavin, right? He left without any explanation and moved back to wherever it was he was from. So, Jack was trying to find a new deputy and ended up finding a wife instead."

Ivas blinked in surprise. "What? In your last letter you said he was just dating someone."

"And now he's getting married."

"After *four* months?"

"Told you, complete doofus. No one from town either. New girl, fresh from the police academy. Every time I tried to get Jack out for coffee, he would claim he had a long night at the office. Guess they were getting to know each other *real* well."

"You sound kind of bitter," Ivas said. "Did...did you like Jack?"

"Not in that weay," Tess said honestly, "but it did make me think. Remind me just how small this town is. How little there is for me..."

Ivas frowned. "What do you mean? Are you okay?"

The truth was that Tess wasn't okay, not fully. For a while she had been, or at least thought she had, but even during Christmas she had been unable to relax, always watching the fog. Underneath her clothes was a bottle of sun-blessed water.

Even with Marlene keeping her ear to the sea, assuring her that things were quiet on that blue horizon, Tess still took her boat out on foggy, icy evenings to see for herself.

Through the cold months, Tess had found herself with little else to do. Her landlord's flower shop was empty except for the greenhouse where she was keeping the plants safe for the winter. Now that the holidays were over, Tess was in the midst of the slow season, and she was starting to wonder if it was time to take her own trip. The small town was making her feel claustrophobic and paranoid.

"Tess?" Ivas stood up, adjusting the bundle under his coat, and stared at her. Tess stared back.

I'm fine. I'm just tired. All the usual excuses rolled through her mind, but they had been through too much to lie. Ivas was the one person she felt she could actually tell the truth to, who would really understand.

"I've been on edge lately," she said. "It's hard getting to sleep at night. And every time a fog rolls in, I can barely breathe…"

"I'm sorry." Ivas's eyes were squinted against the wind, but they were full of sympathy.

"I love this town, and I'd hate to leave my parents, but…"

"You want to leave?"

"I need to, Ivas." She looked at him ruefully. "Isn't that why you left?"

"Yeah."

"And do you think you'll stay?"

Ivas ran a hand through his hair. "I'm not sure," he said. He had thought about it, thought about just staying in his new mountain home. But he had a package to deliver first. What happened from there… Well, he would just wing it.

∽

*R*uby wound her way through the cobblestone streets toward the docks. It was freezing cold, and no one else was outside in their little town. Lights and evergreen branches were still out, leftover from the holiday season. Icicles glinted from the rooftops and frost bordered the windows.

Ruby ran out onto the dock, hugging herself. Even the layers of wool coat and cardigan weren't enough to keep out the wind. Despite this, she was smiling wide as the *Ocean Scorn* pulled into the harbor. She waved to Tess at the wheel, then to Ivas, who was leaning against the rail. He had something small and white bundled in his arms, and Ruby started to squeal.

She clapped her hands to her mouth as the boat approached, and Ivas grinned. It was the most she had ever seen him smile.

"Oh my *gosh*…"

Tess set out the platform and Ivas disembarked, handing over a little white puppy. Blanc walked by his side, looking very proud.

"It's so sweet. I'm so glad you saved one!"

"He's all yours," Ivas said.

Ruby bounced on the balls of her feet, too excited to speak. She hugged the tiny Suisse Blanc, who stared at her with shiny black eyes, little ears pointed up in curiosity. "Really? He's for me?" she whispered.

"I didn't want to sell them all," Ivas said. "Gotta keep one in the family."

Ruby buried her cold nose into the puppy's soft fur.

"He had a little trouble on the boat, so you'll want to give him plenty of rest and probably a bath," Ivas advised.

"A bath sounds pretty good," Tess said, hopping off the boat after them. "I'm freezing."

"I told you to just drive," Ivas said.

"We both know that truck wouldn't have survived the trip." Tess gave Ruby a wink. "How are you, Ruby?"

"I'm good," Ruby said. She hadn't seen Tess much over the past few months. The sailor had kept herself busy on the water, and Ruby had been wrapped up in the chore of returning to school.

"What was Switzerland like? I want to hear everything!" Ruby demanded.

"Well, if it's a story you want to hear, then I know the place we should go." Ivas motioned them to follow, and they made a short trip to the little house down the road where an eccentric bookkeeper eagerly invited them inside for warm tea. Everyone settled in, Ruby with her new puppy in her lap, rattling off name ideas. "What about Frost? Or North?"

The puppy seemed uninterested in his new name, instead giving his attention to a warm bowl of milk Old Popper provided him.

Tess drank in a steaming cup of tea, shivering with relief. She pulled down one of Old Popper's many travel books and began to leaf through the pages.

Ivas took up a comfy chair with Blanc curling up at his feet. She immediately drifted off into a warmth-induced nap, happy to be home. Once everyone was settled, Old Popper, happy for the company, built up a fire and took a seat, hungry for new stories.

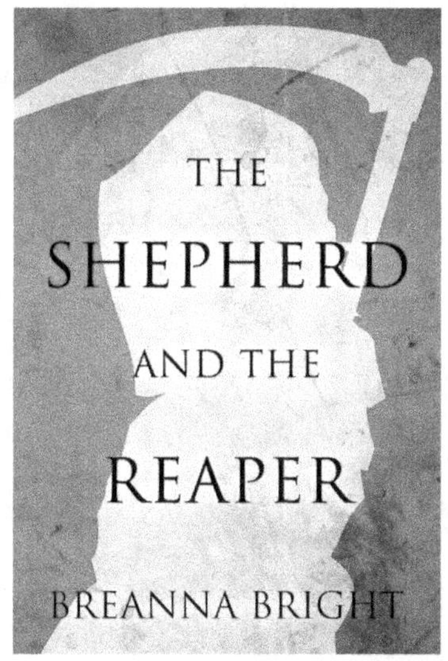

books2read.com/u/m0a65y

Don't go in the woods...

Desperate for respite from the horrors of their past, the Ivas and Ruby seeks refuge in the serene mountains away from the seaside, hoping to leave their troubles behind. After narrowly escaping the clutches of supernatural scavengers from the sea, Ivas and Ruby find sanctuary on a secluded mountain farm. But tranquility proves elusive as they soon discover that the monsters they sought to escape are lurking in the shadows of this new wilderness.

As Ruby, finally free from her cursed horns, begins to embrace her newfound sense of safety, a sinister presence emerges from the depths of the forest. A legendary monster, responsible for the countless disappearances haunting the woods, sets its sights on the unsuspecting duo.

With danger closing in from all sides, Ivas and Ruby must summon all their courage and ingenuity to survive the relentless pursuit of this ancient terror. As they unravel the mysteries of the mountain and confront their darkest fears, they realize that the true battle for their lives has only just begun.

Join Ivas and Ruby on another heart-pounding adventure fraught with peril and suspense in *The Shepherd and the Reaper*, the thrilling next installment in this spellbinding series of fantasy horror.

ABOUT THE AUTHOR

Breanna Bright lives in Missouri, working as a technical writer by day and a fiction author by night. When she's not writing she's traveling the world and going on adventures, looking for her next story. You can learn more about her and her other works by visiting her website, breannabr.wixsite.com/website

Make sure you never miss a new release. Subscribe to our newsletter, http://redempresspublishing.com/subscribe/

f facebook.com/authorbreannabright

ABOUT THE PUBLISHER

***VISIT OUR WEBSITE
TO SEE ALL OF OUR HIGH QUALITY BOOKS***:

http://www.redempresspublishing.com

***Quality trade paperbacks, downloads, audio books, and books
in foreign languages in genres such as historical, romance,
mystery, and fantasy.***